# THE Wishing GARDEN

*a novel*

# ANITA STANSFIELD

Covenant Communications, Inc.

Cover image: *Wendy's Roses* © Al Rounds. For print information go to www.alrounds.com

Cover design copyright © 2012 by Covenant Communications, Inc.

Published by Covenant Communications, Inc.
American Fork, Utah

Printed in the United States of America
First Printing: May 2012

18 17 16 15 14 13 12    10 9 8 7 6 5 4 3 2 1

ISBN-13: 978-1-62108-120-3

# Chapter One

MARY JANE CRANFORD-BEWKES KNEW SHE should be sleeping. She always felt sleep deprived, and by all the rules of logic, her sleep-starved body should have succumbed to slumber within minutes, given any possible opportunity to lie down. But Mary had learned long ago that very few things in her life could be added up with any degree of logic. In that respect, her inability to sleep was consistent with a typical pattern for her—in an illogical kind of way. The lure of a sleeping pill was tempting, but knowing it might inhibit her ability to be roused if she was needed, she knew it was better to resist. She consoled herself with the theory that lying down was still some form of rest, and it would surely sustain her. But she knew well enough that a human body needs good hours of REM sleep on a regular basis in order to function properly. However, she had far too many things to worry about to preoccupy herself with her lack of REM sleep. Ironically, her worrying about not getting enough sleep only contributed to her not getting enough sleep. She was inherently a worrier; she'd gotten that trait from her mother. And even though she'd seen firsthand how much grief her mother had experienced from her worrying—whether or not her worries were well grounded—Mary just couldn't keep herself from doing so. The need to worry felt as ingrained in her DNA as the fact that her eyes were hazel-green and her hair was dirty blonde. She'd gotten those things from her mother as well.

Mary looked around at the bedroom in which she was attempting to sleep. It was the room she'd slept in through all her growing-up years. The decor was simpler now and had lost its childish appearance since her mother had redone it many years earlier so it could be used as a guest room. But Mary could close her eyes and remember the pink floral curtains at the windows and the matching bedspread that was folded back each night when she slept under softer, more comfortable blankets. Some of the furnishings were the same, but the queen-sized bed where she now lay had replaced the twin bed she'd used as a child. Still, the room had the same feel to it in most ways. The way the moonlight came through the windows, the angles of the shadows, the position of the doors that went into the closet and into the hallway were all exactly the same. Mary could look at her surroundings and feel her childhood creep eerily close to the surface. Perhaps a little *too* close. She shut her eyes quickly against the memories, like slamming a door on them. But in her mind they became even clearer, and she was unable to force them away.

*Mary liked knowing that her parents' bedroom wasn't terribly far down the hall. She knew that her mother was close by if she might need her for any reason. But there were times when the closeness of their rooms was a severe disadvantage. And now was one of them. Perhaps if the doors to the rooms had been closed, the sound of her father's shouting might not have been so loud. But Mary usually preferred having her own bedroom door open just slightly, and it was evident her parents' bedroom door was wide open, judging by the sheer volume of her father's voice.*

*Mary was nearly twelve and certainly old enough to understand the nature of her father's insults when he spoke to her mother like that. His shouting and degrading remarks had been a part of their lives for as long as Mary could remember, and it had only been recently that she'd fully realized that not* all *girls her age had fathers like that. Since she'd become old enough to actually think about talking to her friends instead of just playing with them, she'd been stunned to realize that most girls liked their fathers, had fun with them, and weren't afraid of encountering them in the house. Once Mary had become aware of this difference, she had talked to her mother about it when she'd been certain her father was out of the house. Mary's mother was sweet and kind, and Mary had always known she could talk to her about anything. But she'd never been more nervous about bringing something up than she had about that. However, her courage had been fueled by the simple need to know the reasons why a woman as good and gentle as her mother was married to such a difficult and frightening man. Loretta had been vague regarding the reasons for the marriage, but she had made her reasons for staying very clear. "For all of your father's faults," Loretta had said with a soft voice and kind eyes, "he provides a very good living for us, and it's best that we stay here with him and simply remain patient."*

*Mary had learned a great deal about patience from observing her mother's interaction with her father. But she still felt confused, and at times like this, she felt frightened. Her father had never physically harmed Mary or her mother, but, oh, how he could yell! And sometimes the things he said were so cruel!*

*Mary finally slipped out of her bed, dashed quietly to the door and closed it, and scurried back beneath the covers, as if some kind of monster might devour her if she were not safely in her bed. She covered her ears with her hands, which made it impossible to hear the words that were being said, but she could still hear muffled shouting. She cried on her mother's behalf until the shouting finally ceased and she was able to relax. A short while later, Mary knew the door to her room was being carefully opened. She pretended to be asleep, not wanting her mother to believe that she'd heard all the awful things that had been said, but it became difficult to keep pretending when Loretta sat in the chair near the window and wept softly. Mary wanted to bolt out of bed and put her arms around her mother; she wanted to assure her that she understood and it was all right. But Mary resisted, afraid her mother might be embarrassed, and even more afraid that her father might find them there, crying together, and begin his tirade again. She didn't understand why her father was the way he was, but she instinctively knew that if her mother had been unable to tame him, Mary certainly couldn't. The best solution was to simply avoid encountering him as much as possible, and then to follow her mother's example and be patient.*

Mary sat up abruptly, forcing away the memory that had overtaken her so vividly that she'd felt as if decades had vanished. She was stunned by how quickly her heart was beating and how dry her mouth had become. She wondered if this was some kind of post-traumatic stress disorder, given the fact that she was actually sleeping under the same roof with her father again. However, she had plenty of other things to be traumatized over; she didn't need *him* adding fuel to *that* fire!

Mary swung her legs over the edge of the bed and hung her head, surprised at how difficult it was to take a deep breath. In forcing away the layers of difficult memories related to her father, she was assaulted instead by mental images of the recent car accident that had instantly altered her life. She was still reeling from the impact of that event, and wished that she could find a place in her mind where she could experience peace and tranquility, a place where she could completely block out all of the ugly things that had happened in her life so she could just find joy.

Mary sighed and got out of bed, making *another* trip to the bathroom. Then she ambled quietly into her daughter's room and found Adrienne sleeping peacefully, looking as beautiful as an angel. Mary sat on the edge of the child's bed and gently brushed her thick, dark hair back off of her face. She sighed and glanced toward the bedside table that held the photo of Adrienne and her twin sister, Isabelle. The picture was barely visible in the mild glow of light emitting from the hallway, enhanced only slightly by a nearby Cinderella night-light. The girls looked far too much alike for most people to be able to tell them apart, but Mary could tell the difference at a glance. Even in the photo she could look at each face separately and instantly know which child was which. But Mary was their mother, and mothers were like that. Even though Mary hadn't actually given birth to the twins, they had been put into her arms and into her care when they were less than nineteen hours old. She was the only mother they'd ever known, and in every possible way that mattered, she *was* their mother. The thought provoked familiar tears, but since Adrienne was sleeping soundly, she made no effort to hold them back. They slid silently and painfully down her face, reminding her of the loss in her life that was still too fresh to fully comprehend. It had only been a few weeks since the funeral, and Isabelle's absence still felt like a bad dream, an experience that was completely surreal. After having Isabelle as a part of her daily life for more than four years, living without her felt impossible.

Mary wiped her tears and pressed a kiss to Adrienne's cheek. The child's breathing remained even, and she didn't stir. Mary felt grateful beyond words to still have Adrienne in her life. If she didn't feel needed, if there wasn't still someone here with her who called her mommy, she felt certain she would curl up in bed and never get out. Of course, her father needed her as well. But he didn't *think* he needed her. Hired nurses had been caring for him for years, and her presence in the house likely wouldn't be terribly missed by him or the people who cared for him. But Adrienne would notice Mary's absence. In fact, since she'd lost her sister and her father in one fell swoop, she'd become especially clingy. Mary was fine with that, however, because she felt rather clingy herself. As long as she and Adrienne could cling to each other, they might be able to get through this.

Mary went down the hall and around a corner at the top of the stairs to peek into her father's room. His snoring let her know that he too was sleeping peacefully, and she crept back to her own room, the same room she'd slept in all through her growing-up years, when her own mother had been her only real stability in life. But Loretta Cranford had lost her life to cancer the same year that Mary and Simon had adopted the twins. Mary had never quite gotten used to Loretta's absence. Since she'd been living with her new family in another state, it had always felt as if her mother were just miles away and might be available for a visit at some time in the future. Mary had avoided coming home for two reasons. One reason was knowing that if she did, she would have to face the fact that Loretta was no longer there, and the other was that her father's cantankerous attitude had magnified since Loretta's death.

The people who worked for Walter Cranford, whether as employees of his hugely successful company or as part of the minimal staff in his ostentatious home, did so only because they were well paid. It wasn't because anyone actually respected him or enjoyed his company. In fact, Loretta had never seemed to enjoy his company, either. Mary certainly hadn't. It was desperation that had brought her back home to help care for her ailing father. There had been no life insurance, and even before her husband and daughter had been snatched from her, finances had been much worse than Mary would have ever let on to her father. And now she was having to live under the same roof with him—an option much better than being homeless, but she certainly paid a very high emotional price.

Being charitable in the company of Walter Cranford took a great deal of effort—and patience, which was one of many reasons that Mary enjoyed the time when he was sleeping. Since she'd come home, he'd insisted that nurses still come in on two eight-hour shifts—from 6 A.M. to 2 P.M, and from 2 P.M. to 10 P.M.—because he didn't want Mary having to do anything for him that would embarrass either of them. Mary was grateful for that, but *she* had insisted that it was silly for a nurse to be paid for simply being on hand through the night when Mary could certainly handle whatever needs might arise—whether it embarrassed either of them or not. She'd quickly realized, however, that whether or not a nurse was available, her father seemed to take some kind of perverse pleasure in having Mary nearby, available and willing to do his bidding. It seemed like some kind of continual testing, as if her doing whatever he asked of her might somehow prove that she loved him. Well, she *did* love him. But it was a dutiful kind of love based on the simple fact that he *was* her father, and he'd been there day in and day out throughout her life, providing an abundant living for his family, if nothing else.

Mary finally slept, but not deeply. She drifted in and out of sporadic slumber, strange dreams laced eerily into brief stretches of unconsciousness.

She came awake to hints of light peering through the curtains. Bizarre images of Simon and little Isabelle clung to her mind, bringing the memories of her dreams to a place where images of the accident and the funeral were ever present. She'd not personally witnessed the crash where her husband and daughter had died on impact and supposedly had not suffered. She took some consolation in believing that it had happened so quickly that there had not been time for them to experience much fear or pain. But since Mary had seen the police report and the coroner's report, her imagination had filled in the gaps, and the accident haunted her as if she had been in the car herself when a drunk driver in the wrong lane had collided head-on with the vehicle transporting half of her family of four.

"Mama?" she heard a quiet voice say, and for a tiny second she wanted to believe it was Isabelle calling to her through the veil between life and death. She rolled over abruptly to see Adrienne outlined in the doorway of her room.

"Come here, precious," she said, reaching out a hand, relieved by the distraction from the hideous scenes in her mind. Adrienne ran and jumped onto the bed, worming beneath the covers and into Mary's arms. "How long have you been awake?" Mary asked, glancing at the clock. It was nearly seven, which meant the day-shift nurse would be here by now, sitting with her father. That alone always gave Mary a feeling of relief. The baby monitor on her bedside table near the clock had a light on that indicated it was working, but its silence was evidence that her father had not yet awakened, and the nurse was likely sitting quietly in his room or in the hall, reading a book or crocheting—depending on which nurse it was. Since shift assignments varied, Mary couldn't always keep track of who was coming when. She only knew it would be one of four women employed by the home health care company. She had barely become acquainted with them in the short time since she'd been back home, but they all seemed friendly and competent. Whatever their personality or skills, if they were willing to put up with her father, she owed them great admiration.

"I woke up at 6:42," Adrienne said in a voice that bragged about how she was learning to read her numbers.

"Did you have any bad dreams?" Mary asked. It had become a standard question, since Adrienne had been severely traumatized by the loss of her father and sister, and nightmares had been one of the symptoms. Thankfully they were not frequent, but they were still a concern.

"No," Adrienne said, and Mary sighed, comfortingly relieved as she pressed a kiss to the top of her daughter's head and stroked her thick, dark hair, tangled with natural curl.

"I'm so glad," Mary said.

"Did *you* have bad dreams?" Adrienne asked with great maturity.

"I had very strange dreams, but they weren't frightening."

"I'm so glad," Adrienne said, mimicking her mother's tone. She was unusually mature for her age, and also very tender and sensitive to her mother's feelings.

They snuggled in silence for several minutes before sounds on the monitor indicated that Walter was waking up and the nurse was speaking to him. Mary reached over and turned off the monitor, then got comfortable again. A minute later Adrienne asked, "Can I go with you to talk with Grandpa after breakfast?"

Mary took in her breath slowly and let it out even more slowly, measuring her words and trying not to betray any of the fury she felt. Still, she was determined to be honest with her daughter and not sugarcoat the situation. "I wouldn't think you'd want to after the way he treated you last time."

"You said that just because Grandpa was being unkind to me, it didn't mean anything was wrong with *me.*"

"Yes, I said that."

"Then it doesn't matter if he's unkind to me," Adrienne said with an amazing self-confidence that Mary envied. If she could have felt that way about her father's treatment when she'd been a child, she likely wouldn't be nearly as messed up as she felt now.

"No, it doesn't matter," Mary said, "but that doesn't mean you have to be around him when you know that he likely *will* be unkind. Do you understand?"

"I understand," Adrienne said, "but I want to go with you."

Mary thought about it, trying not to be affected by how deeply hurt she felt at the way her father treated her daughter. She wondered if Adrienne was hoping that her own kindness would eventually soften her grandfather. Mary would like to think such a thing might be possible, but she knew better, and she hated to think of the disillusionment the child would face when she had to accept that it never would. Still, she couldn't dispute the child's desire to be charitable when it was so perfectly noble. Mary finally said, "Very well. You may come in with me, but if he's unkind I want you to leave."

After Mary and Adrienne were both dressed and ready for the day, they shared breakfast, made their beds, and tidied their rooms. When Mary couldn't think of any other reason to put off checking in on her father, she took Adrienne by the hand and went to her father's very large bedroom, which was more like a hotel suite. Besides the bed—which was surrounded by medical equipment and cluttered bedside tables—there were two dressers, a table and four chairs, two couches, and an enormous entertainment center, which was fully equipped. There were large sliding glass doors that opened out onto a lovely deck, which looked toward the distant hills of Los Angeles. But Mary's father never wanted the drapes opened, let alone the doors. Off of the bedroom was a huge bathroom with a sunken tub *and* a shower. Walter Cranford never left his posh and comfortable *suite*. He had nurses and servants who saw to his every whim, but only because he paid them well.

The door from the hallway was open, and Mary stepped inside, holding tightly to her daughter's hand. She recognized the nurse sitting on one of the couches with her crocheting.

"Good morning, Doris," Mary said cheerfully.

Doris offered a smile that indicated she had a strong resiliency to having to spend long hours in the same room with her employer. "Good morning, Mary," she replied. "And good morning to you, little miss," she said, turning to Adrienne.

"Hello," Adrienne said.

"He's just finished his breakfast," Doris announced a little more loudly, as if to alert Walter to the fact that he had company.

Mary tried to keep a bright outlook foremost in her mind as she stepped into the room. "Good morning, Daddy," she said brightly, knowing that no attempt at putting forth a positive attitude would have any effect on him. But it would help *her* to contend with whatever he might throw at her.

"It's no good morning for *me*," Walter growled. "It'll be a good morning when I don't wake up."

"I suppose that all depends on whether or not you believe in life after death," Mary said.

"And which place you end up," Doris said in an attempt at humor. Mary chuckled, but Walter glared at the nurse, who returned an apologetic expression, then nodded at Mary as she said, "I'll take a little break while you're with him."

"Take your time," Mary said and opened the drapes over the sliding glass doors as Doris hurried from the room.

"Don't do that!" Walter snarled.

"Five minutes of daylight won't hurt you," Mary insisted. "I only want to visit with you and be able to see you while I do. I won't stay long if that's what you prefer."

"I don't know what there is to talk about," he said with spite in his eyes that was sharper than the spite in his voice. Mary wondered what in his life had made him so bitter and angry. He'd always been a hard, unfeeling man. But everything negative in his character had been amplified since Loretta's death. Since Mary's parents had never been close in any way as far as Mary had ever been able to see, she couldn't see how Loretta's absence should have made much of a difference. But it had. Mary wished there was something she could say or do to soften him or make a difference, but she'd made up her mind upon returning home that she would not make that a condition for herself. If she spent her days in this house with the continual goal of trying to accomplish something that could never be accomplished, she would drive herself mad.

Walter then noticed Adrienne standing just behind and to the side of Mary. His face tightened into a deeper scowl, and he actually made an effort to lift his head away from the pillows propped behind his head. "What is that child doing in here?"

"She's my daughter," Mary said and took Adrienne's hand. "For reasons I cannot understand, she actually wanted to come and see you."

"Well, I don't want her in here," he said, glaring at the child as if he were the villain in a melodrama. "You may consider her your daughter, but she's no granddaughter of mine. No child with—"

"Don't you dare say it!" Mary said, knowing he was going to utter some deplorable comment about Adrienne's ethnicity. She and her sister had been born in Mexico; her dark skin and black hair immediately made it evident that Mary shared no DNA with the child. But Mary saw nothing but beauty in both of her daughters, and she loved and honored the people and culture of the land of their birth. Her father's unreasonable bigotry was one of the widest chasms between them. She didn't care that her father disagreed with her beliefs. But she did *not* want Adrienne to be an innocent victim caught in the crossfire.

"If you don't want her to hear my opinions on having a little wetback under my roof, then don't bring her in here."

Mary heard Doris gasp and turned to see that she had returned and was hovering in the doorway. Mary turned back to her father and said with firm indignation, "It's amazing how such an educated man can be so ignorant. Even *if* a decent person used such a word—which he would not—he would know that it infers coming into this country illegally. Adrienne is legally and lawfully my daughter."

Mary could see her father trying to articulate a retaliation, and she knew she needed to get Adrienne out of the room. But she didn't want to back down and make a hasty exit that might make her look weak. She felt inexplicably grateful when Doris stepped forward, holding out a hand toward Adrienne. "Come along, dear," she said. "I think I know where Janel has hidden the cookies she baked yesterday."

Adrienne looked at Mary, asking silently for permission to go with the nurse. Mary was amazed at the apparent unruffled innocence on her child's face, as if the conversation had gone right over her head and she had no idea what had been said and had no comprehension of the derogatory inferences in regard to herself.

"Go along," Mary said to her. "I'll come find you as soon as I'm done here." To Doris she added, "Thank you. I won't be long."

Doris and Adrienne left the room. Mary took a deep breath to strengthen her own resolve, then exhaled her father's words with her well-rehearsed inner conviction that they could not truly affect her. She didn't care what he thought; she didn't care what he said. She was living here on his charity, and she was determined to be charitable in return. Simple as that. Fortunately, he never left this room, and it wasn't difficult to avoid him. She simply had to make an appearance at least once a day to assure herself that she was making every possible effort to be charitable and gracious.

Now that Adrienne was out of the room, Walter leaned back against the pillows stacked against the headboard. He apparently had no further interest in expressing his obnoxious, prejudiced attitudes now that only Mary was here, since he knew they would have no effect on her.

Mary sat on the edge of the bed, which brought a glance of annoyance from her father, but no comment. She wanted to tell him that she was thankful he was allowing her and Adrienne to stay here, but she knew that any attempt to express her gratitude would only bring on a lecture about the horrible situation she'd gotten herself into that made it necessary to live on her father's good graces. Or if he was in a really bad mood, he would threaten her with ending up on the streets and tell her how he'd written her out of his will when she'd married the wrong man and adopted children that had brought shame to his good name and reputation. So Mary kept her appreciation to herself, knowing that in some warped kind of way he respected her more for not acknowledging her dependence on him. Instead she brought up a point that had been on her mind since she'd moved in less than a week earlier.

"Daddy, I want to talk to you about the garden."

"What about it?" he asked in a tone that implied she had better tread carefully. As if that were not already clear on a continual basis.

"It's been completely neglected since Mother died, and—"

"And why wouldn't it be?" he countered. "It was *her* garden. I've got no use for it."

"I know, but . . . it really looks awful. It's so overgrown, and the weeds are terrible. I wonder if you've considered how it appears to your neighbors. And there is some concern that if the weeds get too overgrown, the seeds from them can blow into the neighbors' yards and cause problems for them." She saw the tiniest hint of interest in his eyes and felt gratified at her prediction. He *didn't* care about the garden, but he *did* care what the neighbors thought. Her motivation in this matter was a combination of honoring her mother's memory and creating a place where Adrienne could play and be comfortable—a place where Mary had spent many hours of her own childhood. But if she even implied her own reasons for wanting to restore the garden, she would never get the permission she was seeking, so she stuck to the perspective of keeping up appearances.

"I've spoken with Mr. Lostin," she said, and her father's eyes widened, bordering on anger, as if she had no right to speak to his accountant without his knowledge, but she hurried on. "He agrees that the state of the yard and garden is cause for concern, and your financial resources would never feel even a hiccup from the cost of hiring a gardener to put the grounds in order and maintain them." She hurried to add Mr. Lostin's argument, certain it would speak to Walter's kind of thinking. "He pointed out that having the grounds in pristine condition is mandatory should you decide you want to sell the property—which is something you've considered."

Mary didn't know who he planned to leave all of his money to; she only knew it was *not* her. But she knew that he prized his own net worth, and the value of his property only added to that. She was grateful that Mr. Lostin was someone she'd known well through her growing-up years. He was a certified accountant, but specifically he had been employed by her father's corporation for many, many years to oversee every matter of business on her father's behalf. He even mediated between her father and his attorney and the board of directors that was in charge of Walter's business endeavors since his retirement due to illness. Mr. Lostin was one of many who put up with Walter because he was paid well, but he still held a deep respect for Walter and had learned to see through the crustiness of the old man and appreciate his strong business sense and deep intelligence. But he had admitted to Mary his disgust for Walter's bigoted attitudes and his lack of kindness to his family. In this way, he was a great ally for Mary, especially since Walter knew that Mr. Lostin was a trustworthy advocate who would always represent him fairly.

"So, what do you say?" Mary hurried to ask before her father had time to think too deeply over the matter. "Are you all right with my hiring a gardener?"

"What about Melvin?" Walter asked.

"What *about* Melvin?" Mary countered. "He comes by now and then to fix things when you need it, and he mows the lawn. He has a lot of other responsibilities elsewhere. Even if he had the time to do more, he doesn't have the skills to restore such an enormous garden and take care of it. If we have a full-time employee to see to all of the yard work, Melvin will not be put out. He has plenty of work elsewhere to keep him busy. And we can still call on him if there's something that needs fixing."

"Fine," Walter said with an impatient flourish of his hand. "Hire a gardener. Just make sure it's someone we can trust to be loitering around the yard all day every day."

"He'll be working, Daddy, not loitering."

"You know what I mean."

"Yes, I know what you mean," she said. "I can assure you that I have the intelligence to hire a decent gardener." He didn't argue with her, which she took to mean some kind of compliment. Silent insinuation was the closest thing to a compliment she would ever get from her father. But then, his silent insinuation could also be very cutting, depending on the context of the conversation.

"Take care of it, then," he said. "I'm tired. I need some rest. And shut those blasted drapes!"

"Fine," she said and stood. "I'll leave you to your darkness."

Mary resisted the urge to dutifully tell her father she loved him, or to kiss his face in some silent expression of that duty. But it would have been more duty than anything, and she knew he wouldn't respond well anyway. So she just closed the drapes and left the room, saying over her shoulder, "I'll check on you this evening."

"No need," he called back, and Mary thought of a hundred things she'd rather do this evening than engage in another such conversation with the surliest man she'd ever encountered in her entire life. The problem was that he had been at the center of her life for most of her life, and she wasn't sure she could ever recover from the impact he'd had on her. She was proud of herself for being able to stand up to him, but deep inside, his attitudes made her churn with an unsettled bitterness that she knew affected her outlook on life, and especially the way she regarded herself. It was a conscious hourly battle to keep her father out of her head, but she was determined to fight that battle, and perhaps eventually she would win.

Mary almost felt as if she needed to take a shower to rinse away the negativity she'd been exposed to in her father's presence. Instead she just paused some distance down the hall to shake out her hands as if she could shake it off. She took a deep breath in a conscious effort to relax and see the good in this day, then she breathed out the memory of her father's ugly words, knowing they had no bearing on her. Just getting through *any* day with the grief of losing Isabelle was a challenge in itself. She didn't need to carry around the burden of her father's bad attitude.

Mary went down the stairs and into the spacious kitchen, looking forward to the project of hiring a gardener and seeing what a skilled man could do with the neglected remains of her mother's favorite place in the entire world. She found Doris and Adrienne having milk and cookies at the table, and Janel wiping out shelves in the fridge. Janel was in her early fifties and had worked in the household for many years. She'd worked closely with Loretta, and they had in fact been friends. Janel pretty much ran the house and did the cooking so that Walter and the nurses could have nice meals. Since Mary had arrived, she'd pitched in some with the cooking; she liked to cook when the mood struck her, and she enjoyed cooking with Adrienne, who loved to get involved in projects in the kitchen. Beyond the handful of nurses that came and went on assignment from the home health care company, the only other person who worked in the household was Kristi, who put in about fifteen hours a week doing the cleaning projects that Janel didn't care to do—"jobs that are more suited to someone younger and more fit," Janel had often said. Kristi *was* young and fit. In fact she was rather beautiful and currently going to college at UCLA. She was the daughter of a friend of Janel's and therefore came highly recommended and from a trusted source. Mary was glad for the things that Kristi did to keep the house clean, and she knew her father was very fussy about strict cleanliness. Even though he never left his room, it was as if he could sense if something wasn't clean according to his standards, which were—quite frankly—much too rigorous for Mary to adhere to. She too liked cleanliness and order, but she didn't want to devote every waking moment to it. Therefore, Kristi was very much appreciated, even though Mary had assessed through their minimal interactions that they had absolutely nothing in common and nothing to talk about. The same was not true of Janel. She reminded Mary of her mother, and they were quite comfortable together. Janel had declared that her employment had become much more enjoyable and fulfilling since Mary and her daughter had come to live here.

Adrienne jumped up and hugged her mother at the same time that Mary was saying to Doris, "Thank you. You're a saint."

"Glad to help," Doris said.

"Whatever they're paying you," Mary added, "it's not enough."

Doris laughed softly and stood up, taking a cookie with her. "Believe it or not, he's not the most ornery patient I've worked with, and I actually enjoy what I do. Don't you worry about me."

"Like I said," Mary chuckled, "you're a saint."

"Amen," Janel said, and Doris went back upstairs.

"How did it go?" Janel asked as Mary sat down at the dining table and urged Adrienne onto her lap. The kitchen was at one end of a very large common room, with comfortable couches and a television at the other and a lovely dining table in the center. Glass doors near the table looked out over a patio, beyond which was the yard and garden that were ghastly to behold, but the view added to Mary's gratification over answering Janel's question.

"We have the go-ahead to hire a gardener," she said triumphantly.

"Oh, that's marvelous!" Janel said, stopping her work long enough to clap her hands together. "I never dared even ask."

"Now, how exactly do I go about hiring the right person?" Mary asked.

"On the chance that he agreed to it," Janel said, "I looked up some numbers for you and wrote them down. Employment agencies."

"Oh, wonderful," Mary said, then she asked Adrienne if she wanted to go out and look at the garden. They went outside and wandered around the perimeter of the overgrown shrubberies and out-of-control rose bushes intermixed with waist-high weeds and unpruned trees. The air was cool even for March in Los Angeles, but they huddled into their sweaters and enjoyed their time outdoors. Mary told her daughter how it had looked when Adrienne's grandmother had been alive, and how much fun she'd had playing there when she'd been a little girl. They speculated how it might look when it came to life again, and Mary said a little prayer that she would find the right person for the job. She felt almost as if she were hiring a plastic surgeon to repair some kind of hideous scar. It was a fragile, sensitive job. At least it was to her. She felt as if her mother's spirit was somehow encompassed in this garden, and bringing it back to life would help her feel closer to the only true strength she'd ever known in her life.

* * * * *

A week later, Mary felt downright depressed about finding a gardener. This undertaking in regard to her mother's garden had become hugely important to her for reasons she didn't fully understand, and she had to find the right man for the job. She'd talked to multiple agencies and interviewed several applicants. But not one of the men she'd spoken to had felt right. In all but one case, the incompatibility between their views and what she wanted done was obvious. The only one that seemed even a remote possibility just didn't feel right, and no matter how Mary looked at it, she just couldn't feel comfortable about hiring him.

Mary continued to feel intense grief over Isabelle's absence and guilt over the fact that she felt practically no grief at all over the absence of her husband. She was glad to see that Adrienne was doing as well as could be expected. She missed her sister desperately, but she had a simple faith that her sister was not forever lost from her, and they found ways to stay occupied. Adrienne missed her father as well, but he'd not been actively involved in his daughters' lives, and it was the absence of her twin sister that was more difficult. Sometimes Mary took her father's Mercedes out, and they drove to the beach or went shopping. They cooked and baked sometimes, did some craft projects, watched movies, and completely avoided going into Walter's room. Mary continued to go in once a day to make her presence known and reassess that he was as ornery as ever. But she refused to let Adrienne go anywhere near that man after what he'd said the last time. She'd talked plainly to Adrienne about the situation and did her best to make certain the child understood how beautiful and wonderful she was, and that Walter Cranford's attitude and behavior didn't change that. Adrienne seemed to understand, and Mary was glad the child wouldn't be exposed to Walter day in and day out as Mary had been during her own childhood.

On a rainy afternoon while Adrienne was occupied with a computer game that helped her learn her numbers, Mary hovered in the kitchen, talking to Janel about her dilemma of finding a decent gardener.

"You know," Janel said and stopped slicing cucumbers for the green salad she was making, "I remember a man we hired off and on many years ago to do some work in the garden. He was amazing! A Mr. Eden, I believe was his name. But oh, that was a long time ago!"

"A gardener with the name Eden?" Mary laughed. "That's cute."

The humor seemed lost on Janel. "I think it was Claudia who knew him . . . recommended him. Do you remember Claudia?"

"I do, of course," Mary said, recalling fondly the woman that Janel had replaced. Janel had worked in Kristi's position while Claudia had been in charge of the household through much of Mary's childhood.

"Anyway, he died . . . oh . . . several years ago, but I've kept in touch with Claudia, and I believe this man's son inherited his gift. Would you like me to call Claudia and see if he's around?"

"It's worth a try," Mary said, not feeling hopeful. The friend of a friend who wasn't likely to even *need* a job seemed like a poor prospect, but it was better than *no* prospect.

While Adrienne was still occupied, Mary put some time into organizing the personal things she'd brought with her, then she got on the computer and answered several e-mails, wrote a lengthy post for her blog, and composed a letter to the director of an orphanage in Mexico in regard to a project they'd been working on together and the progress she'd made from this end. With her obligations in that regard under control for the moment, Mary found Adrienne and they went for another walk through the garden, which looked more like an overgrown jungle. But the fresh air and exercise were good for both of them, and Mary's incentive to find the right man to fix this mess was refueled.

The following morning Janel told Mary to check her email. She did and found an impressive resume from a man named Whit Eden—impressive as far as gardening, at least. She didn't see any evidence of much education. But it wasn't a college degree she was looking for. She wanted a man who had a natural touch for growing things, and his resume made it clear that he did. She printed out the résumé and called the cell phone number she found there. It went to voicemail, but she left a message, saying simply that she would like to set up an interview if he was interested in the job. He called back less than ten minutes later and was very polite on the phone. They set up an appointment for later that afternoon, and Mary made certain that Janel was available to look after Adrienne while she met with Mr. Eden. She hoped his name was a good omen, and she hoped he was the man she'd been looking for.

# Chapter Two

MARY SAT DOWN BEHIND HER mother's little desk while she waited. She had left the door to the room open so she could hear the doorbell. She was incredibly glad that her father had closed the door to this room at the time of her mother's death, and that he'd not opened it since. This was the only room in the house that had truly belonged to her mother. Her father had never come into this room, which was probably the biggest reason it had been her mother's sanctuary. If Walter had had something to say to Loretta while she'd been in here, he had thrown the door open and bellowed it from the doorway. In this room, Loretta had kept her books, her sewing projects, and all things personal and precious. She had written letters at this little desk, and had often sprawled out on the little sofa near the window to read from a variety of books that filled the shelves covering one wall. She loved novels and nonfiction alike, depending on her mood, and if she liked a book she never got rid of it. Mary loved to just look at the titles on the spines of the books and consider how they represented her mother's personality.

As soon as Mary had returned home, she had meticulously removed the dust from this room while doing her best to keep everything where it had been. The only exception had been that Mary had taken advantage of a bare section of wall to hang a few of her own things that held meaning for her. Now she enjoyed coming here either alone or with Adrienne. The child enjoyed hearing stories about her grandmother, and Mary loved to tell them.

Mary had been conducting her interviews in this room for two significant reasons. First of all, she felt more confident in this room than she did anywhere else in the house, as if her mother's spirit was closer to her here and gave her added strength. Also, since the gardener was being hired to care for her mother's garden, it seemed appropriate to interview the candidates here in her mother's room. Not to mention, it was a lovely room with a nice desk that was suitable for a one-on-one professional appointment. Mary had her laptop computer on the desk, and this was also where she'd been doing her own business and correspondence. She'd become very comfortable at her mother's desk.

While Mary listened for the doorbell, she knew that Janel was close to the intercom in the kitchen that connected to the outside of the front gate, which had to be opened either by the visitor punching in a code or by someone inside the house pressing the appropriate access button. Mr. Eden had been forewarned of the gate, and Mary knew that Janel would push the button to let him into the driveway once he arrived.

The doorbell rang right on time. Mary straightened her hair and glanced down to make sure she hadn't spilled anything on herself at lunch that she'd not noticed earlier. She hurried into the front hall and pulled open the door. Her first surprise was to find that the man standing on her porch was dressed in a dark suit, a white shirt, and a tie. All of the other applicants had come dressed very casually. Her next surprise was that he had such startlingly good looks that she imagined he could hardly go anywhere without turning women's heads. He had dark eyes and dark, wavy hair combed back somewhat haphazardly off of his tanned face. It was long enough to hang over his collar, but not long enough to look rebellious or sloppy. He wore sideburns that were even with the top of his earlobes. She knew from the application that he was twenty-nine years old, but he looked younger than that. She wondered how he'd managed to remain unattached. She saw the absence of a wedding ring, but the application had also said that he was single. Given the fact that she was a decade older than he was, she forced her mind away from any thought in regard to his marital status and held out a hand in greeting.

"Mr. Eden?" she said, and he shook her hand firmly.

"That's right. Mrs. Cranford?"

"No, actually . . . I used to be *Miss* Cranford, but . . . then I got married, but . . . I'm not married anymore so . . . just call me Mary."

"Okay, Mary," he said. "I'm Whit."

"I saw that on the application," she said and motioned him inside. "Is it short for something?" she asked and closed the door.

"Whitmer," he said, "but one syllable is just easier."

"It's nice," she said, wondering why the name sounded familiar when she couldn't recall ever before meeting anyone by that name.

"Thanks," he said, and she led the way into her mother's room and closed the door. "Have a seat," she added, motioning to a chair on one side of the desk, and she took the chair on the other side where she'd been sitting before—the one where her mother had always sat.

While Mary was glancing again at his application and thinking what to ask him first, he said, "You're a Mormon."

"What?" she asked, looking up. She'd not even heard the word in years and couldn't imagine why he would have said such a thing.

He nodded while looking above her head and said, "You have a picture of a Mormon temple on your wall. Naturally I just assumed that . . ."

"Oh." Mary glanced at the picture, then back at him. At least his statement made sense now. "My mother was a Mormon. This was her room. She . . . died a few years ago."

"I'm sorry to hear that," he said and seemed to mean it. "So you're not, then? A Mormon?"

"No. Well . . . yes, sort of."

He chuckled comfortably. "Either you are or you aren't," he said, and she wanted to ask exactly who was conducting this interview.

"My mother lived her religion very privately because my father disapproved of any organized religion. I was baptized as a child, but it was done without my father's knowledge, and since my mother and I were rarely able to go to church, it just kind of . . . fizzled out. So . . . technically I guess I'm a Mormon."

"That's sad," he said. "I mean . . . it's not sad that you're a Mormon. It's sad that it . . . fizzled out. Is your father still alive?"

"I'm afraid he is," she said and saw one of his eyebrows go up. "I'll be frank with you, Mr. Eden, I—"

"Whit."

"Whit. My father is likely the most difficult man on the planet. He is in very poor health and never leaves his rooms upstairs. He has a nurse with him during the days, and I try to avoid him as much as possible. If you take this job, I would advise you to do the same."

"I'll take that advice to heart," he said and nodded.

"Are you, then?"

"Am I what?" he asked.

"A Mormon."

"Oh, yeah," he said with an easy laugh. "Although it's more correct to say that I'm a member of The Church of Jesus Christ of Latter-day Saints. It's a mouthful, but that's the name. We usually say *LDS* for short. Contrary to the belief of some, I am a Christian."

"That's good to know," she said and actually felt impressed. While she knew very little about Mormonism in actuality, she knew enough to know that people who belonged to this church and lived their religion were generally good people. And she liked the way he'd declared himself with no embarrassment or hesitation.

Mary briefly explained her reasons for hiring a gardener, being very frank with him about the situation, then she asked him questions about his experience and his work ethic. She listened very closely after she asked the question, "Do you enjoy your work, Whit?"

"I do," he said. "I enjoy being the guardian, so to speak, over growing and living things. I like seeing them grow and evolve. I like getting my hands in the dirt. It makes me feel . . . grounded."

Mary was so impressed that she found herself staring at him. Good-looking, religious, sharp, polite, and *grounded*. She knew he was the right man. She could just feel it, but he smiled in response to her staring at him, and she glanced down quickly, embarrassed. Seeking a reason for buying some time to gather her thoughts, she looked over his application again and made a contemplative noise. Then she noticed something she hadn't noticed before. She looked at the address on his application, looked at his face, then looked at it again. "I know this neighborhood," she said. "It's predominantly Hispanic."

"Yes," he drawled with caution. "Is that a problem?"

"No, of course not," she said. "I just . . ."

While she was trying to think of a way to explain, he said, *"How* do you know this neighborhood?"

"Our housekeeper," she said as she made the mental connection. Claudia. Janel had phoned Claudia. This was the son of a man who used to work here, who knew Claudia. "When I was growing up," she clarified, "our housekeeper . . . lived in this area, and I . . ."

"So you know that people like me tend to work for people like you."

He didn't say it with any malice or bitterness; not even a hint of it. But there was something in his eyes that alerted her to some kind of disdain over the statement. She hoped some clarification might help her understand his reaction. "People like you?" she asked, taking a good, long look at him.

His wavy hair was almost black, and his eyes were dark. Beyond that, he didn't *look* Hispanic. His skin had the look of a dark tan—something she'd expect from someone who worked outdoors in Los Angeles. But his features and overall appearance would never make her think he would come from a neighborhood that she had known to be *very* dominantly connected to a particular ethnic group. He also didn't speak with any hint of an accent, or in a way that she might have associated with growing up in such an area. She could guess from that fact alone that for some reason he had made a conscious and diligent effort to develop a refined speech and manner. But she was only guessing.

When Mary had shared a somewhat comfortable relationship with Claudia, the Hispanic housekeeper, she had heard stories of how whites were not looked upon favorably in her neighborhood. The conversation had come up when Mary, being the naive child that she'd been at the time, had asked if she might come to Claudia's house sometime to visit her. The housekeeper had insisted it wasn't a good idea. But Mary recalled very well when Claudia's husband had passed away, and Loretta had insisted on going to visit her, taking a lovely basket filled with breads, cheeses, and a large ham. Mary had begged to go along, and the visit had left an impression on her. For some reason, she clearly remembered driving down the street that Whit Eden apparently lived on. She remembered because she'd been reading the directions to her mother from the notepad where she'd written them down. She remembered because driving down that street had exposed her to a world that she'd never imagined existed. And she remembered that their visit had been very brief.

"Mary?" Whit Eden startled her from her reverie.

Recalling the last thing he'd said, she countered, "People like you?"

"Hispanic and poor," he said, again with no agitation in his tone, but something subtly defensive in his eyes.

"You don't look Hispanic *or* poor—not that it matters; I'm just curious."

"I'm half Hispanic," he said. "My mother was born and raised in Mexico. I'm not poor anymore; at least I don't see myself that way. Although compared to people like you, I might be. I grew up very poor, but now I make more than an adequate living to care for myself and my mother, and we always have enough to eat." Without missing a beat he added, "Is this relevant to the job interview?"

Mary looked down again at the application, if only to avoid his eyes. "No, of course not," she said. "As I said, I was just . . . curious."

"Fair enough," he said, sounding completely relaxed.

"May I ask why you're looking for work now?"

"You may ask me anything you like," he said. "I've been working for a landscaping company, but it's turned out to be mostly digging trenches to install sprinkler systems. I've been looking for something more . . . fulfilling. When I heard about this position, it sounded promising."

"Well, as far as I can tell, it's—"

The door opened suddenly, and Adrienne ran into the room and crawled onto Mary's lap before she looked up at her mother and asked, "Can I have a popsicle, Mommy? Please? I ate all my lunch." She then looked up at the stranger sitting across the desk and became very quiet.

Mary saw Whit look at Adrienne, then at her, his eyes full of questions. She waited for him to verbalize them, figuring he had his own right to curiosity. She sensed that he didn't want to ask in front of the child, so Mary said to Adrienne, "Yes, you may have a popsicle. Tell Janel I said it was all right. But eat it out on the patio so you don't leave sticky drips in the kitchen."

"Okay," Adrienne said and ran out in an unusually cheerful mood.

Once Adrienne had left the room and closed the door, Whit said, "Your daughter?"

"That's right."

"She's . . ."

"Hispanic? Yes."

"Then her father is—"

"My husband was more blonde than I am," she said. "Adrienne was adopted." She debated whether or not to add more explanation than what might be necessary, then opted to do so. He had a way of making her feel comfortable talking about it; perhaps it was the way he'd been so forthcoming in answering her questions. "I've always had a fondness for Mexico—and its people." She didn't tell him that her intrigue had begun that day she'd gone with her mother into *his* neighborhood. The overt plight of those people had inspired her. She added for the sake of further clarification, "I took a year off college to live in Mexico; I worked in an orphanage. Many years later when Simon and I realized we couldn't have children, it seemed the obvious route to take—since he and I *met* in Mexico." She took a deep breath and decided to just get the rest out of the way, since she had every intention of hiring him. "I was in my middle thirties by the time we adopted Adrienne and Isabelle—twins.

They turned four last summer."

"And you're divorced?" he asked, and if she didn't know better—given their age difference—she might have thought he was asking in a tone that hinted at flirtation. When she hesitated he said, "At the door you told me you weren't married anymore. Forgive me if I'm being too straightforward. I tend to be that way."

"It's fine," she said. "Better to just . . . clear the air, since you're going to be working for me."

"Am I?" he asked.

"If you want the job."

"I do," he said and laughed with genuine relief and delight. "Thank you."

"You might not feel the same way once you've seen the garden."

"Oh, I think I will," he said. "But . . . you were clearing the air." He seemed genuinely interested. "About your husband."

Mary cleared her throat. "Simon was . . . killed in a car accident last month," she said and saw Whit lean back in his chair a little as if something invisible had struck him. She knew the feeling. "Isabelle was with him. She died as well."

After a long moment of silence, Whit said, "I'm so sorry. I don't know what to say."

"Tragedies happen. Life goes on."

"Yes, they do. And yes, it does. But that doesn't mean it's easy."

"No," she said and forced a smile. "Thankfully, I have Adrienne. And thankfully my father allowed me to come back here to live for the time being, given that there was no life insurance." She chuckled tensely. "My goodness, I'm just sitting here telling you absolutely everything about myself. Way too much information, for sure."

"Not at all," he said. "Since I'm going to be working for you, I'd probably worm it all out of you in no time anyway."

"So . . ." Mary chuckled again, "given that you now know practically everything about me, would you like to see the garden?"

"I'd love to," he said, and they both stood at the same time.

Mary stepped toward the door, then realized that Whit had stopped and was looking at the wall that had been behind him while he'd been sitting down. She saw his eyes glance over the three framed diplomas she had hung there.

"Impressive," he said, and she felt a little embarrassed. She'd hung them on *that* wall so that she could see them from where she sat at the desk as a reminder of something valuable she'd accomplished in life. She'd never expected anyone else to ever see or notice them. Whit Eden was apparently more observant than her other applicants had been.

"I suppose," she said. "They're mostly useless when it comes to finding a practical occupation, but I very much enjoyed the things I learned, and I believe that my education contributes to the things I enjoy being involved in now."

Mary was hoping to remain cryptic, usher him out of the room, and move on with talk of his new job, but his eyes moved over to the large bulletin board she had hanging there, covered with the faces of many dark-skinned children; some were Mexican, and some African. But all of them were children that she had personally been able to help in one way or another. Being able to see their faces inspired her each and every day, but she'd never expected to be talking about them to a stranger.

"And is *this* what you enjoy being involved in now?" he asked. She hesitated, not certain how to answer, and he added, "You don't have to tell me, but . . ." He looked again at the pictures as if he were looking directly into the eyes of each child. "This is . . ." She expected him to use a word like *impressive*, as he'd used in regard to her diplomas. But he finished by saying, "very precious."

The word *precious* tugged at her; it was a word she often used in reference to *her other children,* as she often thought of them. "They *are* precious," she said. "I . . . uh . . . well . . ." She wondered why she felt embarrassed to be talking about it, when she knew it was a huge part of her life and certainly a great endeavor. She reminded herself of that and just spit it out. "Once I became a stay-at-home mother, I still wanted to be able to make a difference in such causes. I've always had a passion for the children of the world who go without. So . . . I do a blog that I use to drum up awareness for the cause, and I have some fund-raising projects going on, and . . . well, stuff like that. I do most of it by phone and computer so I can be with Adrienne, but . . . these are the children that have had special meaning to me."

Mary's embarrassment deepened slightly when she found Whit staring at her as if she'd broken out with purple spots. She sensed admiration in his expression, but she didn't know him well enough to be sure. All she knew for certain was that the moment had become very awkward.

"Anyway," she said, moving toward the door, giving him no choice but to follow, "that's what I do with my spare time." She led the way through the house toward the patio doors at the back of the common room, seeking to change the subject. "The name *Whitmer* is very interesting," she said. "Is it—"

"It's actually the surname of a family that's quite prominent in Mormon history."

"Oh," she said with enlightenment, certain that's why it sounded vaguely familiar. Her mother had told her many stories from the Book of Mormon and about the history of the Church.

"So," he said as they went out the patio doors and past Adrienne, who was contentedly sucking on a red popsicle. The day was more pleasant than the last several had been, but the child was still wearing a sweater, and Mary wished she'd grabbed hers before coming out. "What were you—"

"Hold on," she said and left him there while she hurried back inside to get one. She returned to find Whit asking Adrienne her favorite color.

"Purple," Adrienne said.

"I like purple too," Whit said. "Would you like some purple flowers in the garden?"

Adrienne nodded with enthusiasm, then said, "Mama likes lavender. Some people think that lavender and purple are the same color but they're not."

"That's right," he said. "Big difference between lavender and purple. Did you know there's a flower called lavender?" Adrienne shook her head, and he went on. "It has a very nice smell and people use it in soap and candles and stuff like that."

"Mama likes the color lavender. She has a lavender scarf that used to be her mama's, and it's her favorite."

"How very sweet," he said and smiled at Mary, who tried not to feel embarrassed. As if it weren't bad enough that she'd impulsively spilled her entire history to him—including her financial situation—now he knew her favorite color and her sentimentality over one of her most precious possessions.

"We're going to look at the garden," Mary said to her daughter. "Go inside as soon as you finish your popsicle, and Janel will help you wash your hands."

Mary stepped off the patio and across the very small patch of lawn toward the massive shamble that covered nearly half an acre. "*This,*" she said with a huge flourish of her arm, "used to be a garden." They stepped carefully between some overgrown shrubberies and weeds, and she added, "Maybe you don't want to come out here wearing that suit."

"The suit will be fine," he said and looked around contemplatively. "It has great potential. I assume I have a budget for supplies."

"Yes, of course. We can discuss that when you start. When do you want to start?"

"Tomorrow, if that's okay," he said.

"Oh, that would be great," she said and laughed softly. They were silent for a minute while they walked a little and he continued to look around and assess the situation.

"It's terrible isn't it," she said, wondering if she should break his studied concentration of his surroundings.

"I've seen worse," he said, still studying. He walked a little farther and she followed him. He stopped in front of a deteriorating three-tiered fountain, overgrown with weedy vines. "Do you want a new fountain? The sound of running water is nice, don't you think?"

"Can you do that? The water . . . the electricity? All that?"

"Oh, yeah," he said as if it were nothing, and he moved on. "Just tell me what you want."

"A fountain would be nice. I know my mother loved that. Although, having it a little closer to the house might be nice. I don't know. Whatever you think. Nothing too big."

"I can give you some options to choose from," he said.

"That would be great." She followed him in silence for a few minutes through nearly half an acre of neglect, and finally couldn't keep herself from voicing her thoughts, "You were saying something when we came outside and I interrupted you."

"Oh," he said. "I was just wondering what you might have been doing during those years before you adopted the twins and became a stay-at-home mother. You got three college degrees, but I don't see you as the kind of woman to just sit around and wait for life to happen, and I wonder what you meant when you said that you *still* wanted to make a difference in such causes."

Mary looked at him in surprise, then remembered him saying that he had a tendency to be very straightforward. She actually liked that about him, even if she wasn't quite sure how to handle it when he seemed so interested in *her*. "That's . . . kind of a long story."

"Give me the short version," he said.

"Well, we . . . mostly lived one year at a time. We lived in Mexico about half the time . . . off and on. We both had a lot of different jobs. We kept being drawn to working in orphanages or getting involved in projects of one sort or another. We didn't really settle down until the girls gave us a reason to."

"Amazing," he said, looking right at her.

"Is it?"

"Yeah, I think it is."

Mary felt suddenly uncomfortable and couldn't quite discern why. She hurried to say, "You're welcome to look around all you want. I should . . . get back inside. I'll see you tomorrow morning at nine, if that's all right."

"Perfect," he said. "I'll be here."

Whit watched his new employer walk away and wondered how his life had managed to take such an enormously favorable turn in so short a time. It had been years—literally—since he'd really felt like his prayers were being heard, since he'd had any evidence that God was really listening. He'd been overcome with a warm swelling in his heart when his mother had told him that Claudia had heard of a possible job opportunity. And now he knew why. He actually had a job that would be enjoyable and fulfilling, and he would be working for the only woman he'd felt even remotely intrigued with in years. He reluctantly left the Cranford estate and drove home, feeling more hope and happiness than he'd felt since he'd returned from Mexico nearly six years earlier.

\* \* \* \* \*

Mary went to her father's room to inform him that she had hired a gardener who would be starting work the following day. Walter was caught up in some crime drama on television and more or less ignored her, entirely disinterested in her enthusiasm over restoring and maintaining her mother's garden. She was glad to be able to make a quick getaway from her father, and was relieved that this information had not instigated some kind of argument. She phoned Mr. Lostin to inform *him*, and he was very pleased. She gave him the personal information on Whitmer Eden so that he could add him to the payroll as soon as Whit filled out the necessary tax forms. She also discussed a budget for materials for the garden and asked Mr. Lostin how to go about funding it. Mr. Lostin indicated that he would set up an account with a debit card that Mr. Eden could use for this purpose, and he assured her the card would be active by the following week.

Through the remainder of the day, Mary became completely preoccupied with the garden. Memories of how it had once been meshed into her vision of what it might become, and she felt an inner thrill to imagine walking beneath healthy trees and between neatly manicured shrubberies. She visualized the variety of flowers that might grow under the tutelage of Whit Eden's hands. And against all will and reason, she kept thinking about Whit Eden himself. He was young and attractive, but she couldn't see how that was reason enough for her to find it difficult not to think about him. She'd encountered many attractive men throughout the course of many years in a loveless marriage. It wasn't in her makeup to engage in unfaithful or inappropriate actions, and she never would have. But any normal widow, only a few weeks beyond her husband's death, would not be preoccupied this way with a man she'd just met—especially when he was so much younger, and likely very different in many respects. She convinced herself that her intrigue with Whit had more to do with his impressive answers in regard to his attitude about her mother's garden. She had a good feeling about him being the right man for the job, and she anticipated his arrival in the morning so he could get started. Beyond that, she was just lonely and bored and had way too much time on her hands.

The following morning Whit arrived five minutes early, looking entirely different than he had the day before. He was wearing a forest-green T-shirt that wasn't too tight but couldn't hide the fact that he was in very good shape. He also wore sunglasses, faded jeans, and lightweight, lace-up work boots.

"Hello," he said with a smile when he saw her. "How are you this morning?"

"I'm good, and you?" she asked, telling herself that her pleasure at seeing him was entirely due to his potential gardening skills.

"I'm great," he said with firm enthusiasm.

He removed his sunglasses as if to see her better, and Mary couldn't help noticing a ghastly burn scar on his right forearm that had been covered the previous day by his long sleeves. Before she could check herself, he noticed that she'd seen it. He seemed to be used to getting a reaction to it when he said, "It's hideous, I know."

"Whatever happened, it must have been painful," she said, hoping to imply that he didn't have to tell her.

"Let's just say it reminds me not to make stupid choices."

"We all make some of those, don't we," she said and changed the subject to the work she'd hired him to do.

Mary showed him a neglected garden shed where the lawn mower and a variety of tools were kept. Only the lawn mower had been used recently. He told he had also brought some of his own tools, but he would clean up the shed first thing. She talked to him about the arrangement with his salary and budget, and told him that the accountant would take care of everything.

"I keep my cell phone with me most of the time," she said, patting it in the pocket of her jeans. "Let me give you the number and if you have a question . . ."

"Oh, great," he said and took out his own cell phone to put the number in. "Set on speed dial," he said, and she caught a distinct sparkle in his eyes as he added lightly, "since I'm certain to have a lot of questions."

They agreed that he could come and go as he wanted for lunch and breaks, as long as he put in forty hours a week. He told her he would more or less keep a schedule of nine to six with only minor variations most of the time.

"You trust me to keep track of my own time?" he asked.

"Is there a reason I shouldn't?"

"No," he said. "It's just that . . . most employers aren't so trusting."

"Well, unless you give me a reason not to, I trust you. Which reminds me, you'll need the security code to the outside gate."

"You *are* trusting."

"How else are you supposed to get in and out of the yard? You can just come in the front gate, then the driveway splits and you can drive straight to the backyard."

"Thank you," he said. "That will make it easier. But you're giving me my own debit account as well?"

"That's what I said, isn't it? You sound so surprised."

"I am," he said. "But *pleasantly* surprised. I won't let you down."

"I wasn't worried that you might," she said. "I have a good feeling about you."

He smiled in a way that she was sure had melted the hearts of many women. "That's good," he said, "since I have a good feeling about *you.*" For a moment she could have sworn he'd intended some kind of hidden meaning, but he chuckled and looked away, and she felt sure she'd imagined it.

"I'll let you get to work," she said and went into the house.

Inside, Janel was standing at the sink and watching Whit out the window. "He's a nice-looking young man," she said.

"Yes," Mary agreed. "And he's very . . . polite. I'm sure it will work out well."

At lunchtime Mary watched from an upstairs window when Whit left in a midsize black truck that appeared to be fairly new and rather nice. She didn't see him come back, but she knew that he had when she heard the distant sound of a weed trimmer. Their paths didn't cross during the remainder of the day, but the following morning she caught a glimpse of him from an upstairs window, hard at work just past eight-thirty. She was glad that the view out of her father's windows faced the other direction—as if he would even get near a window or care to look out.

Days passed, and it quickly became impossible for Mary to imagine what it had been like to live in this house and not have Whit Eden coming and going five days a week. Weekends felt longer, and she wondered why she felt somehow safer when he was on the premises. She purposely tried to avoid crossing his path for the most part, simply because she found herself uncomfortably fascinated with him, and she didn't want to be around him enough that he might pick up on what she might not be able to hide. Occasionally she took him a bottled water or a cold soda, just often enough to ask him how he was doing and if he needed anything. He was always kind and gracious, and he seemed eagerly pleased when she made such an effort. After he'd been there a little more than two weeks, he gave her a brief tour of the progress he'd made so far, during which he declared, "To the untrained eye it might not look like a big difference, but it's kind of like an archaeological dig."

"Well put," she said.

"How long has your mother been gone?"

"She died the same year we adopted the twins, but she was ill for a long time, and the garden looked dreadful even before she . . . left."

"Well, perhaps her spirit will come here once in a while to enjoy the beauty when it's finished."

Mary felt unexpectedly choked up. "What a lovely thought."

"Maybe she'll even help me make it the way she would want it," he said, as if the idea was very matter-of-fact.

"You believe in angels?" she asked.

"I sure do," he said, looking at her firmly. "Don't you?"

Mary forced herself to gain composure. "I've wanted to believe that my mother has had some awareness of us since she's passed, but I wonder if that's just wishful thinking."

"I don't think it's wishful thinking at all," he said, holding her gaze firmly in a way that caused her stomach to flutter. She looked away, scolding herself for such childish thinking, at least in regard to her feelings about him. As far as his belief in angels, she found it endearing and comforting.

"You're very kind, Whit," she said.

"Just telling you what I believe," he said.

Mary left him to his work and went back to the house to find Adrienne and get her engaged in some kind of productive activity. They both did better in handling the absence of her sister when they kept busy and weren't alone. Janel had been wonderful in taking Adrienne under her loving wing. Janel had seven grandchildren, but five of them lived out of state, and she and Adrienne had taken well to each other. It was nice for Mary to be able to run some errands, or even have some alone time away from the house, knowing there was someone to look out for Adrienne and keep her safe and secure. Mary herself had come to find some solace in Janel's company. She was a kind and compassionate woman, and helped make up somewhat for the absence of a mother in Mary's life.

Janel also took well to the new gardener. More than once Mary had found them taking a break and talking and laughing together. Kristi too, although not around nearly as much as Janel, had quickly gotten to know Whit. Sometimes they all had lunch together. On some days Whit insisted that he had things to take care of on his lunch break and he needed to leave, but on others he seemed very pleased to join them for lunch, even though most days they just had sandwiches or leftovers. He was very complimentary about the food—whatever it might be—and always appreciative of every little offering of kindness.

Adrienne apparently liked Whit very much. Whenever they crossed paths or shared lunch, he would tease the little girl and make her giggle. Mary also heard him tell her more than once how beautiful she was, which Mary considered a lovely compensation for how Adrienne had heard her grandfather criticize the very color of her hair and skin. Adrienne had decided that at least once a day she needed to take Whit something to drink, or sometimes even a popsicle. Mary often sat on the patio and observed from a distance. They apparently had some important things to talk about while he stopped working for a few minutes to visit with the child. And Adrienne always came back to the house cheerful and pleasant after her little interactions with Whit.

Mary grew to respect Whit more every day, which didn't help at all in trying not to think about him. She felt sure that with time her brain would figure out that being attracted to a younger man was ludicrous, and this would all pass. In the meantime, she felt like a girl in high school, always excited with the possibility of running into a particular cute guy in the hallways or cafeteria. When she realized that Kristi obviously had an interest in Whit, and was in fact flirting with him now and then, the absurdity of Mary's feelings became more evident.

Mary kept herself distracted by staying involved with work on her humanitarian efforts via the Internet. She devoted at least a few hours to it every day while Adrienne played nearby. On top of that, Mary had been putting a concerted effort into going through her mother's things, a task that she'd been avoiding. Janel had told Mary that soon after Loretta's death, Walter had asked her to box up everything of his wife's and get rid of it. Janel had felt that some things were obvious charity donations, but there were a lot of things that she felt Mary should go through herself, so she'd hidden boxes in the basement and in the closet of Loretta's private room with the hope that eventually Mary would have cause to come home, and then she could go through her mother's things. Now seemed a good time. She often cried to see and touch things that brought back memories—some good, others not at all good. But she felt like the process had a  healing effect on her, and in a strange kind of way, grieving more fully over her mother's death helped lessen her grief over losing her daughter. As for losing Simon, she mostly just felt guilty over the fact that she felt no grief at all, but rather relief. She reminded herself often that their emotional separation had not been her doing. He'd engrossed himself in anything and everything except her for as many years as they'd been married. She'd tried repeatedly to express her needs and feelings, but to no avail. The twins had taken his attention away from other things to some extent, and he had been a good father, although not a very involved or attentive one. But adopting the twins had not changed the way that Mary had remained completely invisible to him except during rare moments when interacting with her beyond the necessary exchanges of living under the same roof seemed to suit his mood.

Mary made an obligatory visit to her father's room once a day, and rarely stayed more than a minute. It wasn't that she didn't have the fortitude to endure his presence any longer than that; he simply showed no apparent desire to have her there. As much as she preferred to avoid him and his unfathomable negativity, she thought that it would be nice to feel like her father loved her and that he might enjoy spending some time with her—even if they didn't agree on anything.

Through her communication with the nurses who came in to care for him, Mary knew that her father's condition was terminal, but he wasn't so bad off that he couldn't get out of bed more than to use the bathroom and shower with assistance. He seemed to prefer being confined to his bed, and never venturing beyond of the four walls of his self-appointed prison cell. When he needed a doctor's attention, he even managed to bribe a physician who was also a family friend to make house calls. He had no reason to leave his sacred space, and Mary didn't try to convince him otherwise. Having his ornery attitude and belligerence confined to a small space in the house made it easier to avoid having it become contagious. She knew that Walter had never laid eyes on the new gardener, and Mary felt certain it was better that way. If Walter even suspected that Whit had Hispanic origins, he would find a way to deride and belittle him. He had tolerated a Hispanic housekeeper for many years, but he'd always made certain that Claudia knew her place, and much of her place included staying out of his way. Mary didn't know and couldn't understand the source of her father's deep-seated bigotry, but she hated it, and she had to work very hard at not hating *him* for being that way.

Knowing she could do nothing about her father's behavior or attitudes, Mary focused on the good in her life. She was grateful that, for all their differences, her father was allowing her and her daughter safety and security in this house. She was grateful to have Adrienne in her life, and as time passed farther beyond the death of little Isabelle, she felt a deep sense of gratitude that was difficult to define. She knew little about religion beyond what her mother had taught her, but she knew her mother believed that God's hand was in the lives of His children. Mary found comfort now in a vague belief that God had known Isabelle's life would be brief, and that's why He'd led Mary and Simon to adopt twins, so that Mary wouldn't be left alone. Such a belief could not take away her aching and emptiness over Isabelle's loss, but every day she found a reason to live and a reason to count her blessings due to the very presence of her beautiful Adrienne.

# Chapter Three

WHIT HAD BEEN EMPLOYED IN the Cranford household for nearly two months when he reached a day that forced him to face the facts of how this job had changed his life. Over breakfast his mother kept smiling at him with a suspicious twinkle in her eye.

"What?" he finally asked with a chuckle.

"You like your new job very much," she said.

"I do," he said in Spanish. For all the years his mother had lived in the United States, she still struggled with English and mostly chose to avoid even trying to speak it. "It's the best job I've ever had."

"I know you enjoy that kind of work," Ida said, "and I know you prefer working alone. But I wonder if it's the little girl you've fallen in love with, or her mother."

"What?" he asked again, pretending to be utterly astonished.

His mother just smiled. "I've never seen you like this before. Sometimes I've wondered if it would ever happen, but you're practically glowing."

"Am I?" he asked, not seeing any point at pretenses. He couldn't deny that what she'd said was true.

"Why don't you ask her out to dinner or something?" Ida suggested.

"It's . . . complicated," he said.

"How complicated can it be?"

"She's white, she has a rich daddy who's a bigot, and I work for her." He hesitated admitting to the biggest complication of all, but he and his mother had never had secrets from each other. "And she's older than me."

"I'm older than your father," she said as if he didn't know.

"Not *this much* older," he said. "I'm afraid she'll think I'm just a silly kid."

"Do you have some reason to believe she would think that way?"

"I have no idea what she thinks," he said.

"You haven't talked to her?"

"We talk about the garden mostly, what little we talk at all. We talk about her daughter. I wouldn't know how to begin to tell a woman like that how I feel about her."

"A woman like that?"

"She's . . . amazing." He knew he didn't have to expound, because he'd already shared with his mother the many fine attributes of his employer—and her little daughter. The truth was that he'd fallen in love with both of them. Adrienne was a beautiful child and he wanted instinctively to look after her and to fill the emptiness her father had left behind. But he had no business assuming that such an option would ever be a possibility. There were so many reasons he could think of that a woman like Mary would be wise to have nothing to do with him. He felt sure if she knew the whole truth about him she would promptly end his employment. Considering any romantic interest was simply ludicrous.

Throughout the day, Whit couldn't help contemplating his mother's words and her insight. She was frequently having moments of senility and he felt concerned for her on a regular basis, but this morning at breakfast she'd been perfectly lucid, and she'd hit the nail right on the head. He just didn't know what to do about it. He caught a glimpse of Mary on the patio with Adrienne. She was wearing a floral-print skirt and a lightweight sweater and sandals, sitting in the sun with a wide-brimmed hat shading her face. She looked like something out of a fifties movie, perfectly feminine and picturesque. The woman had a great deal of class! The contrast of her blonde hair and fair skin to those of her daughter was fascinating. Mary was a good mother. He could see it all the way across the yard, and he enjoyed every opportunity he had to interact with them. Tuna fish or peanut butter and jelly had never tasted so good as it did when sharing sandwiches with Mary and Adrienne. But it all felt like a fantasy that was destined to erode away in the face of practicality and wisdom.

When Mary brought him a cold drink, as she did occasionally, he had trouble keeping himself from staring at her. But something about his mother's questions at the breakfast table made him more prone to just stare rather than trying to avoid getting caught looking at her. He almost wanted her to question him. In fact he *did* want her to do just that. She met his eyes in a way that had happened many times, but he was purposely more bold in his gaze and felt gratified by the way she visibly blushed before she turned away. His heart quickened at the realization that he'd been so concerned about suppressing his own feelings that he hadn't bothered to notice that she was attracted to him too. He watched her walk away after a few minutes of conversation, secretly thrilled at the thought that eventually they were going to have to acknowledge these feelings. Whatever might happen beyond that was impossible to know, but he was willing to take it one step at a time. Just knowing there was even the slightest possibility of his association with Mary broadening into something larger made him almost giddy.

* * * * *

Mary was in the kitchen cleaning up the lunch mess while Janel was rinsing dishes to go into the dishwasher. The phone rang, and Janel reached for it according to her habit, and answered as she always did, "Cranford home." Her expression immediately became panicked, and she quickly added, "Wait. Wait. Hold on. I can't . . ." Janel then held the phone out toward Mary. "I have no idea who it is. She's speaking Spanish, but I know she said something about Whit."

Mary snatched the phone, overcome with her own panic. She hurried to say in Spanish, "This is Mary Cranford. Tell me what's wrong." A moment later she had to say, "Slow down," when the woman on the other end of the phone was speaking in such a frenzy. Mary was finally able to conclude that this was Whit's mother, and she was having some kind of pain that was making her afraid but she couldn't get hold of Whit; he wasn't answering his cell phone. While Mrs. Eden repeated the same information again, Mary asked Janel quietly, "Do you know where Whit is?"

"Doctor appointment, I think; something like that."

Mary then coaxed Mrs. Eden to answer some very specific questions that would help her determine if this was a 911 emergency or something that Mary could deal with herself. Once she felt confident that Whit's mother might need a doctor but it wasn't an emergency, Mary told her that she would come over and stay with her until Whit was finished with his appointment. Mrs. Eden was immediately calmed down by Mary's promise. The fact that Mary could speak to her in fluent Spanish didn't hurt. Mary asked for the address and wrote it down. She knew the street, and she knew how to get there, and she could have looked up the house number on Whit's employment application, but she needed to hurry. She also wrote down the phone number from the caller ID in case she needed to call en route from her cell phone. Janel was happy to look after Adrienne and to explain why her mother had left in a hurry.

A minute after she hung up the phone, Mary was backing her father's Mercedes out of the garage. It took her nearly twenty minutes to get to the neighborhood she remembered so well from her childhood. In fact, it felt so eerily familiar that it was like stepping back in time. If not for the newer models of cars parked on the streets, she might have believed that absolutely little had changed here in thirty years. The houses were small and close together, and some of them were painted in very bright colors. Overall, the neighborhood looked rundown and crowded and a little scary. She felt some skeptical eyes on her as she drove past porches and yards where small groups of pierced and tattooed Hispanics were gathered. Mary ignored them, said a prayer, and quickly found the right house, not surprised to find that it had the neatest yard on the street, and that it also had the most flowers planted in front of the porch and along the chain-link fence.

Mary parked the car and went through the gate and up to the door. She noticed then that the door and all of the windows had wrought-iron bars over them. She rang the doorbell, wondering if Mrs. Eden would be able to answer the door. If not, what would she do? She obviously wasn't going to be able to break in. She might end up calling 911 anyway. She rang the bell again, then prepared to dial the Edens' phone number from her cell phone, wondering if Whit's mother might answer the phone even if she couldn't get to the door. Before Mary pressed the button to dial the number, she heard multiple locks being undone on the other side of the door. She put the phone in her pocket and met the cautious eyes and worried expression of Mrs. Eden.

"I'm Mary Cranford," she hurried to say in order to soothe her concerns. "Tell me what I can do to help you."

Mrs. Eden opened the door and invited Mary in, but she seemed to want her to come in quickly so she could hurry and close the door and lock it. Mary wondered if her father's car would still be in one piece when she left. Whit's mother was shorter than Mary, and she looked a little too thin. Her hair was completely gray, and she was slightly stooped over, shuffling a bit when she walked. She led Mary to the couch, muttering all the while about how sweet Mary was to come and sit with her, and that it was probably not necessary because she was feeling better now. Mary sat beside her and took her hand, offering assurance that it was no trouble and she was glad to come and meet her. Mary couldn't see any visible resemblance to Whit in this woman, but when she turned to look at pictures on the wall, pictures taken in years gone by, it was readily evident that this was indeed his mother. She was older than Mary had expected, which meant that she must have been on the older side of her childbearing years when she'd had Whit.

By pressing her with specific questions, Mary determined that Mrs. Eden had been feeling some chest pains that had been alarming. She reported that she'd once had a mild heart attack, but she'd also had many of what the doctor called panic attacks that mimicked a heart attack. She admitted that she was prone to anxiety and nervousness, and not being able to reach her son by phone had increased her stress. Once Mrs. Eden started talking, Mary found it easy to get information from her. She tended to worry excessively, but she hinted at a history of violence that seemed to make her concerns warranted. Mary couldn't tell if she meant violence in the neighborhood, or specifically in her family. Perhaps both. She wondered what that meant about Whit.

The house phone rang, and Mrs. Eden got up to answer it. Mary could hear her saying that everything was all right now and there was no need to worry. It was likely Whit. But Mary didn't hear his mother saying anything about her being there, and she wondered if it might be best to leave before he came back. Mrs. Eden returned to the couch and began talking in a way that made it difficult for Mary to make any attempt at an exit. She seemed to enjoy having someone to visit with who spoke her native language. She admitted that she knew a little English but she wasn't very good at it, since her friends and family and the people she went to church with all spoke Spanish.

Mary noticed then the evidence of what Whit had told her when they'd first met. It was obvious from the framed picture of the Sacred Grove, and another framed picture of the temple in Salt Lake City. Mary commented on them, and Mrs. Eden said that Whit had told her about Mary's mother being a Mormon, and that Mary had been raised on good teachings, as she put it.

"You should come to church with us sometime soon," Mrs. Eden said.

Mary had to admit, "That sounds lovely. I would like that very much. Perhaps we can—"

She stopped when the sound of a key turning in a lock could be heard from the direction of the kitchen, which Mary assumed was a back door. Mrs. Eden said that Whit was home; only he had keys to the door.

Half a minute later Whit came into the room, his eyes focused on Mary. He didn't even acknowledge his mother. "What *are* you doing here?" he demanded, showing an angry side that she'd never seen before. "Are you out of your mind?"

"Your mother couldn't get hold of you and—"

His mother broke into the conversation, frantically telling her son that it was her fault that Mary had come and he shouldn't be angry with Mary. Mrs. Eden actually started to cry, as if it had just occurred to her that she might have put Mary in danger. Mary tried to assure her that there was nothing to worry about, but she wouldn't be convinced. She turned to Whit for help, but he only said—in English, so his mother wouldn't understand—"She's right, you know. Did you see those packs of wolves you drove past, looking at you as if you're a stray rabbit?" She knew it must have been a constant element in the neighborhood for him to have pegged it so accurately. "They don't just act that way for show, Mary. They're serious. They'll do whatever they have to—or want to—in order to make a buck or catch a thrill. And you drive down the street in a *Mercedes*." Mary realized she was sufficiently frightened even before he added, "Now you go get back in that car and leave! Make sure you're not being following until you know you're very far away from here. Do you understand?" She hesitated a moment, and he added, "No, I'm following you out. Come on." He grabbed his keys and grabbed her arm with the other hand, saying to his mother in Spanish that she needed to lock the door behind him and he'd be back soon. Mary barely had a chance to say a hurried good-bye to Mrs. Eden as she was dragged out the door.

"Don't look at anything or anyone," he said. "Just get in the car and drive. I'll be right behind you."

"Okay," was all Mary said and followed his instructions. She drove randomly for about ten minutes, seeing Whit close behind her in the rearview mirror. Her heart was still pounding when she pulled into the empty parking lot of a mortuary and Whit pulled in behind her, apparently confident that they hadn't been followed.

Whit turned off his truck but left the keys in the ignition. He gripped the steering wheel and hung his head, attempting to steady his breathing before he had any further interaction with Mary. He didn't want her to know what she'd triggered inside of him, and he certainly didn't want her to know how much danger she'd really been in. But he also wanted her to understand why he'd gotten so angry. He reminded himself that her intentions had been completely charitable. He sat up straight and took a deep breath, then was startled when she opened the passenger door of his truck and got in. She looked straight ahead and put her hands in her lap. He noticed they were shaking.

"I need you to tell me what just happened," she said, "and I need you to be honest with me."

Whit sighed and pushed the button to lock the doors. "First of all," he said, "I want to thank you for helping my mother. You're a good woman, Mary. I'm not angry with you. I was just . . ."

"Scared?"

"Yeah," he admitted readily, then noticed her hands were still shaking. "Are you all right?"

"I'm fine," she said. "Apparently you don't think I would have been without your intervention."

"Not likely," he said. "You were being watched. A car was waiting to follow you, but pulled back when they saw me."

"What would they have done?" she asked. Now her voice was trembling.

"I don't know," he said. "Bottom line? This neighborhood is smack in the middle of the territory of a Chicano gang. They hate whites. They hate the rich. Officially what they do is called hate crime. Theft, rape, assault, vandalism, sometimes murder. The more they can get away with, the more they have to brag about, and the more power they hold over other gangs in the city. Every time I leave the neighborhood, *especially* when I'm going to work, I have to absolutely make sure I'm not being followed, because I don't want to bring any trouble to your door."

Mary took a moment to digest what Whit had just told her and made a valiant attempt to maintain her dignity. She'd never been this scared in her life; not even when she'd been in undesirable places in Mexico. A thought occurred to her and she said, "But you're half white."

"Which is *exactly* the reason my father was shot down in the street when I was eleven."

"What?" Mary gasped, and Whit looked the other way, wishing he hadn't let it slip out, or that he might have at least delivered it more tactfully. "Why do you stay there? Isn't your mother in danger? Don't you—"

"My mother refuses to move. She's lived in that house too long. She has family in the neighborhood. It's home to her. It's comfortable. Believe me, I've tried."

"They don't mess with you," she stated.

"No, they don't mess with me."

"Why?" she asked.

"Is this conversation going to put my job in jeopardy?"

"Of course not!" she insisted. "I'm just . . . trying to understand."

Whit sighed. "I suppose this was bound to come up eventually, but I would have preferred to avoid it." As soon as he said it, he realized how ridiculous it was to think that he *could* have avoided it if he truly hoped to have any kind of relationship with her. Or perhaps it was most ridiculous that he'd even considered that he could have *any* kind of relationship with her, given the truth about who he was—and what he'd been.

"Just tell me."

Whit drew a hesitant sigh before he lifted one shirtsleeve, then the other, revealing the hideous tattoos that labeled him as permanent property of the gang he'd been fighting for more than a decade to leave behind. Mary inhaled sharply, then glanced at the burn on his lower arm. "The scar?"

"Yeah, I burned that one off. It was the only one I couldn't hide with a short-sleeved shirt. I couldn't very well go on a mission to a warm climate with *that* on my arm."

"*You* burned it off."

"Kids like me don't get plastic surgery."

"So . . . you . . . belonged to this gang and then . . . went on a mission. You didn't tell me you'd gone on a mission."

"Didn't I?" he asked. "I guess I'm used to most people not knowing what that means. Yeah, ironically I served in Mexico."

"Really?" she said as if that was something she would love to talk to him about. He would love to talk to *her* about that, but now wasn't the time.

"Some other time," he said, wanting to get the present conversation over with and out of the way. "I *still* belong to the gang . . . officially speaking . . . in a strange kind of way. I'm sort of . . . emeritus status. I was punished pretty badly when I burned off the tattoo and declared my intentions."

"Punished?"

"A few broken bones. Lots of stitches."

Mary gasped again and put a hand to her stomach, wishing she could calm her growing nausea.

"But I held my ground, and eventually I made it clear that I could live and let live. We have a kind of grudging respect. They know if they give me or my mother any grief, I know way too many of their dirty secrets. As for a random white woman showing up in the neighborhood, that's not part of the deal." He took a deep breath, rubbed his forehead, and added, "I'm sorry, Mary."

"Sorry? Why?"

"Sorry that . . . you have to know all of that. Sorry that you got involved. I'm sorry if my working for you has caused you any grief, and if you want to let me go I understand, and I won't be—"

"I'm fine now, right? It's over, right?"

"Yes," he said firmly.

"Then it's over. This has nothing to do with your job, or . . . anything else."

"Anything else?" he asked cautiously.

She looked away. "We're friends, aren't we?"

"I hope so," he said. "At the very least." Whit wanted to clarify exactly how he felt about being *friends*, but given the information he'd just spilled in her lap, he figured it was just about the worst time to try to declare his attraction to her. He knew that his feelings had contributed to the depth of his anger when he'd realized the situation she'd gotten herself into. He also had to admit that he admired her and respected her more now than he had earlier today. Her efforts on his mother's behalf meant a great deal to him—even if it had been a foolish move. And she wasn't exhibiting any judgment or anger toward him over what he'd just confessed about his life. If she did, that would likely be the end of any hopes he might have in getting to know her a whole lot better than he knew her now.

"Thank you again," he said.

"For what?"

"For being so kind to my mother. I . . ." His cell phone rang. He glanced at it and smiled slightly. "She must have known I was talking about her."

"Or she's worried because you said you'd be right back," Mary pointed out.

"So I did," he said and answered the phone, immediately assuring his mother that he was fine and he would be home in a while. Since Mary spoke fluent Spanish, she could understand everything he said, and it was evident his mother felt terrible over what had happened and he was trying to soothe her. He glanced at his watch and told her to turn on the television because one of her favorite programs would start soon. When he hung up the phone, he turned to Mary and said, "I was going to tell you that my mother is showing signs of dementia. Her heart problems are minor. Her anxiety can be a big problem sometimes. I can usually be available by phone and calm her down, but it's impossible to answer the phone when a dentist has his hands in your mouth."

"Cavities?" she asked.

"Not anymore," he said.

Their eyes met, and he knew he was staring, but then she was staring right back. He really wanted to kiss her. It wasn't the first time he'd been tempted, and it was likely far from the last time he would talk himself out of it.

"I guess I should . . . get home," she said.

"Are you sure you're all right?" he asked, putting his hand over hers. He was glad for an excuse to do so. "You're not shaking as badly, but you're still shaking."

"I'll be fine," she said. "Thank you . . . for being there. I shudder to think . . ." She didn't finish that sentence, and he was relieved.

"I'm going to follow you home," he said.

"There's no need for you to do—"

"I'm going to follow you home," he repeated. He knew she wasn't in any danger, but he would feel better just to see her pull into her own yard, with its gate and high fences.

Whit followed Mary home and breathed more easily after he'd seen her father's Mercedes go through the gate and watched the doors close behind her again. He drove home and had supper with his mother, who couldn't stop fussing over her guilt about putting Mary in a bad situation. Whit listened and tried to be patient, hoping that it might be one of the things she would quickly forget.

That night Whit had trouble sleeping. He couldn't stop thinking about all of the possibilities of what might have happened to Mary if she'd left this neighborhood without him watching out for her, followed by vultures with nothing but evil in their intentions. He'd long ago stopped judging the lost boys of his neighborhood and the unspeakable crimes they committed. They had never known any other way, which didn't make it right, and he knew that they would have to face the consequences for their actions sooner or later, one way or another. Still, it wasn't for him to judge. That was God's place; no one else's. All he could do was protect himself and the people he cared about. And if he hadn't come home when he had and Mary had left the house unescorted, it could have been disastrous in so many ways.

Sometime between three and four in the morning, he determined that he would be a fool to think that their worlds could ever connect without bringing things into her life that she didn't deserve to have there. Tears actually crept from the corners of his eyes and trickled into the hair at his temples as he considered the fact that he needed to let go. It was the most humane thing he could possibly do.

Whit's resolve about letting go completely vanished the following day when he saw Mary from a distance across the yard soon after he'd arrived. Later in the day he had the chance to talk with her privately for just a minute. He asked if she was all right, and she assured him that she was. He couldn't keep from staring at her for a long moment, but it was readily evident that she had the same problem.

The next day was Saturday, but Whit enjoyed his weekends less since he'd been working for Mary. He helped his mother with some extra cleaning, as he often did on Saturdays. And he mowed the lawn and pulled weeds in the yard, his mind always on Mary. The following day wasn't fast Sunday, but he fasted anyway, feeling the need for some extra guidance as to whether it was right to pursue his feelings for Mary. He wanted to do what was right and best for everyone, and since Mary had only gotten a little glimpse of the true reality of his past life, he couldn't count on her to have the proper perspective on whether or not it was right to bring her life closer to such things. As much as he'd done his best to leave it behind and separate himself from his past, he had relatives who were actively involved in gang activities, and his mother still lived in that neighborhood. His tattoos and the burn on his arm were constant reminders that for all his efforts to repent and forgive and put the past away, the consequences would always be with him. However, if he had the confidence of knowing that God was behind him in these feelings, and that pursuing Mary was a righteous endeavor, he could move forward and trust that God's hand would be in their lives, and they would be protected and guided.

By Sunday evening Whit felt a calm peacefulness in acknowledging how he felt about Mary and an assurance that he needed to move forward in exploring those feelings. That wasn't to say that he knew whether she was the right woman for him to settle down with completely, but he knew that for now he had to at least get to know her well enough to figure out if it was a possibility.

Whit woke up Monday morning eager to see Mary, thinking he might be so bold as to ask her out on a date. His mother had a bad morning, and it took him longer than usual to make certain she had what she needed and to know that she was calm and settled. She kept muttering about strange noises outside in the night, and he had to accept that her dementia was worsening. He assured her that they lived in a rough neighborhood and there were always strange noises in the night. He suggested over breakfast that perhaps they should move. His hope was that if her memory started failing her, she might forget why she was so determined to remain in this pathetic little house in this poor excuse for a neighborhood. Neighborhood? According to Jesus' description of a neighbor, this was a sorry place to live. But they lived in sorry times that were getting sorrier, and there was nothing he could do about it.

Whit finally left the house, locking the door behind him, glad that Mary was flexible with his work hours. He didn't want a late arrival to make him look bad, especially when it meant so much to him to be responsible and respectable. If he couldn't be responsible and respectable, who was he? And even if he weren't trying to impress her on a personal level, he needed to be firm in his character. It was who he needed to be!

Whit stopped at the edge of the driveway when he saw that the windshield of his truck had been smashed dead center with a heavy object, probably a baseball bat. He just stood there for a full minute, willing his temper to be calmed, and reminding himself of what was *truly* important in life. Any time or energy he wasted on being upset or thinking he might somehow retaliate was simply fruitless or more likely to cause problems. He turned around and went back into the house, locking the door behind him. He had no choice but to tell his mother what had happened, and naturally she became upset again—so much so that he had to devote several minutes to just getting her to lie down and breathe deeply so that she wouldn't catapult herself into a panic attack. With his mother resting, he called Mary's cell phone, hoping to just get voicemail so he could leave a message and tell her he'd be a little late, but she answered and he had to talk to her. Too late, the thought occurred to him that he should have texted her.

"Is everything all right?" she asked.

"Yeah," he said. "Yeah, everything's fine. I just . . . my truck needs a repair and I've got to take it in to get it fixed. It's . . . drivable, but barely. I'll get there as soon as I can get a ride, and—"

"Would you like me to come and get you . . . meet you . . . somewhere?"

She asked the question eagerly, but he recognized her correction in *meeting* him somewhere as a recollection that she couldn't drive into his neighborhood. Only then did it occur to Whit that getting a ride to work might be difficult. There were people he went to church with who would be glad to do it, but getting hold of the ones he felt comfortable with wouldn't necessarily be easy. There was no relative or neighbor that he would dare give even a hint of where he worked.

"Um . . ." he said to give himself another few seconds to think. "I . . . hadn't gotten to figuring that part out yet," he added truthfully to give himself a few more seconds. "I don't want to put you out or—"

"I'd be glad to," she said even more eagerly. Given his feelings for her, and what he suspected she was feeling about *him*, he couldn't dispute that he would have done exactly the same thing if the situation were reversed.

"Are you sure?" he asked, reminding himself not to be too proud to accept her help. Besides, it would give them some time together—and maybe an excuse to take her out to dinner as repayment for her kindness.

"Yes, yes. Of course."

"Okay, well . . . I've got to make some calls and see where I can take the truck. I'll give you a call when I know where and when I can meet you. How's that? And I'll make up the hours. I promise."

"I'm not worried about the hours. You probably have many extra hours already stored up if you were really keeping track in any fairness to yourself."

"I don't know about that," he said, and there was a long pause of awkwardness.

"So . . . call me and I'll come and get you."

"Talk to you in a while," he said. "Thank you."

Whit had to steady his breathing after he hung up the phone. The reality quickly settled in. How would she feel to know what exactly was wrong with his truck—and why? He had to be crazy to think that asking her out on a date was a good idea. Didn't he?

Whit focused on the problem at hand and made some phone calls. The insurance would cover the *vandalism* damage with a minimal deductible. He'd purposely gotten good insurance for this very reason. It was one of many reasons it cost him more to live in this neighborhood, even though the house was paid for and the utilities were low. He found a glass repair place that would be able to replace the windshield that day, since they had the right make and model on hand. He called Mary and gave her the address and an approximate time when he would be ready. He then made certain his mother was all right and went back out to his truck, wondering if the broken windshield had anything to do with his escorting Mary out of the neighborhood the previous week. He only had to wonder for a moment to know the answer. Of *course* it did. There was always payback. Always some kind of hypersensitive radar out there, looking for any and every reason to commit a violent act. Since no reason at all could be reason enough, he knew there was a connection.

Whit was glad for safety glass, which meant there wasn't actually any broken glass to clean up that had come loose from the windshield. And he was glad that he could see well enough to drive safely to his destination to have it repaired. He spoke with a guy at the counter, gave him all the pertinent information, and handed over the key before he walked outside to see Mary sitting there in her father's Mercedes, wearing sunglasses and looking as gorgeous as ever. He got into the car, and his terrible day melted away when she smiled.

"Everything okay?" she asked.

"Yeah. I really appreciate your coming to pick me up."

"No problem," she said and backed out of the parking place. "Glass?" she asked. "A problem with a window or—"

"The windshield," he said and saw her expression register suspicion as she pulled out onto the highway. It didn't take a rocket scientist to figure out that a rock chip or a crack would not make the vehicle *barely drivable.* He decided to just go for honesty and get it over with. "Vandalism," he said, hoping to keep it simple. "Probably a baseball bat."

He was hoping she would just take it at that, but he knew the wheels of her mind were turning, and he wasn't surprised when she asked, "Does it have something to do with what happened last week? With my coming to your home and—"

"I don't know," he answered. Even though he strongly suspected that the two incidents were related, he could honestly say he didn't *know.*

"Is that kind of stuff . . . common . . . in your neighborhood?"

"Yeah, it is," he said, able to be completely honest with the added incentive of making it clear to her that she should never go back there again—for any reason, ever! "Let's talk about something else. How's the lovely Adrienne this morning?"

"She's great," Mary said. "In fact, I've felt a shift in her grief over losing her father and sister. She seems more at peace over it. I can't explain why or how, really. I just feel it. She's completely stopped having bad dreams, and she's not nearly so clingy or sad."

"I think you've guided her very well through all of this."

"You really think so?"

"I really do," he said, and they spent the rest of the short drive talking about the adorable things that Adrienne did. She'd become one of Whit's favorite people, and therefore one of his favorite topics of conversation. And it was a topic that made Mary smile. He loved it when Mary smiled.

# Chapter Four

IN THE MIDDLE OF THE afternoon, Mary went into the garden, noticing signs of improvement even though it still looked rather bland. She had no trouble finding Whit. She just had to follow the sound of the shrubbery trimmer—and the long cord attached to it. When she *did* find him, she almost felt ashamed of herself for the way she just stood there and admired him for a good minute or more while he was unaware of her presence, mostly due to the noise. It occurred to her as it had earlier that he made her feel like she was in high school again, smitten with a crush on the cutest boy in a boring class where there was nothing better to do than just look at him and try to not get caught. The difference was that he was way too young for her—or she was way too old for him. It amounted to the same thing.

Once again, she was convinced that any normal woman recently widowed would not feel this way about a younger man. Or *any* man, for that matter. But then, she'd been emotionally separated from her husband long before his death. In fact, she would probably guess that the emotional separation began sometime during the honeymoon. So she was a love-starved widow with a handsome gardener that she found attractive. Standing there in the garden would be no different than going to see a movie just because it had Hugh Jackman or Alex O'Loughlin in it. Except that this man was actually standing here in her garden, and when she moved just a little he caught sight of her in his peripheral vision. He turned off the noisy machine, put his safety glasses up on his head, and smiled at her. The combination of his smile and a certain sparkle in his eyes made her stomach flutter, but she ignored it and stuck to her purpose.

"You thirsty?" she asked, holding out a cold bottle of water.

"Thank you," he said and took it, removing a glove so he could twist off the cap. After swallowing about half of the larger-than-average bottle, he said, "You came all the way out here to give me a drink? You're very kind when you do that, but I know where the water is if I need it. Not that I'm complaining," he hurried to add along with another smile, "but . . . your behavior is suspicious."

"Is it?" she asked, looking at the ground, hoping that didn't mean he suspected that she felt attracted to him. The very idea mortified her! "Actually," she drawled and looked at him again, "I just . . . I've been thinking about what happened the other day, and . . . more specifically, I've been thinking about what you told me."

"And now you've decided I should find another job?" he asked, not entirely serious. But his eyes told her that he did have at least a little concern that she might let him go.

"Not at all," she said. "On the contrary, I want you to know that I admire your courage in making such dramatic changes in your life."

"Really?" he said and chuckled.

"Is that . . . a problem?"

"No. I just . . . uh . . . no one's ever told me that before. It seems more like no matter what good choices I've made, the bad ones will forever haunt me."

"I would think that eventually the good will keep getting stronger and diminish the past."

"That's a nice thought, Mary. I hope you're right."

"I also wanted to say that . . . I'm sorry about your father. I can't imagine how horrible that must have been for you."

"Yeah." He looked down and cleared his throat. "Unfortunately it's the kind of thing that can make a kid turn to violence . . . especially when it's everywhere he turns."

"You saw it happen?"

"I did," he said and cleared his throat again before he looked up. "But that was a long time ago."

"It probably doesn't seem so long."

"No, it really doesn't," he said.

"And it happened because he was white?"

"That was the word on the streets."

"Why did your parents live in that neighborhood if interracial marriage was an issue?" She laughed with tension. "I'm sorry. You don't have to answer that. I'm probably being far too nosy."

"You can ask me anything you want. We're friends, right?"

"Right," Mary said.

"My mother's sisters both lived in that neighborhood; one of them still does. It meant a lot to my mother, since she was never really comfortable away from her home in Mexico. My father was always patient with the harassment he got, and over time it died down and people respected him. But obviously *someone* didn't like it. On the other hand, there could have been a number of possible reasons."

"Like what?" she asked.

"There's no reasoning to the violence, Mary. Someone looks at you wrong, or takes your parking spot, or it's Tuesday, or it's raining."

"That's horrible!"

"It is," he said, "but it's a battle that will rage until the Millennium. It's too deeply ingrained to reverse it."

"You reversed it in yourself."

"I can control my own actions. I can't do anything to stop the machine."

Awkward silence made them both aware that they were surreptitiously glancing at each other, then they both chuckled awkwardly and glanced away. Whit hoped he wouldn't increase the awkwardness when he said, "Can I ask you something?"

"Sure," she said with an eagerness that hinted at validating his suspicions. He'd been so preoccupied with his attraction to her that it hadn't even occurred to him until she'd given him a ride earlier that she didn't exude the aura of a recent widow. She'd told him the day they'd met that it hadn't been long since her husband had been killed, along with her daughter. In their bits and pieces of conversation, he had heard a great deal about the grief she'd been dealing with in regard to her daughter's death—Adrienne's twin sister. But he hadn't heard a word about the difficulty of losing her husband; on the contrary, she reflected an attitude that would never imply that she might be grieving over losing the man she'd loved.

He prided himself on having good instincts about people, but he'd never once connected the fact that she'd recently lost a husband to the fact that she was romantically fascinated with him. If she had been putting off vibes that she was grieving for someone she deeply loved, he would have sensed it and he would have respected that completely. But now he realized that what he'd felt from her had been contrary to that. And he couldn't help being curious over the reasons. He *suspected* the reasons, but he needed to hear it from her. He couldn't be sure if she had any suspicions over his interest in her, but he couldn't move forward without knowing exactly where she stood in regard to her deceased husband. If he'd been reading her wrong, he needed to know. It didn't change how he felt or what he knew was the right course for him; he just might have to be more patient.

"Ask away," she said while he was trying to gather his thoughts.

"If I'm being intrusive just say so. Maybe it's too personal, but . . . I can't help wondering."

"You'll never know if it's too personal unless you ask."

"Okay," he said and set the trimmer aside, folding his arms over his chest. "You've talked a lot about how difficult it's been to lose your daughter—and how difficult it's been for Adrienne to lose her sister *and* her father. But I've never once heard you say anything about how losing your husband has affected *you.*"

Mary looked down, caught off guard. She didn't know what she'd believed he was going to ask, but it wasn't that. They'd become comfortable in their brief little chats. But that was it: their chats had been brief and little. She'd been very open about Adrienne's grief, and about her own feelings in losing her little girl. It was only natural that he would wonder about her absence of grief over her husband. She just hadn't expected him to bring it up in such a straightforward way. But then, they had established a pattern of being straightforward with each other, so why not about this? She cleared her throat and looked up at him. She had no problem telling him the truth. Even if he thought less of her, anything short of the truth would serve no purpose.

"I'm not trying to keep any great secrets," she said. "I'm surprised it hasn't come up before." She sighed and folded her arms much the same way he had a minute earlier. "The truth is that Simon and I hadn't really shared much of a marriage for . . . well . . . I'm not sure we ever did. We were completely emotionally separated for a very long time. We worked together to take care of the girls. Beyond that our lives were very separate, and to tell the truth . . . I had stopped being comfortable around him years ago. It always took patience to even be in the same room. I've struggled most with feeling guilty over the fact that I don't feel any grief. I feel badly about Adrienne having to lose her father and about him losing his life. Beyond that . . ." She let the thought fade, knowing she'd already explained sufficiently.

"Why didn't you divorce him if it was that bad?" he asked with more concern than curiosity.

"I've wondered about that," she said, "but . . . we were always committed to the same causes, always involved in the same charitable organizations. And then there were the girls. I'd always hoped that children would bring us closer together. All it did was give us another common cause. There wasn't anything *bad* in the marriage. He was decent and respectful. He didn't cheat on me or abuse me. He wasn't even unkind. Well . . . perhaps in a passive kind of way. I felt completely invisible. That always felt like some form of unkindness, but I could never quite define it." She chuckled tensely and looked at the ground. "Now, I'm probably getting way too personal."

"If I hadn't wanted a personal answer, I wouldn't have asked a personal question."

"Why?" she asked, looking at him.

"Why what?"

"Why are you asking personal questions?"

Whit hesitated, wondering if this should be the moment to express the truth of his feelings—or at least offer a big hint at them. But he held back, feeling that minimal information was best for the moment. "I just want to know more about you," he said.

"You're very kind to me, Whit Eden."

"That's very easy," he said. "I actually think it's more the other way around."

"That's very easy too," she said and added, "I should . . . get back . . . to Adrienne. If you ever . . . need anything . . ."

"I know where to find you," he said and watched her walk away. The part of him that had been concerned that she was simply keeping her grief very private felt relieved to know that he was not competing with her dead husband for her affection; nor was he intruding into a tender territory. Now, he just had to hope that she might reciprocate some degree of what he was feeling.

At the end of Whit's workday, Mary drove him back to where he'd left his truck. He made a call on his cell phone while they were en route and was assured that the vehicle was ready to go, with a new windshield in place. After he got off the phone, he said, "I'm sorry if I got too personal earlier."

"You didn't," she said and actually smiled at him. He loved it when she smiled. "I just hope you don't think badly of me to admit that I don't miss my husband—even a little."

"I would say your feelings are a consequence of the way he treated you."

"I believe that," she said, and he was surprised when she added, "I really tried. As long as we're getting personal, I want you to know that I really tried to be a good wife. I'm not sure at what point I gave up. The sad thing is that he didn't even notice that I *had* given up."

"I'm sorry," he said and hoped she knew he meant it.

"You're very sweet," she said and smiled again just as she pulled into the parking lot where she'd picked him up earlier. "Is there anything else I can do for you?" she asked.

"No, thank you. I'm good. It's very kind of you to give me a ride." He opened the door and got out, then he leaned down to say, "Have a good evening."

"You too," she said, and he closed the door.

\* \* \* \* \*

That night Mary had more trouble sleeping than usual. She kept rewinding her encounters with Whit and wondering what—if anything—her obvious preoccupation might mean. She felt a continual battle in her mind as she bounced back and forth from her right brain to her left. The logical part of her that had deducted firmly there was nothing to even justify the energy of thinking about him completely contradicted the emotional part that was undeniably drawn to him. And no amount of trying to put her logic in the driver's seat could eradicate the feelings.

Whit's questions about her marriage also spun around in her head, making her think of Simon more than she had in a long time. Her mind went to one of the visits she and Simon had made to Los Angeles to stay with her parents for a few days. Such visits had happened far too rarely in her opinion, and yet they'd always seemed such a burden to Simon. Coming up with the money to travel to LA wasn't always easy, but a couple of times Walter had actually purchased plane tickets for them so they could be home for Christmas or Thanksgiving. Holidays had meant little to Walter, although Mary could say that he had generally been a little less cranky during holiday celebrations, and therefore some of her most pleasant memories were associated with them.

Loretta was always thrilled to see Mary and was always very kind to Simon, even though she had told Mary privately that she really didn't think he deserved Mary and that she could have done better. Mary had always kept to herself the belief that she'd done a lot better in marriage than her mother had, but now she knew that wasn't saying much.

Mary nestled more comfortably into her bed and found herself more relaxed as she pondered a specific memory of coming through the front door after not having seen her mother in more than a year. Loretta had met her in the hall, laughing with excitement, and the two of them had shared an embrace that felt literally warming to Mary's heart. Loretta had gotten tears in her eyes as she'd surveyed Mary and told her how beautiful she looked and that seeing her was the highlight of her life.

It was typical during such visits that Simon would spend a lot of time in front of the television or reading; he would occasionally chat with Walter if they could find some tiny bit of common ground on which to base polite conversation. Mary hovered almost constantly with her mother, either in the kitchen while they were cooking together, or walking through the garden for a lazy chat, or holed up in her mother's special room for deep conversations. Mary treasured these  memories, and she loved the way that those memories of her mother now warmed her as much as sharing an embrace had warmed her years ago.

Then Mary's mind wandered to a situation in which her father and Simon were discussing something about discrimination laws in regard to regulations Walter's company had to meet in their hiring. Of course, her father didn't hold back on his bigoted opinions, but what had astonished Mary was how Simon was boldly agreeing with him to the point where he was actually lying about his own personal convictions. She had felt queasy to realize that her husband had so little backbone or integrity that he would talk like that just to please his father-in-law. She'd brought it up to Simon later, and told him that she could understand the need to be somewhat passive in a conversation in order to avoid an argument, but his lies had been aggressively dishonest. Simon had accused Mary of making a big deal out of nothing, but as years had passed, she had seen more and more evidence of his lack of integrity, and it had bothered her deeply. Ironically, Walter had probably sensed the same thing. She knew he had no respect for Simon, and even if they'd argued over something, Walter would have at least had some admiration for a man who stood up for his own opinions.

When one negative thought of Simon led to another and another, Mary had to roll over abruptly in bed and shake her head before she settled it back onto the pillow, as if doing so might make the thoughts go away. She blew out a long, slow breath and thought instead of Whit Eden. She knew for a fact that he was a man of integrity, and she certainly didn't feel invisible around him. Beyond that, she considered her thoughts to be a silly crush. But they made her smile, and she was finally able to drift off to sleep sometime after two.

Mary was awakened around four when sounds on the monitor in her room alerted her to being needed by her father. He was having an unusually difficult time breathing and felt afraid. On such rare occasions when he genuinely needed her and felt extremely vulnerable, he was actually cooperative and not so difficult to be around. She wouldn't go so far as to say that he was kind to her, but he wasn't nearly so grumpy. She turned up his oxygen, gave him a dose of the recommended medication, and sat with him, encouraging him to relax and breathe deeply. He finally went back to sleep, and she returned to her own room after checking on Adrienne, but it was too close to morning now for her to be able to go back to sleep. She read for a while instead, then got a jump-start on her day.

Mary was disappointed to learn at breakfast that this was one of the days that Kristi was coming in to do housework. Even though Mary managed to avoid her most of the time, she felt mildly awkward around the younger woman. They simply had nothing in common and had very little to say to each other. On the days when Kristi came in to work, she usually joined them for lunch, and Mary thought it might be a good day to take her daughter out to lunch—for that very reason.

A little after ten, Mary tried to be polite when Kristi came to do a thorough dusting of the common room that bordered the kitchen. Mary and Adrienne were at the dining table working on a craft project, so Mary couldn't avoid Kristi without creating an awkward situation with her daughter. Mary managed to politely respond to Kristi's attempts at making conversation, but she was thinking of excuses that might pave the way for her escape. Mary's disappointment deepened when Kristi seriously began trying to make polite conversation. And she did it in a way that emphasized something that Mary had noticed before. Kristi usually managed to avoid or completely ignore Adrienne—unlike Whit, who always sought out ways to help Adrienne feel included and noticed. Mary's efforts to be polite became increasingly challenging when she felt mostly annoyed by having her time with Adrienne intruded upon by absolutely meaningless chatter.

Mary was already tense when Kristi paused in her dusting to look out the window. Mary didn't notice until Kristi let out a long, almost dramatic sigh and commented, "Whit is certainly very handsome."

"Yes, he is," Mary agreed with forced calm. She could never debate *that*. But she wondered why her most prominent emotion was jealousy. It only took a moment to determine that her jealousy was more a wish to be younger, to have the chance to start over, to have the innocence of falling in love for the first time. She wanted to say that if she was Kristi's age, she would be trying to figure out how to get the handsome gardener to take her out on a date. In fact, it wasn't at all difficult for Mary to imagine that Whit and Kristi could be suited for each other. But she would prefer that he not start dating someone who worked in the same household. She convinced herself it was due to possible complications in regard to their work, but she couldn't avoid being honest enough with herself to know that her reasons were much more personal. Ridiculous, but personal.

"Come along, Adrienne," Mary said and stood up, holding out her hand. "We'll finish this project later. We have some errands to run."

Mary tidied their things enough so they wouldn't be in the way, then she informed Janel that she and Adrienne were going out to lunch, since they had some shopping to do. She was glad to leave the house, and was delighted with Adrienne's excitement over having an outing. They had a wonderful time together, and Mary made certain that she didn't return until Kristi would have left. In fact, she made certain that Kristi's car was no longer parked on the street before she punched the numbers of the gate code into the keypad. As she drove in, the gates closed behind her and the garage door opened so she could ease the car inside.

Adrienne ran up to her room, anxious to use the inexpensive Barbie accessories they'd purchased while they were out. Once she was alone, Mary almost felt angry with herself for how her thoughts went immediately to Whit—but then she had to acknowledge that her thoughts had been with him throughout most of her outing. She couldn't get him out of her head, and she had to wonder what was wrong with her. She found herself wandering out to the garden in search of him, even while she told herself it was better to avoid any interaction with him that might risk his picking up on her feelings. It took some exploring to find him where he was pulling up a cluster of dead shrubbery. Sweat made his shirt cling to his back, and his hair looked curlier where the sweat from his neck clung to it. Her heart quickened, and she scolded herself for it.

Whit turned when he realized he wasn't alone. He smiled and tossed the dead foliage from his hands before he removed his gloves and wiped sweat from his brow. "Hello," he said.

Mary handed him a bottle of water and wondered what she might say now that she'd gone to so much trouble to find him. He thanked her for the water and drank some at the same time Mary heard herself saying, "Kristi seems like a very nice girl."

Whit choked on the water and coughed. Mary wondered where on earth such a statement had come from, but she added nonchalantly, "Maybe you should ask her out." His silence made Mary glance away from her perusal of the surrounding garden to see *both* his eyebrows arched high, scrunching his forehead into furrows. "What?" she asked.

"Kristi and I have nothing in common," he said and folded his arms over his chest, as if to add an exclamation point to the comment. "She's much too young for me."

Mary hated the way she wished that such a comment meant what she wanted it to mean. She forced the notion away and pointed out, "She's twenty-four. And you're . . . what? Twenty-nine? How is that—"

"She's much too immature," he corrected. "I have no interest in a woman who thinks that a trial in life is having the power go out right when you're trying to blow dry your hair."

Mary snorted a little laugh, and then laughed outright when she realized how unfeminine her snort had sounded. Whit laughed too, and she felt surprisingly comfortable over something that should have been embarrassing. She turned more toward him and asked, "She really said that?"

"She really did," he said. "Went on and on about it . . . as if I had even noticed that her hair looked different than it usually did. Heaven forbid that there might be a trucking strike on hair products and she couldn't get her hands on the right brand of hairspray."

Mary laughed again. "Okay. Point taken. You're right. She's too immature for you." She realized then that whatever she had subconsciously been trying to accomplish in perhaps wanting to draw his attention away from her and more toward someone closer to his own age, she had accomplished the opposite. But it was the way she found him looking at her that made her stomach suddenly lurch into a violent flutter. He'd looked at her that way more times than she could count, but only then did she realize the implication. If Kristi was too young for him, why would he gaze at her with such overt adoration? *He was attracted to her!* Suddenly the whole thing felt ridiculously complicated, and just plain ridiculous.

While she was struggling with what to say, how to handle this, and some form of escape from the moment, Whit put his gloves back on and began tugging at more dead shrubbery. "Now that we have that settled," he said, "you can stop trying to line me up."

"Okay," she managed to spit out.

Whit wished he could tell her what he was really thinking, and how he really felt. But it was too soon, too fragile, too unfamiliar. Still, he watched her closely as he said, "I'm already quite preoccupied with a remarkable woman."

"Really?" Mary asked with polite intrigue in her voice. But the disappointment in her eyes was unmistakable. It made his heart quicken, and he couldn't hold back a smile.

"Have a good afternoon," she said and hurried away.

"You too," he called and smiled. With any luck they could soon get past this game of guessing and pretending. He was hopelessly in love with her, and he was tired of trying to hide the fact.

Mary actually ran once she got past his view, as if she could run from what she'd just realized. Once she was back in the house she checked on Adrienne, then went to her own room where she could be alone with her thoughts. She paced back and forth alongside the bed while she wondered what she had done to bring this on. Had he sensed her attraction to him, in spite of how hard she'd tried to hide it? Had *her* attraction spurred the same in him? Whatever had happened, it had to stop. There was nowhere for this to go, and she knew it. For a minute or two she indulged in how it felt to have such a man attracted to her. She felt giddy and breathless, and she wanted to bask in the sensation for the rest of her life. Then she forced herself to her senses and to the fact that this was a dreadful situation that had to be remedied. The only way to stop what had inadvertently gotten started was to address it with him, clear the air, clarify the practicality of the situation, and move on in a healthy working relationship.

Mary kept talking to herself about what she needed to do all through a sleepless night and into the next day. After breakfast she realized that she needed to get it over with so she could stop stewing about it. She considered it fortunate that Janel had to go grocery shopping and had offered to take Adrienne along. Kristi wasn't working today, and that left Mary alone except for the nurse that was upstairs and on the other side of the house with her father. She wondered if she should go and find Whit and just do what needed to be done. While she was stewing over this dilemma, Whit came in through the patio doors. She looked up from the book she was pretending to read at the dining room table. He held up his hand to show a spot of blood and said, "Just . . . looking for a Band-Aid."

"Oh, is it serious?"

"Not at all," he said. "Just . . . shouldn't mess with rose bushes without my gloves on."

"Just a minute," she said and hurried to get a Band-Aid and some antibiotic ointment. She came back to find him near the kitchen sink, drying his freshly washed hands with paper towels. A small amount of blood was oozing onto the towel as he pressed it there. "Here," she said and put the ointment and Band-Aid on the little wound, much like she would have done for Adrienne.

"Thank you," he said. She looked up to meet his eyes, which were far too close. She took a step back and knew she would never get any better opportunity than this to say what needed to be said. She drew a deep breath for courage to speak before he could leave the room. "I think we need to clear the air about something."

Whit looked mildly surprised. But a more studied glance at his eyes revealed that he wasn't entirely nonplussed. "Okay," he said and leaned against the counter, folding his arms over his chest. She both hated and loved it when he did that. He was completely oblivious to the way the muscles in his arms emphasized his perfect masculinity when he took up such a comfortable stance. His life of manual labor was readily evident, but the very fact that he was utterly clueless over his own startlingly good looks made him all the more attractive. At least it did to her. But that was the very thing they needed to clear the air about. The thought of talking about it made her stomach swarm with nervousness, but it was becoming increasingly difficult to be in the same room with him and not feel a growing tension that she didn't understand. Even now, there was a subtly dazzled light in his eyes that completely threw her off-kilter.

She took a deep breath and got straight to the point. "Why are you looking at me like that?"

"Like what?" he asked while he continued to look at her in the same way.

Mary tried to return his stare until she became unnerved by it and looked away. But she couldn't bring herself to renege on the question. She was growing tired of the strain between them, and of trying to figure out precisely what kind of man he was and what exactly his interest in her might be. She cleared her throat and absently straightened the cloth napkins on the counter in front of her. "I don't know that it's wise to look that way at a woman who is so much older than you."

He cocked one eyebrow up slightly, and the hint of a smile showed at one corner of his mouth. "Exactly what does *so much* older mean?" he asked.

"What?" she countered, having no idea how to answer such a question.

Whit took a moment to assess this opportunity. He'd been praying for days about how he might approach her and get these feelings into the open, but no moment had felt right, and he'd had a complete stupor of thought on what he might say. Now *she* had opened the door, and he felt immeasurably relieved. Now he knew *exactly* what to say. "I would like to make it absolutely clear right here and now that age has no bearing whatsoever on this relationship, and there is no need to discuss it. Ever!"

Mary looked at him then, so astonished at the implication she could hardly breathe, let alone speak. Even in realizing that she held some attraction for him, she knew now that she was entirely unprepared to have him admit to it. After a long minute of sharing a gaze with him that made her heart threaten to beat its way from her chest into the open air, she finally found her voice enough to echo back the one word in his declaration that had left her most stunned. "Relationship?"

"You say it like it's a dirty word," he observed. "And I know you're not the kind of woman to ever let a dirty word pass through your lips."

Mary turned her eyes down and attempted to defend herself. "It's . . . ridiculous. You look at me as if you're a little boy with a crush on a schoolteacher."

"Is that how you see me?" he asked. "As a little boy?"

Mary still couldn't look at him, but her heart quickened at her own silent appraisal of how she *did* see him. "Of course not," she muttered quietly, "but . . ."

"But what?"

"It's sweet, Whit, but it's not . . ."

"Not what?" he demanded when she hesitated, and she heard a hint of anger in his voice that drew her attention back to him.

Mary saw the same hint of anger flash in his eyes, but now that they were actually engaged in this conversation, she was determined to set the record straight and move past this. "It's not practical, Whit. It's not realistic."

"I'm not sure that your perception of what's practical and realistic is the same as mine."

"Which is evidence of a complete lack of compatibility," she insisted.

"Or evidence of a complete lack of communication," he countered, even more insistent.

"Which is exactly why we need to clear the air," she said, realizing even as she said it that clearing the air was not going to be nearly as simple and uncomplicated as she'd expected it to be. What had she believed he would say? That his interest in her had no romantic implications and she should ignore it? Or that he knew he just had a silly crush on her and it would never amount to anything, given their age difference?

"So, clear it," he challenged. "Say what you have to say and get it over with."

Mary wondered *what* to say now that she had the opportunity. This was *not* going the way she'd intended, and she stammered her declaration. "Just because I'm utterly love-starved and you are . . . a very attractive man who has . . . some . . . *bizarre* . . . fascination . . . with older women . . . does not mean that we have . . . *any* solid basis for a . . . *relationship*."

"That was an awfully hard sentence for you to spit out," he observed with disconcerting accuracy. "So, why don't you tell me why this is making you so uncomfortable?" Before she could come up with an answer he asked, "Is it because I'm Hispanic?"

"You know it's not! That's ridiculous."

"Yes, it is. And I know that's not the reason. I just wanted to hear you say it. Is it because I'm a lowly gardener and you have a rich daddy?"

Mary gasped. "That's even *more* ridiculous!"

"Yes, it is. And just so we're clear, I know *that's* not true, either. So, what is it?"

"What do you mean?" she asked, growing increasingly flustered.

"What is it that makes you so uncomfortable?" Again she couldn't answer, and he pressed on with growing vehemence. "You want to clear the air? Let's clear it! This conversation is way overdue. First of all, I do *not* have a bizarre fascination with older women. You make it sound like some kind of psychosis. What I *have* is a very sincere fascination with *you.*"

Mary could hardly breathe. The intensity of his words was echoed by a firm resolution in his eyes that made her realize he had been giving this a great deal of thought—probably long before it had ever occurred to her. Now that his feelings were becoming evident, she hardly knew how to wrap her mind around it.

"And secondly," he went on, "what makes you think that you find me attractive only because you consider yourself utterly love-starved? So, your father never made you feel loved, and your husband didn't either. That doesn't mean *you* have some kind of psychosis. Has it occurred to you that the reason we feel attracted to each other is because we're *supposed* to be? I think you're beautiful, Mary, but I'm not shallow enough to think that your physical beauty alone is what makes it impossible for me to keep myself from thinking about you every waking minute."

Mary gasped aloud, then turned her back to him, hoping to maintain some dignity. She squeezed her eyes closed and put one hand over her quivering stomach, and the other over her pounding heart. She felt more than heard him step closer, and the sensations inside of her increased when he spoke softly behind her ear. "And I know you well enough to know that you're not shallow enough to fall for the gardener because you're looking for some kind of fling with a younger man. Why don't you just admit that it's our age difference that bothers you, and the only thing shallow about this *relationship* is your believing that the years between us make any more difference than our financial status or the color of our skin?" He hesitated, and she heard him sigh loudly. "Look at me, Mary," he insisted gently. She turned around slowly and met his gaze, almost fearing she would hyperventilate. Maintaining the same intensity, he said, "Why don't you just admit that you're falling in love with me the same way I'm falling in love with you? Clear the air, Mary. Admit it!"

When he stopped talking, Mary realized she'd been holding her breath, and her chest began to burn for want of air. She forced herself to breathe, but taking air into her lungs also allowed his words to fully penetrate her clouded brain, stirring a surge of emotion that she hadn't predicted and couldn't hold back. The quiet fierceness in his expression faded into tender compassion when he saw tears spill down her face. She wanted to turn away. She wanted to look anywhere but at him. But she couldn't force herself to break her gaze that was locked onto his any more than she could stop the flow of tears that came from a source far too deep and overpowering for her to consciously control.

She knew he expected her to say something, and she suspected he would stand there and stare at her until she did. Her most prominent thought finally escaped her lips. "How can it be possible?"

"There's only one reason you would ask such a question," he said as if he'd already given it a great deal of thought, as if he'd predicted it with perfect accuracy. "You've spent your whole life seeing yourself through the eyes of a father who can only see you as a failure and a disappointment, and a husband who couldn't see you at all. You can't imagine seeing yourself the way *I* see you. But you'll get used to it."

"Will I?"

"You bet you will!" he said with such determination that she trembled from the inside out.

"How *do* you see me, Whit?" she asked, a part of her wanting to be convinced that he was wrong. The concept he'd just presented felt so entirely foreign to her that she couldn't even imagine it being true, let alone believe it. If he said something to convince her that he had it wrong, she might be disappointed, but somehow more comfortable. The very idea of embracing everything he had just laid out before her felt utterly terrifying—but in a thrilling, supernal kind of way.

"Oh, Mary," he said on a lengthy exhale, as if he'd been holding his breath for weeks, wanting the opportunity to express this very thought. "You are the most remarkable woman I have ever encountered." He paused to take a deep breath, as if he might hyperventilate otherwise. "I've spent weeks trying to convince myself that this is entirely impractical for a number of reasons, but there's nothing that can talk me out of feeling the way I do. You are too amazing, too sincere and genuine, too *beautiful* in so many ways for me to ever find an obstacle daunting enough to keep me from doing everything in my power to make you a part of my life."

The intensity of his words—if not the words themselves—forced a sharp sob out of Mary's throat, but it came out sounding more like a loud hiccup that made her laugh as she frantically wiped her hands over her cheeks in a futile attempt to dry them. She looked up to see that he'd stepped closer, and his gaze had become even more impossible to ignore.

"Have we cleared the air enough, do you think?" he asked.

Mary let out a tense laugh that contradicted her ongoing flow of tears. "This is not how I expected this conversation to turn out."

"I've been waiting a long time to have this conversation," he said, "but I didn't think it would be today."

He helped wipe away her tears, and Mary felt an actual tingling on her face from his touch. "I am a decade older than you," she felt the need to point out again.

"And I'm your lowly gardener who grew up in the ghetto." He took hold of her chin with his fingers and said in a softening voice, "Get over it."

Mary could hardly breathe, given the fact that their noses were almost touching. "As long as we're clearing the air," he said, almost in a whisper, "do you have any idea how long I have wanted to kiss you?"

"How long?" she asked.

"Almost as long as I've known you," he said.

Mary felt deeply comforted by his confession and validated in her own feelings. All her attempts to convince herself that all of this was ridiculous couldn't hold a candle to the unmasked adoration in his eyes just before he closed them and lowered his lips to hers.

# Chapter Five

MARY COMPLETELY LOST HERSELF IN the experience of his kiss in a way that made her question how such a thing could be possible. Whit's kiss was meek and guarded, as a first kiss should be. But she felt something in the connection of their lips that she'd never felt before in four decades of life. The experience of the kiss was enhanced by the way he looked at her when his eyes came slowly open. Not only had she *never* felt such perfect sweetness in a kiss, she'd *never* been looked at like that. It was as if the kiss had had the same effect on him as it had on her. His eyes practically glowed with unmasked adoration, as if she'd just transported him to some celestial sphere and he might fall to his knees and worship her. She reassured herself that she was projecting her own feelings onto him, and yet she couldn't deny what she could plainly see in his eyes. If the eyes were the window to the soul, his were wide open, holding nothing back, expressing clearly an emotion too deep to express with words, as if he believed that she was the *key* to his soul.

"Mary," he whispered, and the soft sound of his voice enhanced her emotions the way his eyes had enhanced the effect of the kiss. The combination made her heady, and she had to put a conscious effort into remaining steady on her feet to prevent turning this perfectly blissful moment into an awkward one. She wanted to speak his name in return, or ask him what he was feeling, but her voice was restrained by her own emotional overload. She figured that was best, given that words would likely just cheapen what words could never express. He took hold of her upper arms as if he sensed her need for some support in order to remain steady, but he leaned toward her slightly, and she wondered if he was struggling with the same need to be sustained. She took hold of his arms the same way, and she felt more safe and secure than she ever had, simply by the evidence of his strength. But as their gaze continued, she knew his physical strength was the least of what made her feel so thoroughly cared for. This was *not* how she'd expected to have their conversation turn out. He closed his eyes and kissed her again, soothing her every concern into a place in her mind where they could remain quiet while she put her entire focus into simply experiencing a sweet and beautiful aspect of life that she'd never allowed herself to fully admit had always been missing.

The second kiss was better than the first, if such a thing were possible. Again he opened his eyes to look at her, and again she was struck with an overload of impressions and emotion that she knew would take hours—or days—for her brain to fully download. Or maybe she would *never* be able to fully understand it. Maybe she would never get used to feeling this way. A part of her found appeal in that. She could spend the rest of her life feeling like this, and swirling with the intrigue of trying to comprehend that it was real.

They heard the garage door opening on the other side of the kitchen wall and knew that Janel had returned with the groceries. They both let go and stepped apart from each other just before the door from the garage came open and Adrienne ran excitedly to find her mother. Mary squatted down to receive her daughter's embrace, accompanied by several sentences of excited explanation about her outing with Janel and how Janel was going to let Adrienne help cook supper, since they'd picked out the food together. Mary looked up over Adrienne's head to see Whit still staring at her, almost as if he were in a trance. She smiled at him, and he smiled back, a smile that accentuated the dazzled sparkle in his eyes. The trance was broken when Adrienne turned her attention to him and said, "Can you eat supper with us?"

"Thank you," he said, "but I can't tonight. I need to fix supper for *my* mommy."

Adrienne made a whining noise that clearly expressed her disappointment. Whit picked her up and grinned at her, saying, "I'll stay another time . . . when it's okay with your mom."

Mary was taken aback to look at Whit with her daughter, given what had happened since the last time she'd watched him interact so tenderly with Adrienne. She looked like him! Not only in their common Hispanic coloring, but in a subtle similarity of their features. Mary had always been seen as an adoptive mother because of her dramatically different appearance. But if anyone were to see Adrienne with Whit, they might automatically assume he was her father. Something about that gave her a tentative hope that the possibility of sharing a relationship with him might actually have some substance to it. Seeing them together had a mild glow of destiny about it. While it was extremely difficult to imagine herself in a romantic relationship with Whit Eden, it wasn't at all difficult to imagine him taking on the role of Adrienne's father.

Mary was startled from her thoughts by the sound of Janel coming in with groceries. "Oh, it's okay with me anytime," she said. Whit smiled at her and set Adrienne down before he went to help Janel bring the bags in from the car. Adrienne helped Mary get the groceries from the bags and put them away. Some went to the basement, some to the pantry closet, and some into the refrigerator. She was aware of Whit coming in and out of the kitchen with more bags, chatting and joking with Janel. Her stomach swam with butterflies to recall that only minutes ago he had been kissing her, looking at her as if she might be the reason the sun came up every morning. She hardly knew what to think or how to feel—beyond a senseless giddy feeling that was wholly immature and impetuous. She wanted to take these feelings and run with them and never look back. But she was far too practical for that. For the moment, however, she put all practicality aside and just relished the butterflies and the giddiness, feeling more alive than she'd felt since her twin babies had been put into her arms.

Whit finished what he called the *heavy lifting*, then he went out through the patio doors, nodding toward Mary as he said, "I'll talk to you later."

Mary nodded in return and resisted the urge to hurry to the window and watch him walk away. She managed to keep busy with some laundry, even though she often found herself frozen midtask, with her mind wandering back to everything Whit had said, the way he'd said it, the way he'd kissed her. She forced herself to get clothes folded and put away, and another load pretreated and into the washer before Adrienne came to tell her that Janel had lunch ready. Mary was disappointed to hear Janel say that Whit had told her he had some errands to do and wouldn't be joining them today. But she thought that it was just as well. With all she was feeling, she felt sure the tension in the air would be overpowering.

By the middle of the afternoon, Mary still couldn't begin to comprehend what was happening or where any of this could possibly go, but she *did* know that she wanted to see Whit, and since he was working in her yard, it wouldn't take much effort to do so. It occurred to her as she went out the patio door that he likely wanted to see her too. The thought made it difficult to draw a deep breath. She saw him as soon as she stepped outside, and her heart quickened. He was kneeling on the ground, pressing dirt around what appeared to be a rosebush he'd just planted. She watched from a distance as his gloved hands pushed down hard on the rich soil to secure the plant firmly. She noted that there were discarded flat stones around him, and she realized he'd pulled them up from where they had once formed a portion of the walkway into the garden. The remainder of the stone walkway was barely visible with the way that grass and weeds had grown over and between the stones. He'd told her he was going to redo it, but she had one obvious question for him. "Why are you planting a rosebush in the middle of the walkway?"

Whit looked up at her through his sunglasses, which prevented her from seeing his eyes. But he smiled and said, "Hello to you too."

"Hello, Whit," she said in a tone she never would have used with him before today.

"Hello, Mary," he said with equal tenderness and came to his feet. He took off his gloves and shoved them into the back pocket of his jeans, then he pushed his sunglasses up onto his head. "How are you?" he asked, his eyes intense as if he would be reading between the lines of her answer.

"Overwhelmed," she said, but she couldn't keep from smiling when she said it. He smiled in response and it warmed her. It was as if they shared a wondrous secret. As long as no one else knew how they felt about each other, it *was* a secret.

"Yeah," he said in a tone of complete agreement. They looked at each other for a long moment in silence before he cleared his throat and looked down at the new little rosebush. "To answer your question, I'm not planting a rosebush in the middle of the walkway. I'm going to make the walkway go *around* it. This bush will be the central focus when you first enter the garden."

"Oh, I see. What color are the roses?"

Since there wasn't so much as a bud on the bush, she felt it was a legitimate question, but he ignored it and said, "Come with me."

"Where are we going?" she asked and followed him deeper into the garden, where the trees were tall and the foliage dense. He took hold of her hand to lead her through the last few steps, then he stopped and turned to face her so abruptly that she almost bumped into him When she tried to step back he pushed his other arm around her waist to keep her close.

"I want to kiss you," he said, as if announcing such a thing should be entirely normal in their association. "And I assumed you wouldn't want me to do so in full view of anyone looking out the window."

"That's probably best," she said and lifted her lips to his so quickly that the last word was nearly muffled by their kiss. It occurred to her that perhaps she shouldn't come across as so eager for his affection, but that thought was squelched by a firm determination to avoid any kind of game-playing in *any* relationship in her life. She couldn't imagine this having the ability to last, but she'd already admitted to him that she was love-starved and recovering from a very bad marriage. How could she possibly resist his attention? Any woman her age would be flattered by this kind of attention from a handsome, younger man. But it was more than that. Thriving on flattery wasn't really what she was all about. It was too soon to know what exactly Whit gave her that made her crave his company, but until she figured it out, she could do nothing but enjoy the moment.

He took hold of her arms as he had earlier, and she did the same to his. Their kiss lasted longer than those they had shared earlier in the kitchen, then he laughed softly and pressed his forehead to hers. "I've been wanting to do that for *hours*." He dramatized the last word so that it sounded as if he'd been in agony.

"Me too," she said, and he kissed her again. "I should get back," she added, trying to maintain some objectivity.

"I want to take you out for a nice dinner," he said. "I can't tonight, but . . . soon. How long has it been since you went out on a date?"

"Feels like decades," she said and chuckled lightly.

"Then it's high time," he said. "Didn't your husband ever take you out?"

"Rarely, and if he did it always felt like he wanted a break in the monotony more than he wanted to do something nice for me."

"Then let me start making up for all that."

"Why should you have to make up for what he didn't do?"

"Because you deserve better," he insisted and rubbed the tip of his nose against hers.

"You're way too sweet, Whit. I'm not sure how to—"

"Get used to it," he said. "Will you go out with me?"

"I don't know what I'd do with Adrienne. Janel's the only one I trust to watch her, and she's not here in the evenings."

"If I can arrange it, will you go out with me?"

"Do you even need to ask?" she said and smiled, returning the gesture of an Eskimo kiss.

"My mother taught me that it's not polite to assume. You're letting me kiss you, but that doesn't necessarily mean you'd want to be seen in public with me."

She drew back slightly, surprised. "Why wouldn't I? If anything, it's the other way around."

"No, never!" he insisted and kissed her. "Will you go out with me?"

"Yes," she said and *she* kissed *him.* "Now I need to get back inside."

She hurried away before she changed her mind, but glanced over her shoulder to see him watching her. *How could this be happening?* she wondered and walked back to the house, feeling about twenty years younger.

Whit stood where he was for a good three or four minutes just trying to assess and mentally accept how his life had changed since he'd gone into the house this morning to get a Band-Aid. He hadn't felt this happy in years—if ever. Thinking about it, he had to conclude in all seriousness that he'd *never* felt this happy. He'd felt a great deal of joy and peace through some spiritual experiences in his life, and his mission had been very fulfilling. But never had he felt so happy! A delighted little laugh burst out of his mouth as if to add a second witness to the truth, and he was glad to be completely alone, which prevented him from having to feel some kind of embarrassment over his behavior.

He forced himself back to work, thinking about how great it would be to take Mary out on a date. He knew exactly where he wanted to take her and what he wanted to do. He wondered if any kid going to prom had ever felt this excited. Since he'd never had any such experiences, he had no point of comparison. He only knew how he felt now, and he loved it.

Before he left for the day, he went into the house, glad to find Janel in the kitchen, with no one else in sight.

"Hello, Janel," he said, coming through the patio doors.

She looked up from where she was working at the kitchen sink and smiled. "Hello, Whit. What brings you in this time of day?"

"I'm looking for you, actually," he said and closed the door behind him before he moved into the kitchen so he wouldn't have to talk so loudly. "I want to ask a really big favor of you."

Janel dried her hands and turned to face him. "I'm all ears."

"I wonder if there might be an evening soon when you would be willing to take Adrienne home with you for the evening so that Mary could get out."

"That's not a favor," she said with a grin. "I'd love to take her home for the evening. She's no trouble at all."

"Oh, that would be great," Whit said with a little chuckle. He knew that Janel was long divorced and her children were grown, but he still hadn't expected her to be so eager.

"But why are *you* arranging this? I'm all for Mary getting out, but . . ."

"I'm *taking* her out," he said. "Or at least I want to. But she tells me the only time she can leave Adrienne is when you're here, which amounts to about the same hours that *I'm* working. She says there isn't anyone else she'd trust to watch her daughter, so . . ."

"You're taking Mary *out?*" Janel asked, looking mildly suspicious. "Like . . . out on a date, out?"

"That's right," he said firmly. "Is that a problem?"

"Not to me, it's not," she said. "I just didn't . . . peg the two of you together . . . like that?"

"Like that?" he asked, not at all defensive. He was prepared to have people raise eyebrows over his interest in Mary. He didn't care what most people thought, but he liked and respected Janel, and he knew she and Mary were close. He didn't want any misunderstanding about the situation *or* his intentions.

"Should I pretend that she's not older than you?" Janel asked, and he appreciated her straightforward approach.

"Not at all. I just want to be sure that it's not any of our other differences that bother you."

"Nothing bothers me, Whit. I'm just surprised." She smiled. "But *pleasantly* surprised."

"Good," he said. "Is there any evening that *won't* work for you?"

"Nope. My schedule is open. I can even do it tonight, if you'd like."

"I can't tonight," he said. "But how about tomorrow . . . if Mary is good with that?"

"I'll look forward to it," Janel said. "Do you want me to bring Adrienne back after—"

"No, we'll come and get her on our way home. We won't be late."

"Doesn't matter." Janel smiled again, and Whit suspected she was actually quite pleased. "I'm flexible."

"Okay, thanks," Whit said and went back outside, greatly anticipating tomorrow evening.

While he was gathering his tools and making certain everything was left in a reasonably tidy condition for the night, he called Mary's cell phone.

"Hello," she said in a tone that indicated she'd known it was him before she answered.

"You said I could call this number if I ever had a question," he said.

"You haven't called it very much."

"I haven't had very many questions. I have a question now, however."

"Okay," she said, and he felt thrilled by the hint of anticipation he heard in that one word.

"Will you go out with me tomorrow night? Janel will take Adrienne home with her, and we can pick her up when we're done."

"You really *did* arrange it," she said.

"Did you think I wouldn't?"

"I wasn't sure how you could manage."

"So, I've managed. Will you go out with me?"

"I'd love to," she said. "Where are we going?"

"Dinner mostly."

"Mostly? What do I wear for *mostly*?"

"Just wear one of those lovely skirts you look so adorable wearing. I'll bring clothes with me to work so I can change and we can leave as soon as I'm done."

"I'll look forward to it," she said, and there was a long moment of silence. "Where are you?"

"Pulling out of the driveway," he said. "I've got some errands to run. Can I call you later? I'm absolutely certain I'll have more questions."

"Adrienne goes to bed about nine. I'm free after that."

"Okay, I'll call you," he said.

"I'll look forward to that too," she said. "Give your mother my best."

"I will," he said, and there was another long moment of silence. "I'll talk to you later," he added, knowing he didn't want to hang up, but feeling also that he was making a fool of himself.

"Okay . . . bye," she said, but there was a long pause before the click, implying that she hadn't wanted to hang up either.

Whit was disappointed by the way that driving into his neighborhood had a way of diluting his joyful feelings when he contemplated the ugliness of his life here. His hope was to eventually ask Mary to be his wife. But then what? He couldn't move her into his neighborhood, and he couldn't see himself living in the same house with her bigoted father. Ironically, he needed his job in order to support a wife, and she was his employer. He was obligated to care for his mother but couldn't get her to leave this neighborhood. The age and ethnic differences between him and Mary were the least of their problems, but as long as he felt God's approval in pursuing this relationship, he was determined to do everything in his power to remove every obstacle. The best things in life didn't come easy, and they didn't come without a price. And he was willing to pay that price, whatever it might be.

* * * * *

Mary's light mood darkened when she went to see her father and found him in an especially foul mood. He was never in *good* spirits, and she had become very skilled at flitting in and out of his room to give him pertinent information, let him know she was there, and keep a smile on her face no matter what he said. But today his grumbling was full of anger toward anything and everything in the world he didn't like. And there was nothing he disliked more than people who were anything but Caucasian. He once again lectured Mary on her stupidity in spending all of those years south of the border, and especially for her decision to take on those children who were *despicable little spics*. Mary wanted to retaliate hurtfully when her father used such horrible words to describe her daughters. But all she could do was tell him that if he was going to talk like that she wasn't staying in the room. He shouted a string of curses at her as she left, then she heard him start coughing and was grateful there was a nurse nearby to attend to him. She had a difficult time in such moments understanding how any human being could be so hideously cruel. Being charitable in return for such abuse took a stoic nature that she wasn't certain she possessed.

Mary went to her room and paced for several minutes, breathing in deeply to make a conscious effort to feel peaceful and calm, while exhaling all of the hurt and anger her father had incited in her. She couldn't deny her gratitude for having a roof over her head, and having her financial and physical needs met—as well as those of her daughter. But the price was high. She was more thankful than ever that her father wasn't capable of leaving his room. If she had to fear running into him elsewhere in the house she would never dare leave her own room, and she certainly wouldn't want Adrienne exposed to him. Her gratitude deepened when she considered all that had happened today, and how she never would have met Whit if she'd not been living here, and if she'd not taken the initiative to restore her mother's garden.

Adrienne distracted Mary from her mixed emotions, and they spent some quiet time together before Mary put the child to bed with a story, a prayer, and a kiss. Adrienne's sweetness and her remarkable ability to see the best in everything was deeply healing to Mary, and she was able to let go of a little more of her hurt and anger.

Ten minutes after Mary had left Adrienne's room, her cell phone rang and she was thrilled to hear Whit's voice on the other end. They talked of simple things and avoided discussing anything that was too personal, including topics that Mary was not in the mood to get into, but she enjoyed every minute of their conversation. She felt even more comfortable talking to him than she had yesterday, which she considered a good sign. If the things that had been declared between them had created awkwardness, she felt sure that wouldn't be conducive to pursuing any kind of serious relationship.

After they'd talked more than an hour and a half, he said, "I wish I was there with you, or that you were here with me."

"Neither is very practical," she said, not wanting to actually bring up the fact that she would probably *never* go to his home again, and his being here under the same roof as her father just made her nervous, given the change in her feelings.

"No, but I can still wish," he said.

"Given the hour and how lonely we both are, it's probably better that we just talk on the phone."

"Probably," he said, and she marveled at yet one more piece of evidence that he was deeply attracted to her. Her! A woman ten years older than he was! But she couldn't think about that. He'd made his point regarding that issue earlier, and she just needed to do as he'd told her and get over it. She had no reason to believe he wasn't being completely sincere.

They both declared that they needed to get some sleep, although she assured him that his boss would understand if he showed up late for work. Mary found it hard to say good night to him and get off the phone, then she laid back on her pillow and stared at the ceiling, wondering how her determination to *clear the air* between herself and Whit had resulted in a day that she never could have imagined possible. She was looking forward to their date the following evening, and was glad to know that she had the opportunity to see him every weekday when he came to work.

Mary slept moderately well; in fact, she slept better than she had since the accident. She couldn't believe that was a coincidence. She was glad that her father slept too, and that she had no need to be in the same room with him before a nurse arrived at six. By the time she and Adrienne made it to the kitchen for breakfast, she could see through the patio doors that Whit's truck was parked in its usual place. Her heart quickened just to know he was out in the massive foliage of the garden somewhere, and she wished she had an excuse to go talk to him. She had just finished her breakfast and was rinsing dishes to go into the dishwasher when her cell phone rang.

She pulled it out of her pocket, smiling to know that it was Whit. With the exception of a couple of friends she'd left behind when she'd come here, no one else ever called her.

"Hello," she said.

"Good morning, beautiful," she heard and laughed softly, glad that Janel was in the laundry room and couldn't overhear. But then, Janel knew that Whit was taking her out this evening, so perhaps that was irrelevant.

"Good morning," she said. "Are you sure you've got the right number?"

"Oh, I'm sure," he said. "Do you think you could come out here for a few minutes? I have a question."

"Okay," she said, feeling giddy. "Where are you?"

"Near the cluster of trees by the south fence," he said.

"I'll be right out," she said and hung up the phone. To Adrienne she said, "I need to go out and help Whit for a few minutes. You just play right here and don't get into anything."

"She'll be fine," Janel said, coming into the room with a laundry basket on her hip. She winked with comical exaggeration and Mary hurried outside.

Mary couldn't see Whit where he'd said he would be, and she wondered if she had understood him correctly. Then he grabbed her waist from behind and laughed when she let out a gaspy scream.

"Good morning, beautiful," he said again when she turned to face him. She barely got a glimpse of his smiling face before he kissed her.

"Good morning to you too," she said, and he kissed her again. As much as she enjoyed it, she felt the need to clarify something that could not be left unspoken. "You're a good Mormon boy, right?"

Whit drew back, and his brow furrowed. "Yes," he drawled. "At least I try to be. Why?"

"Mormons have . . . rules about this kind of thing, don't they?"

"No rules against kissing, as far as I know."

She smiled, then became very serious. "But . . . they have rules about . . . getting involved before marriage, right? I just need to know if you keep those rules because . . . I'm not ready for that kind of thing in my life."

"Yes," he said.

"Yes, what?"

"Yes . . . they have rules, and yes I keep those rules. I would hope you wouldn't be ready for *that kind of thing* in your life unless you were married. That's how it is for me. I hope that's how it is for you."

"Oh, it is!" she said emphatically. "It's just that . . . a lot of people in this world don't agree with that anymore, and . . . I just wanted to be sure . . . that I could trust you . . . that I wouldn't have to worry . . . or wonder."

"You can trust me," he said. Then he kissed her as if a kiss might be all they would ever need to be completely fulfilled.

In a dreamy voice Mary said, "What was your question, exactly?"

"I can't recall," he said. "I just had to see you. And I'm anticipating that I'm going to need a lot more input from you on this garden than I needed before." He lifted his brows and smiled. "It's getting to that stage."

"Is it?"

"Oh, yes," he said.

Mary reluctantly left him to do his work, glad that he would be coming to the house for lunch. Her only disappointment was that Kristi would be joining them, since she was working that day. Whit came in at lunchtime and washed up at the kitchen sink while Mary tried not to look at him, but when she did he was looking at *her*, and they both chuckled.

"There's no need to pretend when I'm around," Janel said.

"Pretend what?" Whit asked, feigning innocence, drying his hands on the towel she passed to him.

"That the two of you aren't all gaga over each other," Janel said. "I'm the babysitter tonight, remember? And it's not like I haven't noticed the way you two have been twitterpated for weeks."

"Twitterpated?" Whit countered, falsely astonished. "Me?"

Mary had to turn away to avoid having them see that she was blushing. Had Janel really been noticing something between them all this time?

"But you said you were surprised," Whit added to Janel.

"Only that you were actually doing something about it," Janel said.

Adrienne ran into the room after washing up in the bathroom. She ran directly to Whit and said, "Guess what! I'm going to Janel's house for supper and we're gonna watch a movie!"

"That's awesome!" he said. "And I get to pick you up at Janel's house and bring you home!"

Adrienne jumped up and down and squealed with excitement.

"My goodness," Kristi said, coming into the room, "what's all the fuss?"

Adrienne repeated her announcement that she would be going to Janel's house for the evening, and she added that Whit would be bringing her home. Kristi looked at Whit as if he should have some explanation for this, or more accurately, as if he *owed* her an explanation. He said nothing, if only to not give her the satisfaction of thinking that she could provoke an answer out of him. She'd been flirting with him for weeks, and he was glad to be able to put an official end to it. He helped Adrienne get situated in her booster seat, then he sat next to Mary and smiled at her.

About halfway through their tuna fish sandwiches with lettuce and pickles, Kristi said, "So, you must be going out this evening, Mary."

"I am, yes," Mary said.

"She's going on a date with Whit," Adrienne announced. Whit chuckled, just from the sheer delight of having Adrienne be the one to set Kristi straight.

Whit smiled at Kristi with satisfaction, then he smiled at Mary with adoration and changed the subject.

When lunch was over Whit helped clear the table as he usually did and took some dishes to the sink. He turned around to find Kristi standing a little too close to his side while she set down more dishes. She glanced over her shoulder to make certain no one was nearby before she said softly, "Getting in good with the boss, I see."

Whit gave her an astonished glare, although it wasn't as astonished or glaring as he might have given her if Mary and Janel weren't just across the room. "That has nothing to do with it," he said.

"Oh, come on," Kristi said, as if it were some personal insult to her, "she's probably old enough to be your mother."

Whit increased the intensity of his glare and stated firmly, "No, she is *not*! But regardless of our age difference, she is an amazing woman with a great deal of class, unlike some women I know." He left her side and smiled at Mary as he approached her, glad to see that she'd not overheard any of that. For good measure he gave her a quick kiss and said, "I'll see you at six." It felt good to be open about his feelings for Mary. From the corner of his eye he knew that Janel was smiling, Adrienne was oblivious, and he could only guess that Kristi, who stood behind him, was appalled.

"I'll be ready," Mary said, and he went outside to resume his tasks in the garden. He found it more difficult to stick to his work when he was continually talking himself out of going to find Mary, just so he could kiss her and look at her beautiful face.

# Chapter Six

A FEW HOURS LATER WHIT was sitting on the ground, pulling weeds from around a rose bush that he'd just cut back with the hope that it would begin to thrive again now that it wasn't so top heavy. He didn't hear any noise that might alert him to not being alone until Mary said, "I heard a rumor that the gardener has lost his mind."

"Really." He jumped to his feet and pulled off his gloves. "Where did you hear that?"

"Actually, I didn't," she said. "I was thinking of *starting* that rumor."

He smiled and stepped toward her. "I didn't take you for the kind of woman to start false gossip."

"Maybe it's not false. Maybe you *have* lost your mind."

"Or maybe *you* have," he said and kissed her forehead. "You haven't changed your mind about going out with me tonight, have you?"

"No, of course not," she said.

"But you have doubts about . . . us?" he guessed, sensing that her facetious comments had an undertone of seriousness.

"Tonight is our first date, Whit. I'm certain we should give *us* some time."

Whit subdued his temptation to argue with her, certain that no amount of time would change how he felt and what he wanted. But he felt no need to *argue*; he knew that time was on his side. In spite of some obvious lack of practicality and logic, he knew in his heart that he wanted to spend the rest of his life with Mary. He just had to convince *her* that she wanted to spend the rest of her life—and forever—with *him*. For the moment he decided to change the subject. "Are you busy Monday . . . during the day?"

"No, why?"

"We need to go shopping." Her eyes widened, and he added, "This is professional, actually. I want you to come with me to the nursery and pick out some new plants and flowers for the garden."

"Oh, how delightful," she said.

"I was thinking we could take Adrienne and go to lunch while we're out. What do you say?"

"I think it will give me something to look forward to once our first date is over."

"I had the same thought," he said. "For the moment I need to get back to work so we can *go* on that first date."

"I'll see you later, then," she said and walked away, but she looked over her shoulder twice while he was still watching her.

At ten minutes to six, Whit got some things out of the truck and went into a bathroom that was near the kitchen where he knew he could clean up a bit and change his clothes. He wore dark slacks and nice shoes and a button-up shirt that was a pale pink with burgundy stripes. His mother had picked it out for his birthday last year, and she'd teased him about how a real man could wear pink because it didn't threaten his masculinity. Maybe. He just knew he liked the shirt. But as he checked his appearance in the large mirror in the bathroom, he actually felt nervous. He'd been completely comfortable with Mary right from the start. Why would he be nervous now? This was more official, yes. But surely there was no need for anxiety. He wanted to impress her. He didn't want her to think he was immature, or to decide after spending some time with him that they were too incompatible to attempt a serious relationship. He said a quick prayer, took a deep breath, and opened the door.

Whit paced the common room for about five minutes before Mary came down the stairs. She was wearing a lavender skirt scattered with cream-colored flowers, and a short-sleeved, cream-colored sweater. A lavender scarf was looped around her neck, and he wondered if this was the one that had belonged to her mother—the one Adrienne had told him about the first day he'd come here. He hoped so. It would surely bring good luck. Mary had a long-sleeved sweater hanging over her arm and a little purse on a long strap over her shoulder.

Their eyes met, and they shared a smile as she descended. "Forgive the cliché," she said, "but you clean up well."

"You look beautiful," he said. "You *always* look beautiful."

"Thank you," she said. "Shall we—"

"Is Adrienne—"

"They've already gone," she said, and he took her hand.

"Let's go then," he said and led her out to his truck, which he had cleaned out to make it presentable for a date.

A few minutes into the drive, she asked, "So, where are we going?"

"My favorite restaurant," he said.

"Ooh," she smiled. "I'm excited."

"I hope you like it."

"I'm sure I will."

When they arrived at their destination, Whit was pleased that Mary had never been there before, because he wanted the evening to be a completely new experience for her. Since the weather was pleasant, the entire back of the restaurant was wide open, stretching out onto a lovely patio that was surrounded by a variety of flowers intermixed with rock formations. Beyond the gardened patio was the beach, and the sound of the waves was prevalent.

"Oh, it's amazing," Mary said with a sparkle in her eyes right after they were seated and she had a chance to look around.

"The food is good too," he said.

"No wonder it's your favorite. How did you find it?"

"I did the landscaping," he said, nodding toward the vast array of flowers surrounding the patio.

"Really?" she said and let out a sweet little laugh. "It's remarkable."

"Thank you," he said. "One of these days soon I hope you can start to see some changes in your garden. Now that I've cleared out a lot of the weeds and dead stuff, I want to start improvements near the house and work out from there, so that the view from the patio will be nice. I should be able to make a visible difference after another two or three weeks."

"How exciting!" she said. "But let's not talk about work."

"It doesn't feel like work to me," he said. "Truthfully, I almost feel guilty getting paid so well when I enjoy it so much."

"You work hard."

"That may be, but right from the start I've considered that I was doing it for you, and it's never felt hard."

They ordered their food, and Mary ignored the very subtle curiosity in the server's eyes, which she instinctively knew was centered in the obvious age difference of the couple he was serving. She figured she would have to get used to that if she pursued any kind of relationship with Whit. She quickly put it out of her mind, and they chatted casually over salads and bread. Then somehow they got into a conversation about the impact of Whit losing his father and of Mary having a father who was worse than no father at all.

Mary listened to the way he spoke about the hard things in life, and she felt amazed and impressed. She wondered if it was perhaps inappropriate to compare him to Simon, but how could she not think of her husband of eighteen years and not see the vast differences? Simon had always been kind about her frustrations about her father, but he was mostly indifferent about it, often saying things like, "It's not that big of a deal," or "You shouldn't let it get to you." Whit was expressing a great deal of compassion about the impact of such unloving and harsh attitudes in a parent. He understood her, even in things that they'd hardly talked about before now.

Their entrees were brought to the table, and they took a few minutes to taste everything and comment on the beauty of the food as well as its deliciousness. They got full quickly but agreed that they could enjoy leftovers tomorrow. After Mary declared that she couldn't eat another bite, she made a point of getting back to their conversation. "How is it that you know so much about such things? You don't talk like a street-hardened, ex-gang member. I should add that you also don't *speak* like one."

"I worked very hard to get over *that*," he said emphatically. "I didn't want to open my  mouth and have people judge me by my speech. As for the other, I've been through a lot of counseling, if you must know. At one point it was forced on me. Court-ordered anger management and anti-violence courses. Initially I was determined not to internalize any of it, pridefully believing that I was justified in my anger *and* my violence. Then something just . . . clicked one day. My mother swears it was the answer to her prayers—years' worth of them. It probably was. I just . . . realized that I didn't *want* to be angry, and I didn't like the violence. It was a long road back, with a lot more counseling. Thankfully, I got some help from people who were eager to see a kid like me turn his life around, otherwise we never would have been able to afford it." He chuckled tensely. "It wasn't easy reversing everything I believed . . . everything I was. I've heard it's like changing the course of a river while the water keeps flowing."

"Is it?"

"No, it's worse than that," he said with eyes that chilled her.

"But you did it, and that's a remarkable accomplishment."

"I've come a long way," he said, "and I'm very grateful." He focused more on her. "But sometimes I worry that my past will catch up with me. It's my primary concern in becoming involved with you. I don't want to bring any of *my* consequences into *your* life."

"Do you think the anger is still inside you somewhere? Do you fear it will erupt?"

"No, not at all," he said calmly and matter-of-factly. "I don't worry about that, because I know how deep the change is inside myself. I can explain that more some other time. I worry about the people who know me, and . . . maybe you could call it bad karma, or something like that. I don't believe in karma exactly, but I do believe in consequences. People can change, but the consequences of bad choices just can't be undone sometimes. The tattoos are a good example of that, but they are the least of it."

"Do you think I should know about your past . . . about those things?"

"I'd prefer that you didn't," he said, "but if you feel like you need to, I'll tell you anything you want to know. I would prefer not to expose you to the ugly details of my past, but it's not because I'm trying to hide anything from you. It's just because it's ugly." He leaned his elbows on the table and looked at her intently. "Listen to me, Mary. In my mind, there is a very clear line in my life dividing the before and after. Everything that took place before that moment is wiped clean in God's eyes, and I've worked very hard to make restitution as far as it's possible, and to forgive myself. Wallowing in it, given those facts, will never accomplish anything good. Do you understand?"

"I can't say that I fully understand, no. But it makes sense. You don't have to tell me anything you don't want to tell me."

"The only thing that matters to me is whether or not *you* can fully let go of my past and not let it come between us, no matter what the future might bring."

"If you can let go of it, I certainly can."

"Can you? Are you sure?" She hesitated, and he added, "More than anything to do with compatibility or values or love, I need to know that we have complete trust. You need to know that even though the past is in the past, I will never be anything but completely honest with you, and I need you to be the same. I need to trust you, Mary, and I need you to trust me. I don't want you to tell me right now whether that's possible. I want you to think about it; think about it a lot. When you're ready we can talk about it some more. As for now," he scooted back his chair and stood up, "I think we've had enough heavy conversation for one evening." He held out his hand. "Let's dance."

Mary glanced around skeptically. "I don't think they do that here."

"There's music, there's plenty of room. What more do we need? I don't think we'll cause a ruckus or anything." She still hesitated, and he said, "Oh, come on. Just a simple little slow dance, Mary. You'll like it. I promise. I know *I* will."

She put her hand in his and he led her past the tables to the open space on the patio where it was easier to hear the sound of the ocean, but where they could still hear the music playing over the speakers in the restaurant. Whit held her hand near his shoulder and put his other hand on her back, easing her into a gentle back-and-forth step as she put her hand on his other shoulder. At first she couldn't look at him; just being so close to him was overwhelming. Then her eyes were drawn to his and she couldn't pull them away.

"This is probably the most romantic song the Beatles ever did," he said.

"It's very nice," she said.

"So dancing with me isn't so bad?"

"It's not bad at all."

Whit smiled. "See, I told you that you'd like it."

"You're really quite a romantic, I think."

"I always thought of it as being kind of sappy."

"Well, whatever it is, I like it."

"My mother will be pleased to hear that."

"Will she?"

"She tells me I get my *romantic nature* from her. She swears it's her Hispanic blood in me, but I'm not sure I have any evidence of a connection. She tells me her father was a romantic, so maybe that's where I got it. My mother likes it because I watch chick flicks with her, and if they don't have Spanish subtitles I translate for her."

"How very sweet," she said.

"I'm glad you think so," he said, "because I'm trying to impress you."

They both laughed, and she said, "It's working. What I don't understand is . . . why."

His brow furrowed. "Why what?"

"Why you would be trying to impress me. First of all, there's no need to *try*. You impress me without trying."

"That's good to know," he said. "What's the other reason?"

"What?"

"You said . . . 'first of all,' so there must be something else."

"Why would you want to impress *me*?"

The song ended and another began, but it had a similar rhythm and was equally romantic so they kept dancing while no one in the restaurant seemed to notice.

"Are you kidding?" Whit asked. "You're the most amazing woman I've ever met."

Mary wondered why she found it so difficult to believe him. She gently laid her head on his shoulder, mostly to avoid his gaze. She felt his lips brush over her brow, as if to echo what he'd just said. "What's wrong?" he asked.

"I don't *feel* amazing, Whit. And I can't decide if you're immature or delusional. Or both."

"I would take offense from that if I didn't know you well enough to know where this is coming from." He tightened his arm around her waist and whispered, "Mary . . . look at me." She lifted her head and met his eyes, not feeling at all like he was significantly younger than she was. In fact, it occurred to her in that moment how very equal they felt in nearly every respect. Except that for some reason she felt completely inadequate in regard to his feelings for her; feelings that radiated from his eyes with a clarity that could never be misconstrued, even before he said, "I love you, Mary."

She wasn't surprised to hear him admit it, especially after everything else he'd admitted to feeling. But it still took her aback.

"Do you believe me?" he asked.

"Yes," she said with no hesitation, and they continued to dance. "I just can't help wondering if love is enough for us. There is a great deal working against us."

"Then we'll need to work around it."

"Do you think that's possible?"

"Yes," he insisted. "If we love each other enough, and we're committed to making it work, we'll make it work. I know you probably have a list of reasons why it *won't* work out; I admit that I'm also well aware of some obvious challenges. But we need to see such things as challenges, not impediments. So, let's talk about it. Let's talk about our concerns; let's be practical."

"Okay, let's," she said, glad that they were continuing to dance, which kept the conversation from feeling as heavy as it might have otherwise. There were several points she could have brought up, but she chose one of her most prominent thoughts. "I can't have children, Whit."

"Yeah, I got that the first time we talked."

"But . . . you're young . . . with your whole life ahead of you. Surely you want children of your own, and—"

"You think I can't consider Adrienne *my own?*" he asked.

"I know you can, but that's not what I mean."

"Then you mean that I couldn't possibly live a fulfilled life unless my DNA is literally passed down to a child?"

"Can you? That's what I want to know."

"You bet I can! We might decide to adopt more children, or maybe we'll decide that the three of us make a nice family. I think that's a decision we can make in the future. I don't see that as a challenge."

"No one should jump into marriage without knowing if they're compatible with their goals and values," Mary insisted. "Give me credit for having some wisdom."

He chuckled, which kept the conversation light enough to not turn into an argument. "So . . . you're old and wise and I'm young and foolish? Is that it?"

"I believe that wisdom is measured by experience," she said firmly. "You have a great deal of life experience, Whit. But I'm the one who spent eighteen years in a bad marriage."

"I won't argue with that, but don't forget why it was bad. In spite of all your best efforts and your mutual goals and values, your husband didn't love you, and he didn't treat you the way you deserve to be treated. If you and I love each other and take good care of each other, everything else is negotiable."

Mary leaned back and sighed. "Maybe."

"Maybe? You sound . . . cynical; skeptical."

"Maybe I am," she admitted. "For someone who came out of such horrors in his youth, you sound amazingly *un*-cynical."

"Any life away from *that* life has the possibility of being a *good* life."

Mary pondered what Whit had just said, and felt his words warm her heart. She smiled at him and said, "I want to believe that's true. If anyone could make me believe it's possible, it would be you."

"I'm glad you feel that way."

"Maybe it all just feels too good to be true." She sighed and wondered if she was ready to be completely honest with how she was really feeling since he'd so boldly declared his feelings for her. She decided that anything short of complete honesty would never help either of them know whether or not this relationship had the ability to last. She sighed more loudly and resigned herself to admitting her deepest fears. "No one has ever treated me the way you treat me, Whit. No one's ever looked at me the you look at me. I just . . ." Her chin quivered and she looked down. "I've never been loved the way you love me, Whit." She looked up, unashamed of the tears in her eyes. "I don't know *how* to be so loved, and I fear that . . . if I allow myself to become dependent on feeling this way, somehow it will fall apart and I'll end up with a broken heart . . . again. But it would be worse this time; this time I've felt things I've never felt before, and I don't want to go back. How can a person live without the sun on her face once she's felt it? I've lived my whole life in the shade, and now that I've experienced sunlight . . . I can never go back."

Whit smiled tenderly and pressed a kiss to her brow before he looked into her eyes. "You don't have to go back, Mary. I will never stop loving you. Never!"

"I want to believe you."

"Just . . . allow yourself to trust me, and I will never let you down. I promise!"

"I want to believe that, too," she said, glad she'd been candid with him about her feelings. As long as she'd gotten that much out, it was easy to say, "I love you too, Whit. I do."

He smiled with a sparkle of emotion in his eyes. "I'm very glad to hear that. You're right, Mary. You said it more perfectly than I ever could have. *You* are the sunlight I've never felt before, and I don't ever want to go back into the shade."

He kissed her while they kept dancing, slowly swaying back and forth in perfect unison. He then put the side of his face to hers, as if to just enjoy the experience in silence. The tip of his nose came to the top of her head, and Mary found his height perfect for her to rest her head against his shoulder, while the safety and security she felt in his presence increased with every minute they were together.

They finally gave up on dancing when the restaurant began to clear out. Their leftovers had been boxed up, and Whit paid the check. Then they put the food in the truck and went for a walk on the beach, carrying their shoes. Mary didn't want the evening to end, but she knew it was time to go get Adrienne. She sat next to Whit in the truck, and he put his arm around her while he drove. She relaxed her head on his shoulder and told herself that this wasn't a dream. She'd wondered many times if true love would simply never be a part of her life. Starting over as a forty-year-old widow, it hadn't seemed like a positive probability to her, but a miracle had happened, and she prayed it would never end.

They found Adrienne in good spirits, perhaps a little hyper from all of Janel's doting and too much sugar. They thanked Janel, and Whit told her that he owed her one, but she insisted that it had been delightful and she would be glad to do it again. "In fact," she said, walking with them out to her driveway, "we should make a habit of it."

"Maybe we should," Whit said.

He helped secure Adrienne in the middle seat of his truck, and by the time they got back to Mary's house, the child was asleep, her head against Whit's side. He kept glancing at Mary, wishing with all his soul that his whole life could be like this. At the house he carried Adrienne up to her bed and watched Mary tuck her in and kiss her little face. He'd never been upstairs before, and he felt nervous just to be on the same floor as Mary's father, but once they knew Adrienne hadn't stirred at all with being moved, Mary walked him back downstairs and kissed him at the door.

"Thank you for a perfect evening," she said.

"The pleasure was *all* mine," he insisted softly and kissed her again. "I'll see you in the morning," he said and left reluctantly.

During the drive home, Whit imagined what his life might be like if it could be exactly the way he wanted it. A year ago, he wouldn't have been able to even put an image to such a thought. But now it was easy. As long as Mary and Adrienne were in his life, he could see a beautiful future—however they might have to work around the challenges.

* * * * *

Mary curled up in her bed and cried. She cried more than she had in many weeks, much the way she had cried in response to her early weeks of grieving over the death of her little Isabelle. She cried for nearly an hour before she figured out exactly *why* she was crying. She found the answer by measuring her experiences with Whit against everything else in her life. And she grieved over the life she'd lived in a way she never had before. The way that Whit treated her, and the things that he'd said, had shown her a more accurate and vivid picture of the way her life had been before he'd entered it. She thought of how he'd told her about the line of before and after in his life, and she could see the same line in her own—life before Whit Eden had walked in the door, and life after. And what she saw now was that life before had been scarce on anything that had given her joy or made her feel valued and loved. She could sum it up on one hand. She'd had a few friends through the years who had been a boon to her; she still kept in touch somewhat with a couple of them. But if she never spoke to them again, she wouldn't feel a deep loss. Their relationships had been mostly based in surface things. She had her humanitarian efforts: her blog, her fund-raisers, and her projects. She found all of that hugely fulfilling and she knew that what she did made a difference, but she didn't have the money to travel to these places, and therefore her work was all done from a computer, and she could imagine that in and of itself being a very lonely life.

Beyond that, her relationship with her mother had been a true and brilliant force in her life. And it was the same with her daughters. She'd adopted the girls about the same time her mother had died; therefore, they had helped fill the void left by her mother's absence. Now Isabelle was gone, and she had only her little Adrienne. Before Whit had come along, she'd convinced herself that living for a daughter was enough, that finding joy through the love of a child would create enough fulfillment. Mary could see now that's what her mother had done. She had lived her religion privately, served others around her zealously, and nurtured her daughter in every possible way. And that was all.

Mary suspected her mother had been very glad to leave this world, and now Mary had gained more understanding regarding the reasons for that. Once Mary had left home and could take care of herself, what had there been to live for? And if Mary had little to live for besides Adrienne, then she would inevitably have to face the same dilemma. But now everything was different. Already Whit had shown her that there was more to live for, more to feel, more to believe in. And she hardly knew how to take it all in.

Mary's tears subsided into a quiet thoughtfulness that kept her wide awake. She considered what she had said to Whit, startled by her own insight as it sank in more deeply with reverberations of truth. *I don't know how to be so loved.* And that *was* the truth. She *didn't* know how to be so loved. Her mother had loved her unconditionally and incomparably. But that was a *mother's* love. Beyond that, Mary had never experienced *real* love. But Whit loved her. She knew he did. She couldn't deny, however, that the very lack of familiarity in such a feeling made her feel unsteady. He'd told her that she could trust him, that he wouldn't let her down, that he would never stop loving her. She wanted to believe him, but a lifetime of experience to the contrary made it difficult to fully accept. She tried very hard to imagine seeing herself through his eyes, but she knew it wasn't working when all she could see was a woman who was starting to show the signs of middle age, who really didn't have much of anything to offer.

Mary's thoughts turned to spiritual matters as she considered the changes that Whit had gone through in his life, and how he clearly believed in God and respected the place of a divine power in his life. She thought of how spiritually strong her mother had been, and of all the things that Loretta had taught her about the gospel that had been so dear to her. Mary believed that the things her mother believed in were true. Mary had always prayed and felt a respect toward God, but it was a passive kind of thing. Her father's objection to religion had required it to be that way, and Simon had held no interest for religion of any kind. Now Mary wondered if learning more about the gospel and taking it more actively into her life would help her find more peace and perspective.

For all that Loretta had lived a difficult life and had had little to live for, she had always been a shining example of peace and perspective. She'd always credited her happiness to knowing that the Savior was there for her, and that she had the hope of better things in eternity. When Loretta had had so many reasons *not* to be happy, Mary considered that a miracle. But she'd gotten into the habit of respecting Simon's wish to avoid religion, the same way she'd done in regard to her father's wishes. It only occurred to her now that she had a choice. She could follow her mother's beliefs, and it seemed a miraculous coincidence that Whit belonged to the same religion that her mother had. She recalled then with a sparkle of excitement that Whit's mother had invited her to go to church with them. Surely going to church wouldn't fall into the same category as going to their home, because she seriously doubted that the gang members Whit feared would be attending church of any kind. She determined that she would ask him about it in the morning, and with that thought she found enough peace of mind to finally sleep.

Mary was awakened by hearing through the monitor that her father was coughing. She hurried to his room and helped him get it under control while she managed to avoid any conversation with him. When he was settled down and relaxed she returned to her bed and was able to go right back to sleep. She woke up to morning light and Adrienne crawling into her bed, but the child was sleepy and snuggly and she was able to relax, half asleep, for a long while with her daughter close to her. Adrienne finally began to get more wiggly as she recovered from being awake later than usual the previous evening. She suddenly jumped out of bed as if she'd been struck with an exciting idea. "Whit is here!" she declared on her way out of the room, as if she had simply sensed his presence on the premises.

Mary's heart quickened at the announcement. She closed her eyes and breathed in the comfort and security she felt to simply know that one fact. *Whit was here.* And more important and amazing than his being the gardener, he was in her life. And he was in Adrienne's life too.

Motivated by a desire to see him, Mary got dressed and helped Adrienne do the same. But before they could get any breakfast, the child ran out to the garden in search of her new best friend. Mary wondered if the very fact of Whit bringing them home last night had shifted Adrienne's thinking about his place in their lives. Or perhaps with her innocent perceptions, she sensed the feelings between him and her mother. Whatever the reason, Mary loved it.

Certain Adrienne would come back soon, Mary talked casually with Janel while she scrambled some eggs and made toast. She liked imagining what kind of exchange might be taking place between Adrienne and Whit.

"Did you have a good time last night?" Janel asked. "You seemed in good spirits when you picked up Adrienne."

"It was very nice, yes," Mary said.

"I'm glad to hear it. Just so you know, I meant it when I said I'd love to make a habit out of taking Adrienne for an evening. It's good for you to get out—whether it's with Whit or not—and I had a great time with Adrienne."

"Thank you. That's very sweet."

"It's probably none of my business," Janel said, "but I think he's very good for you. Whether it works out permanently or not, I think it's a good thing. That's my opinion, anyway."

"Well, I agree with you," Mary said. "I just hope that I can be good for him too."

"Oh, I wouldn't worry about *that*," Janel said. Mary wanted to ask what she meant exactly, but Janel changed the subject. "Oh, Kristi won't be coming in for a week or two. Her mother—who is a friend of mine, as you know—broke her leg rather badly last night, and—"

"Oh, I'm sorry. Is she all right?"

"She'll be fine, but it's quite bad. She fell on the stairs in the middle of the night and is in surgery right now. Kristi will be helping take care of her until she can get around on her own, and she'll also be helping watch the grandkids that my friend tends regularly. I told Kristi we could manage."

"We certainly can," Mary said. "Why don't you give me a list of her responsibilities, and I'll take care of it. I have too much time on my hands, anyway."

"I was going to ask if you wanted me to get someone to fill in, but I guess that answers my question."

"That's settled, then," Mary said. "No point paying for help we don't need. I don't want to leave Kristi without a job if she needs it, but I can certainly take care of what needs to be done. It might not be up to my father's standards, but since he never comes out of that room, he'll never know. I'm capable of keeping things adequately clean."

"Okay," Janel said, then she nodded toward the window. "Looks like Adrienne found him."

Mary's stomach fluttered even before she looked up to see Whit running around the yard with Adrienne sitting on his shoulders while he held tightly to her hands. The child giggled loudly as she bounced up and down, and Mary couldn't recall Simon ever doing such a thing with his daughters.

Mary went outside and interrupted their play by telling Adrienne she needed to come in and eat her breakfast. Whit smiled as he set Adrienne down, then his eyes met Mary's with silent echoes of deep meaning.

"Good morning, Mary," he said.

"Good morning," she replied and tried not to melt into complete emotional incoherence. "Have you had breakfast?"

"Yes, thank you. You go ahead. I've got . . . work to do." He stepped toward her and gave her a quick kiss in greeting. "How are you this morning?"

"I didn't get a lot of sleep, but I'm all right. How are you?"

"The same," he said. "Maybe we should talk about *why* we didn't get much sleep."

"Maybe we should. If you—"

"Mom!" Adrienne shouted. "Come and eat with me!"

"I'm coming," Mary called, then smiled at Whit. "I'll talk to you later, then."

"I'll look forward to it," he said, and she went reluctantly into the house.

They only saw each other for a minute later that morning when he told her that he needed to use his lunch hour to run some errands for his mother; he'd invite her to come along except that he actually had to go home for a few minutes and it wasn't a good idea for her to accompany him there.

"Can we talk later?" she asked.

"Sure," he said, but she preferred talking in person, as opposed to over the phone.

"Could you possibly stay after work? I can fix some supper, although I'm not any great cook."

"I'd like that," he said. "I'll make certain my mother has something for her supper, then I won't have to hurry home too quickly."

"That'll be great," she said. He kissed her quickly and went back to work. She couldn't deny her growing respect for him, considering the fact that he didn't use their relationship as an excuse to slack on his work. In fact, he seemed all the more determined to go the extra mile in his efforts and the time he put in. She devoted herself to her own work, vigorously attacking some of the chores on Kristi's cleaning list. She spent some time with Adrienne, did some laundry, and greatly looked forward to having a long conversation with Whit. She especially enjoyed the thought that he wouldn't be leaving once his workday was finished. She wished it would always be that way.

# Chapter Seven

SOON AFTER JANEL LEFT FOR the evening, Whit came into the house and told Mary he'd brought some clean clothes and he was going to wash up and change. By the time he came out of the bathroom, she was pulling a meatloaf out of the oven, and Adrienne was almost done setting the table. She hadn't mastered getting everything symmetrical, and each place setting varied greatly in its arrangement, but she did make sure that every person had a napkin and all the right utensils.

"Can I help?" Whit asked Mary.

"No, but thank you. I've got it all under control. We can eat in just a minute."

Adrienne tugged on Whit's pant leg and announced, "My birthday is coming. I'll be five years old."

"No kidding?" he asked with exaggerated excitement. "We need to do something super fun, then!"

"Can we, Mom?" Adrienne asked.

"Of course we'll do something fun. Maybe Whit will know how to make it *super* fun."

Mary picked up a platter of meatloaf slices to carry to the table, and she nodded at a plate of baked potatoes, saying to Whit, "Can you grab that?"

"Sure," he said and followed her.

A minute later they sat down, with Adrienne at the head of the table and Whit and Mary across from each other.

"This is nice," he said, smiling at Mary.

"Yes, it is," she agreed, then they both became aware of Adrienne watching them. "Would you mind blessing it?" she asked him.

"I'd be happy to," he said, and they all bowed their heads. Since he'd shared many lunches with them and they always blessed the food, it was far from the first time she'd heard him pray, but she loved it.

After the amen, she said to him, "Your prayers remind me of my mother . . . of the way she prayed."

"I consider that a great compliment," he said, and they passed the food around. While Whit fixed some potato for Adrienne according to her instructions, he said to her, "My birthday is coming up soon too."

"Really?" Mary said as if the idea thrilled her. Her voice then turned facetious. "You'll be *thirty*?"

"That's right," he said with equal humor. "You're not so much older than me, after all."

"We can do something super fun for *your* birthday too," Adrienne said.

"As long as I can celebrate with you and your mother, I'm certain it will be a very happy birthday."

They talked about possible places they could go and things they could do to celebrate, and discovered that the two birthdays were eleven days apart. Mary declared that was just the right amount of days between in order to have *two* parties instead of just one to celebrate both. Mary began to think about how old Whit had been when Adrienne and Isabelle were born—and how old *she* had been when she'd adopted them. Every time she stopped to consider their age difference, she quickly convinced herself that this relationship was ludicrous. But then she looked at him—and the way he looked at her—and she doubted if anything had ever felt so right.

When Adrienne finally stopped chattering enough for Mary to bring up a new topic, she said to Whit, "I was wondering if . . . well, your mother said something about it, and . . ."

"What?" he asked, making her aware that she was nervous.

"I was wondering if we could go to church with you." He looked stunned, and she added quickly, "It's not dangerous for us to go, is it?"

"No," he laughed softly, "it's not dangerous. I just . . . well, I was going to try to talk you into going with me. I didn't expect you to ask, but I'm glad you did. I'd love to have you come to church, and I know my mother would love it as well, but . . ."

"But?"

"We attend a Spanish-speaking branch. I know you can understand what's going on, but Adrienne might be terribly bored."

He glanced at Adrienne, who was humming and stirring her vegetables around on her plate, oblivious to the conversation.

"Actually," Mary said, "Adrienne speaks Spanish." She saw Whit's brows go up and hurried to explain. "Not perfectly, but she understands it fairly well. We taught the girls to be bilingual right from the start."

"That's amazing," Whit said and laughed again, a perfectly delighted laugh. He looked at Adrienne and said in Spanish, "How is it that you are so smart *and* so beautiful?"

Adrienne's eyes lit up as she obviously understood him. In Spanish she said, "You talk in Spanish." Then to her mother, "He talks in Spanish, Mom."

"Yes, he does," Mary said in Spanish. "His mother is from Mexico."

Adrienne let out an adorable little gasp, then a giggle that made the adults laugh. "I was born in Mexico. I'm going to visit there someday. That's why I need to know how to talk the way they do."

"How wonderful!" Whit said as the conversation continued in Spanish. "I lived in Mexico for two years, and I hope to go back there someday. Maybe we can go together."

Again Adrienne giggled with excitement. Whit looked at Mary and said, "I think she'll manage just fine at church." He looked a little sad and added in English, "I wish we could invite you over for Sunday dinner afterward. My mother's Mexican Sunday dinners are superb."

"Why don't we all eat here?" she said. "If you give me a list of ingredients, I can have everything on hand, and we can help her."

Whit smiled as if he could barely contain his excitement over the idea. "We'll bring the food this time," he said.

"That sounds wonderful," she said and meant it. She couldn't remember the last time a Sunday hadn't felt long and dreary. She was already counting the hours.

"May I ask why you want to come to church?"

"You may ask. I hope you won't be deflated if I tell you that it's not just about wanting to be with *you*."

"On the contrary," he said.

"I certainly *do* want to be with you, but some of the things you said last night . . . about the changes you made in your life . . . got me thinking about my mother's beliefs, and the things she taught me. Simon had no interest in going to church, and I had no backbone, but now that I'm in this place in my life, I'd like to learn more. And I think it would be good for Adrienne."

Mary was a little startled to see a hint of moisture glistening in Whit's eyes. She saw him blink several times and the glisten disappeared, but not before she grasped its implication. "This means a lot to you," she said with confidence.

"Yes, it does."

"I know your religion is very important to you. I assume you would prefer to marry someone who shares your beliefs."

"That's true," he said. "Knowing that you're actually a member, and that your mother had taught you things, made a big difference in my believing that I could pursue my feelings. I hope that makes sense and doesn't sound like—"

"It *does* make sense," she said, "and I respect your convictions. I want you to know that. And I want you to know that even if things don't work out between us, I still want to explore making religion a part of my life."

"Good, I'm glad to hear it. But my hope is that we can make a very happy Mormon family."

Mary smiled and finished eating. Whit complimented her on the food with sincerity, admitting that his mother didn't make things like meatloaf, but he was actually quite fond of it. They worked together to clean up the kitchen, then they played a couple of games with Adrienne. The games were suited to her age level, but Whit kept pretending that he had trouble understanding the rules and he needed her to explain. The more that Mary watched them interact, the more she wanted him to be a part of their lives. It all felt perfect until she considered the decade of years between them. She didn't know why it bothered her so much, but it did.

After Adrienne had gone to bed, Whit and Mary sat on the couch in the common room to visit.

"What are you thinking about?" he asked, taking her hand.

"I'm forty years old, Whit."

He facetiously said, "But in a couple of weeks you'll only be *ten* years older than me, not *eleven.*" She glared at him, not finding it funny, and he added, "Are we having this conversation again? Really?"

"I'm still a decade older than you, Whit," she said as if it might never have occurred to him.

"And I'm covered with tattoos that are ugly and disgusting. The difference is that I actually *chose* to permanently defile myself. You didn't choose the year you were born, and neither did I. It's a fact. And it's an irrelevant fact."

"We can't go into public without people looking at us and wondering why we're actually a couple."

"You mean they're wondering how some idiot guy who actually survived life in a street gang ended up with such an incredible woman? Is that what you mean?"

"People won't *see* evidence of that."

"And people won't see our age difference nearly as much as you think they do. What does it matter what anyone thinks, anyway? That's your father talking in your head. The real Mary does *not* care what anyone thinks. It's all just a stupid cultural credence with no substance to it, whatsoever. If our age difference was reversed, no one—including you— would have any issue with it." She looked skeptical, and he added. "If I were ten years older than *you*, would you keep bringing this up?" He answered for her. "No! Because it's not about age, it's about you finding it impossible to believe that *anyone* could love you the way that I love you. Without reservation, without judgment or condition, without adhering to any social or cultural expectation. It's just love, Mary. Pure and simple. It makes the world go round and all that. And it's *real* love, Mary. Just because you've never experienced it before doesn't mean it's not real. Get used to it!"

"I'm trying," she said in a soft voice that calmed him, although it was plainly evident that he was more consumed with vehemence and frustration than with any degree of anger. He looked at her intently, and she added, "You understand what's going on inside of me in a way that helps me know I'm not crazy for feeling the way I do, but . . . I've spent my whole life seeing myself a certain way. I need you to be patient with me while I try to figure this out."

"Of course," he said.

"I can't help wondering if . . . there's something more to this for *you*."

"What do you mean?"

"Are you absolutely certain our age difference doesn't bother you?"

"I'm absolutely certain."

"It could become more obvious as we get older. I could break out in wrinkles any year now. You could end up taking care of me the way you're taking care of your mother."

"And I could get diagnosed with a disease next month and *you* could end up taking care of *me*. That's not the point."

"What *is* the point, Whit?"

"I don't know what you're getting at."

Mary analyzed once more the evidence of what she was *getting at*, and she said, "You keep bringing up the tattoos . . . and your gang history. It bothers you."

"Yes, it bothers me."

"And yet you've declared firmly that it's in the past; that it's not who you are anymore. So *why* does it bother you?"

He kept his gaze firmly set on hers while he was obviously thinking about it. He finally said, "I wonder if—in spite of everything we feel—you deserve better than that."

Mary shrugged. "Apparently we're struggling with the same insecurities for different reasons." He sighed, and she could see by his eyes that he'd perceived her meaning. "Get used to it," she said, clearly mimicking him.

He smiled but said with seriousness, "It's not the same thing. As I have pointed out, what makes you feel insecure has nothing to do with choices you made. The choices I made have consequences that will be with me for the rest of my life. If you marry me, those consequences will be with you too."

"If you're talking about the tattoos, do you really think I would be so shallow as to let them bother me?"

"I don't think you're shallow at all, but you haven't even seen them yet."

"So, show me," she challenged. "Why don't you just show me and get it over with? If they're on your chest and back and arms, it's nowhere I wouldn't see if we went swimming together."

"I wear a shirt when I go swimming."

"You know what I mean."

"Yes, I know what you mean, but . . . not right now."

"Okay," she said. "Whenever you're ready, you let me know."

"Okay," he said as well. "Come here." He put his arm around her and eased her closer. "Tell me why you had trouble sleeping."

"Only if you tell me the same."

"It's a deal," he said and pressed a kiss into her hair.

Mary recounted the huge gamut of emotions she had experienced during the night. She talked about her grief, and how it felt to acknowledge being able to see how devoid her life had been of relationships that had given her what any woman had a right to need and expect. He agreed with her and offered perfect compassion and understanding. Each time they talked, she felt more certain that he truly understood her, and she was surprised at how completely open she could be with him, and how comfortable she had come to feel with such openness in so short a time. She'd *never* felt this comfortable with Simon, and never would have tried to share such personal feelings. Her words would have fallen on deaf ears and only left her feeling more unhappy or upset. She told Whit that as well, and he vowed to never dismiss her feelings, even if he didn't agree with them.

The nurse that had been on the evening shift with Walter came down the stairs and told Mary that her father was sleeping and all was well. "And here's the monitor," she said, handing it to Mary.

"Thank you, Elaine," Mary said and walked her to the door once she'd properly introduced her to Whit.

Mary returned to the couch and sat beside Whit. He nodded toward the monitor as she set it on the coffee table. "I'm in charge from ten at night until six in the morning, except for last night when we went out. The nurse agreed to stay later. They're all very nice. I don't know how they put up with him."

"It's really that bad?"

"It's worse than bad," she said and told him things about her father's attitude that she'd just skirted around previously. She told him how badly he treated Adrienne, and how the child was simply no longer allowed to go anywhere near her grandfather's room. "If he wasn't confined to that room, I would never be able to live here in peace."

"I'm glad you can live here in peace," he said, taking her hand.

"Me too." She smiled. "And I'm glad he didn't protest my idea to hire a gardener."

"I'm glad about that too," he said, "but if you don't live here, there's little point in my employment, and yet I can't imagine me living under the same roof as your father."

"So, we're like a bird and a fish," she said.

"What do you mean?"

"If a bird and a fish fall in love, where will they live?"

"Ah," he said. "If you must know, *that* is the biggest reason I couldn't sleep last night. I want to have a future with you and Adrienne. I want to provide a decent living for you, but my mother won't leave her house and she needs me, and even *if* she would come here, how could I bring my Hispanic mother into a household with a man who believes that anyone not Caucasian is scum?"

"It *is* a dilemma," she said, "but for now I think we should worry about more important things, and just give it some time."

"What more important things?"

"Like planning birthday parties, and which flowers to put in the garden."

"Of course," he said and laughed. "Those are *very* important things." He leaned over and kissed her. "As long as we're doing those things together, I think I'm good with that."

"Yeah, me too," she said, and he kissed her again.

\* \* \* \* \*

Mary slept much better that night, even though she was dreading the fact that she had to face a Saturday without seeing Whit. The last day of the week was his day for cleaning, yard work, and grocery shopping for his mother. They both agreed that it was too bad she couldn't be at his house, since they would have both enjoyed doing such things together, but it couldn't be helped.

Mary used Saturday to accomplish the same sorts of things. She did laundry, took Adrienne out to do some errands and to get a hamburger for lunch. That evening after Adrienne was in bed, she talked with Whit on the phone for nearly two hours before they said good night and went to bed in their separate homes. To Mary it felt as if he were on another continent. The very fact that she *couldn't* go to his home was more disturbing than she wanted to admit. Instead she focused on her anticipation of having a lovely Sunday with Whit and his mother. It would be nice to get to know his mother better in an environment away from the fearful neighborhood in which she lived.

The following morning Mary and Adrienne were both dressed in their Sunday best when Whit came to pick them up at eight-thirty.

"Such lovely ladies," he said, but Mary was more focused on how nice he looked in a suit. She'd only seen him dressed this way when he'd come for his initial job interview, but she liked it.

Ida was standing in the driveway near Whit's truck, visibly excited to see Mary again. "Oh, my dear girl," she said in Spanish and hugged Mary tightly. "Whit tells me so many good things about you."

"He tells *me* good things about *you*," Mary answered, then introduced her to Adrienne. Ida made a fuss over how beautiful she was, and complimented her on how well she spoke Spanish. Whit hurried them along, not wanting to be late. Only then did Mary realize that the extra space behind the seat of his truck was actually another row of seats. Ida insisted that she wanted to sit in the back with Adrienne because they had a great deal to talk about. Whit got them settled, then held the door for Mary so she could sit in her usual place, next to him.

The drive was pleasant, and Mary thoroughly enjoyed listening to Ida and Adrienne chattering away in the backseat as if they were forever friends. Adrienne's precocious maturity was evident, and it was obvious that Ida did very well with children. Whit just kept smiling at Mary now and then, as if he too were enjoying the exchange.

Mary had expected going to church to be a pleasant experience. She *hadn't* expected it to be one of the sweetest experiences of her life. She was overcome with thoughts of her mother so strongly that she began weeping discreetly during the opening hymn, and she hardly stopped crying throughout the entire meeting. She had memories of attending church a few times with her mother, and she remembered just a bit about her own baptism, but she'd known even then that they were doing these things without her father's approval, and there was a tense dynamic of secrecy woven into her memories. Now, she just felt as if her mother was very pleased with Mary being here, and with her desire to bring the gospel fully into her life, and to have it be an active part of her daughter's life.

Whit was mindful of Mary's tears, and more than once whispered discreetly to inquire about what was wrong, and if there was anything he could do. She quietly assured him that what she felt was good, and he just kept handing her tissues from the little packet she'd gotten out of her purse. A few times Ida reached over Adrienne to put her hand over Mary's, as if she sensed the reasons for her emotion and wished to offer silent comfort. Mary felt as if Whit and his mother were already her family, as if it had been designed in heaven a very long time ago, and now they simply had to work out the technicalities to make it official. She wasn't going to jump headlong into marriage based on her emotions of that moment, but the largest part of her believed that it was meant to be and she needed to trust her feelings, trust in God, trust in Whit, and move forward.

After sacrament meeting was over, Mary was touched by how friendly the people were, and she couldn't help noticing how pleased Whit seemed as he introduced her and Adrienne. His love for them was evident. He seemed happy, and she suspected that happiness had not been a strong or constant factor in his life, any more than it had been in hers. Looking at it that way, she felt more prone to believe that she could make as big a difference in his life as he was making in hers, and their age difference felt less and less significant. She sensed some mild surprise from people they spoke to in seeing them together. For all that she could look in a mirror and feel good about her appearance, she still looked her age, and she couldn't deny that some of the difficulties of her life had given her a worn look that she disliked but couldn't change. On the other hand, Whit looked even younger than his years; therefore, the difference between them was evident. But no one they spoke to seemed uncomfortable or judgmental about it; perhaps only a bit curious. Or maybe even intrigued. Mary related to that. She felt amazingly intrigued with the love blossoming between her and Whit, and with the possibility of having it become a permanent part of her life.

Mary wasn't sure if Adrienne would feel comfortable going to the Primary meeting with other children her age, but when Whit explained it to her, she was eager to do so. Her daughter had not associated with any children her age since Isabelle had died and they'd come to stay here in Los Angeles. Since she didn't go to school yet, and they'd not gone to church, there was nowhere to meet other children. Mary had wondered many times if she was doing a disservice to Adrienne, but she hadn't known what to do about it. Now, she hoped that Adrienne might make some new friends, and perhaps it might be possible for them to play together outside of church. She wondered if Adrienne's lack of social interaction with children might make her shy and skittish about being left in Primary without her mother there, but the opposite was evident. Adrienne seemed eager to be with her peers and confident in being independent of her mother throughout the meeting. She took quickly to the teacher when Whit introduced them, and they left Adrienne happily in her care.

Mary thoroughly enjoyed the adult Sunday School class she attended with Whit and Ida. They were discussing the apostle Paul, reading passages from the New Testament that spoke of the persecution he had endured for Christ's sake. Mary noted that Whit and Ida both had beautiful, thick books of scripture from which they were reading. Whit held his book so that she could see it in order to read along when verses were being read aloud. She recalled that her mother had had a Bible and a Book of Mormon, but they had not been nearly so lovely nor of such high quality.

Somewhere in the midst of the lesson, Whit whispered in Mary's ear, "Paul is one of my greatest heroes."

"I'd like to hear more about that," she whispered back.

He smiled at her and nodded, then they focused on the lesson.

After Sunday School, Mary stayed with Ida in the Relief Society meeting for women. Whit went to what he called elders quorum priesthood meeting, and Ida told Mary how proud she was that Whit was a counselor in the presidency for the elders, something that Mary wanted to hear more about.

Mary asked Whit before he left if she should go check on Adrienne, but he said, "They know where to find you if there's a problem. Don't worry. Just relax and enjoy yourself."

"Oh, I will," she said. He kissed her cheek, then his mother's, and walked away.

When the women's meeting commenced, Ida was asked to introduce her guest. She stood up and spoke with sweet pride of how her precious Whit was dating this amazing *young woman*. Mary wondered if Ida's eyesight was failing her, or if she was just optimistic. Mary received a warm welcome, and the meeting proceeded. The lesson focused on the value of women in God's eyes, and how great their potential was when coupled with the power of the priesthood. Mary felt warmed by the messages of the lesson and again became teary, although not as intensely as she had been earlier. Since she'd run out of tissues, she was glad when Ida provided a little packet of them from *her* purse. She noted that for all of the evidence that Ida was getting on in years and struggled with some health issues, she wasn't at all frail. She'd seemed frail when they'd met before, but Mary now realized she hadn't been feeling well that day.

Whit had told her that his mother was showing signs of dementia, and sometimes her memory played tricks on her. For the moment she was lucid and attentive and seemed deeply happy to have Mary there with her. Mary had not felt so loved or valued since the death of her own mother. Her tears increased at the thought of having this sweet woman in her life in some capacity of a motherly role. Did Whit realize that by making her a part of his life, he was also giving her the gift of a mother? She considered that she was giving *them* the gift of a daughter and granddaughter. Their obvious love for Adrienne warmed her. She was startled to think how she couldn't imagine *not* being a part of each other's lives, when a week ago she'd believed that the interest she and Whit had for each other was shallow and meaningless and temporary. Now she believed it truly had the potential to be a permanent part of their lives. She prayed that it could be so!

When the meeting was over, some kind ladies stopped to talk with Mary and Ida, making polite inquiries about Mary. When she said that she was widowed and had a daughter who was nearly five, one of the women enthusiastically declared that she was divorced and had a daughter who had just turned five, and she would very much like to have the girls get together and play. It felt to Mary as if prayers she'd never thought to actually utter were being answered. They exchanged phone numbers and a hug just before Whit found them. He was holding the hand of a grinning Adrienne; apparently Primary had gone well.

On the way home from church, Adrienne chattered excitedly about her teacher, the other children, the lesson, a word game they'd played, and the songs they had sung. She was clearly thrilled at being with children who had the same color of skin and hair as herself, and speaking Spanish at church had apparently given her a purpose in using her second language in a way that connected with her spirit. At least that's how Mary saw it, and the entire thing just made her swelling heart overflow. It was as if she could feel destiny swirling all around her, then settling comfortably over her like a warm blanket.

Ida was thrilled to be going to Mary's home, and Whit had warned her about the fact that Mary's difficult father was in a room upstairs, but he would stay there and they would never have to cross paths. Mary was stunned when Ida began talking about how she remembered coming to Mary's home a few times when her sister, Claudia, had been the housekeeper here.

"Claudia is your sister?" Mary said, astonished.

"I thought you knew that," Whit said, equally astonished by her ignorance of this fact. "Janel talked to Claudia about the job."

"I knew there was a connection," Mary said, "but I didn't realize you were family."

"Now you know," Ida said with a pleasing laugh. "So many lovely coincidences."

"Coincidences, yeah," Whit said with mild sarcasm while exchanging a smile with Mary.

Through the last few minutes of the drive, Mary considered that the dear Claudia she remembered as being the housekeeper during her childhood years was actually related to these wonderful people. "Where is Claudia now?" Mary asked.

"She's in a care center," Whit said. "We usually go see her on Sundays. You're welcome to come if you'd like."

"Oh, I would love that!" Mary said. "Is she doing poorly?"

"She's doing better with proper care," Whit said. "Her children weren't taking very good care of her, to be truthful. She has a number of problems that make it hard for her to take care of herself, but no one thing that is too serious, in and of itself."

"I'm glad she's not too badly off. And you're related! That is so amazing!" Mary said. "I can't believe we overlooked that with everything we've talked about."

"So, you remember Claudia well, I take it," Whit said.

"Very well. She's the reason I remembered going to your neighborhood when I was a child."

"We'll have to talk more about that later," Whit said as he rolled down his window to punch in the code for the gates to open. He drove the truck in, and the gates automatically closed behind them. After he helped what he called *his three ladies* out of the truck, he got a cooler out of the back of the truck, and Mary realized it had food in it for their dinner preparations.

With Mary's help, it only took Ida a few minutes to find her way around the kitchen. She put on a full-length, floral-print apron that she'd brought with her and set to work with Whit's assistance, once he'd removed his jacket and tie. Mary sent Adrienne upstairs to change, then asked what she might do to help.

"Just stay close by in case we can't find something," Whit said, then he added in English, as if he didn't want Ida to understand, "My mother has been very excited about cooking for you. If you help too much it will disappoint her."

Ida said, "I know when you speak in English you don't want me to understand."

"I just told her you want to cook dinner for her," he said, and Ida smiled. He then said to Mary in Spanish, "You and Adrienne can set the table."

Mary enjoyed observing Whit and his mother cooking together as if it were completely common and comfortable between them. She could see evidence of the closeness they'd shared in having only each other due to the absence of his father, and with his being an only child. Then she realized that she had only *assumed* he was an only child. He'd never mentioned anything about siblings, but then he'd never mentioned that Claudia was his aunt, either.

"You've never told me if you have any siblings," Mary said, making herself comfortable in a chair she'd moved to a perfect vantage point where she could observe them while they cooked.

She saw Whit glance warily at his mother, but she didn't seem ruffled by the question, even though it seemed he had expected her to be. Ida answered for him, talking about her sweet daughter Crystal, who lived very far away, and how much she missed her.

Whit said in English, "She made a clean break; had to get out. She lives on a farm in Idaho and has a good life, but she connects *us* with the bad life she had before she left, so we don't hear from her very often. She has three kids, but we don't hear much about them, either."

"Talk in Spanish," Ida said.

"In a minute," he said in Spanish. More lightly he added, "I can't talk about you if I talk in Spanish." He winked at her. "I'm telling her how amazing you are."

She gave him a doubtful scowl, then he said in English, "Just be warned that she might also tell you about my brother Joseph."

"You have a brother too?" Mary asked, realizing that his lines between one side of his life and the other were very clearly drawn.

"He was killed when I was seventeen."

Mary gasped, wondering how they had survived *two* tragic deaths in the family.

"You're talking about Joseph," Ida said, glancing at Mary's expression, which surely gave away that she'd just heard something shocking. "You don't have to pretend you're not talking about him. I miss him, but I know he is in a far better place. He never could have escaped from the evil of his life any other way." She put a hand on Whit's arm. "He was not as strong as you, but he's all right now."

"Yes, he is," Whit said, then he turned to Mary, continuing in Spanish. "We miss Joseph and Crystal, but they're both fine, and we're glad for that."

"Your life has been very difficult," she observed.

He looked at her firmly and said, "So has yours."

"Not nearly so much."

"That's all a matter of perspective, I suppose."

"It will be better now," Ida said as if she had personally been given a vision that the future would be brighter for all of them, the implication being that Whit and Mary being together would make life better for all of them. They exchanged a smile that mutually declared their agreement with that implication.

# Chapter Eight

THE CONVERSATION LIGHTENED WHEN ADRIENNE returned. Mary helped her set the table according to a more orderly standard in light of a very special Sunday dinner. They took their time about it while Mary enjoyed the lovely aromas wafting from the stove and the sounds of busyness as Whit assisted his mother in cooking what she declared was some of the best of her traditional Mexican fare. When the food was ready, Mary took some upstairs on a tray for her father and the nurse who was attending him. Janel was in the habit of leaving food in the fridge that the nurses on duty over the weekend could easily find and heat up on her days off, but since Mary had been there she had helped cover that task on Saturdays and Sundays. Between her and Janel they always made certain something was available; Walter wouldn't tolerate not having a decent meal to eat. She hoped that her father enjoyed the Mexican food in spite of his intolerance of Hispanic people. As long as he believed that she had cooked it, she figured he probably would. And no one told him otherwise.

With that taken care of, they finally sat down to eat, and Mary declared enthusiastically that it was some of the best food she'd ever tasted—even with all of her years of living in Mexico. She urged Ida to share her memories of growing up in Mexico, and she realized that Whit's father had served a mission in Mexico, where he had met Ida and had taught her the gospel and had actually been the one to baptize her. They had kept in touch through letters after the mission, then Whit's father miraculously had been given a job opportunity that allowed him to return to where he'd served his mission. While working there, he'd connected with Ida again and they'd fallen in love.

When he could no longer find work in Mexico, they had moved to Los Angeles, where two of Ida's sisters were already established in the same neighborhood. They had made a fresh start but had quickly realized there were many detriments to living in a dominantly Hispanic neighborhood, where gang activity was becoming more prevalent. The family endured a great deal of persecution before it had finally culminated in the shooting death of Ida's Caucasian husband. And then her daughter had moved away and her sons had become involved in the gang she so detested. Her sisters' children were also involved, and the three of them had lamented a great deal together over the grief of such a life, but they had all been stuck there due to financial limitations. Her sister Claudia was now in a care center, and her sister Sofia still lived in the neighborhood but was mostly homebound due to symptoms of her old age. Sofia and Claudia were both older than Ida, and they were all widows, although Ida's sisters' husbands had not died so violently.

Mary was amazed at how Ida seemed to want to talk about all of that, and how freely she did so. She was also amazed at how Ida had an underlying peace about the challenges of her life. She reminded Mary of her own mother in that way. It seemed the gospel had a way of putting trials and hardships into perspective. Mary wanted to understand that more fully.

After they had cleared away the dinner, they all took a brief tour through the garden so that Ida could see what her son had been doing. He talked about his plans and what it would look like, and Mary felt excited to ponder the results. She was glad to know that restoring and maintaining it would certainly justify a full-time job for Whit for a good long time.

After the tour, they all got into the truck again to go and visit Ida's sister Claudia. Ida wished they could go and visit Sofia as well, but since she lived in the same neighborhood as Ida, it would be impossible. They focused instead on how good it would be to visit Claudia with Mary and Adrienne along. Mary felt excited at the prospect of once again seeing this woman who had been so kind to her in her younger years. She also remembered how unkindly Claudia had been treated by Mary's father. He had made it clear that he preferred Caucasian people as hired help in his household, and Loretta had hired the woman without her husband's knowledge. He had made a great concession in order to please his wife, since she very much liked Claudia. As Mary remembered it, Loretta had apparently not been aware of how deeply bigoted her husband was until she *had* hired Claudia, and it had ignited an enormous argument.

Mary didn't remember that argument; she'd only been told about it later. Walter had conceded that Claudia could retain her employment in the household as long as she knew her place and kept it. Claudia had been a part of Mary's childhood, the same way that Janel was currently a part of Adrienne's. This woman already felt much like an aunt to Mary; to know that she was Whit's aunt just seemed too remarkable to be any kind of coincidence.

"I remember going to Claudia's home," Mary said, speaking in Spanish so Ida could be a part of the conversation. "I was a child, and Claudia's husband had passed away. My mother and I went to visit."

Ida reminisced a bit about when her brother-in-law had died from a heart attack at a fairly young age. She mentioned that it was before Whit had been born, and Crystal had been very young.

"Of *course* it was before you were born," Mary whispered lightly to Whit in English. He just smiled at her and kept driving.

When they arrived at the care center, Mary hung back in the doorway of Claudia's room while she observed Whit and Ida exchanging greetings with her. Of course she'd aged a great deal since Mary had last seen her, which was before she'd left for Mexico nearly twenty years ago. But Mary still clearly recognized her, and it warmed her heart to have this opportunity. Whit motioned toward Mary and Adrienne and quickly explained to Claudia who had come to see her and why. Claudia's face lit up, then she got tears in her eyes as she reached her arms out toward Mary, who bent over to hug Claudia where she was sitting in a recliner. They hugged tightly, and Claudia expressed in English what a great thrill it was to see her. Mary told her that both she and her daughter could understand Spanish, and Claudia looked pleasantly surprised. She then spoke to Adrienne, who approached Claudia with a hug, as if her mother's example had given her a desire to be affectionate. Claudia took obvious delight in the child as they all sat to visit.

They stayed for a long while, and Mary promised Claudia that they would be back. On the way home, Mary asked Whit, "Does she ever get out?" She spoke in English since Ida and Adrienne were deeply preoccupied with their own conversation in the backseat.

"Oh, yeah. We take her out once in a while, and one of her sons does as well. She can't walk much, but she likes to go for a drive or out to eat occasionally."

"Perhaps she can come to our home for a visit sometime."

"That would be nice," Whit said and smiled at her.

"What?" she asked.

"It just feels to me like you're a part of the family already."

"It feels that way to me too."

"We should make that official," he said, lifting his brows.

"We should give it some time," she insisted, but she couldn't help smiling at the thought.

Mary found it difficult to have Whit and Ida leave to go home, but she'd had a glorious day, and she had tomorrow to look forward to. Whit had told her he wanted to leave as soon as they were finished with breakfast to go to his favorite local nursery and pick out flowers and plants.

Monday turned out to be a wonderful day. Adrienne exhibited great childlike excitement that fully expressed how Mary was feeling, but her own maturity dictated that she not be quite so exuberant about it. Mary loved the nursery, and they all had a glorious time exploring it with no need to rush as they admired the different plants and flowers. She was duly impressed with Whit's knowledge over nearly every species. He could tell her what would thrive in the shady parts of the garden and what would do better in the sun. He knew which flowers would offer the most resilient blooms and which plants would offer ground cover that was resistant to weeds.

"How did you learn all of this?" she asked.

"Truthfully," he said with a chuckle, "it was mostly through Google. It's not such a bad way for a kid like me to get an education."

"Learning is learning," she said. "I know *I'm* impressed."

He smiled at her and continued his discussion on what he would like to put in the garden and why. His insights were very much aligned with her own, and Mary felt pleased with his suggestions. He'd come prepared with a diagram of the entire garden that looked much like a blueprint for a home or building. He explained to Mary again how he wanted to start with the section of garden that was visible from the house; he also explained that they couldn't buy too many flowers at once or he wouldn't be able to get them planted in a timely manner. But he would make notes of what she liked and didn't like and would continue working at it. They picked out some rose bushes that he suggested would complement those that were already there that he'd pruned back to compensate for years of overgrowth. "They'll be amazing come next spring," he said, "and if we plant more now, they'll *all* be amazing."

"I can't wait!" Mary said with a childish giggle that reminded her of Adrienne, and it made Whit laugh. "What about the rosebush you put in the middle of walkway—the walkway you're going to rebuild? What color is that?"

"When it blooms, you'll see. I paid for that one, by the way."

"Why?" she asked.

"Because it's a gift for you," he said and kissed her quickly.

"How sweet," she said.

"We'll see if it actually does what I want it to do." He then changed the subject and moved on to a section of bulb flowers. He pointed out that there were some places in the garden where tulips, daffodils, and irises were still coming up in the spring, but he wanted to expand on that and make those areas more dense and colorful. Mary heartily agreed.

The flatbed cart that Adrienne was managing to push around gradually became filled with flowers and plants in a variety of cartons and buckets. Whit asked a nursery employee if they could be watered again before he took them, since they would be in his truck for a while. They gladly complied, and they even let Adrienne hold the hose and help sprinkle them with a healthy drink of water. Whit paid for the goods with the card Mary had given him for this very purpose, then everything was loaded into the truck and they went to eat at a place that had a child's playground. Adrienne had a wonderful time going down slides and jumping into a myriad of colored balls while Whit and Mary ate slowly and talked. Even though they'd talked about it before, she asked him to tell her more about his mission in Mexico, and she told him more about her work there in different cities. They had actually lived in some of the same places, which was one more commonality in their lives that was almost eerie—but in a good way.

After they managed to get Adrienne to eat enough lunch so she wouldn't be starving by midafternoon, they got into the truck again and Whit said, "There's somewhere else I want to take you; something I want to buy for you."

"There's no need for you to buy things for me," Mary said as he pulled out onto the highway.

"I can if I want to," he insisted and smiled at her. With such a smile, how could she argue with him?

Mary was surprised when they arrived at a bookstore, and she realized from the signs in the windows that it sold exclusively LDS products. "Oh!"

she said with glee. "I remember once coming to such a store with my mother, but I'd completely forgotten that such a place existed."

"Shall we go in?" he asked, and she resisted exhibiting that childlike excitement again. Adrienne was excited enough for both of them.

They wandered around the bookstore the way they'd wandered around the nursery. Whit was able to answer all of their questions about the books, music, art, and other products. To Mary it felt like a magical place. She could have spent hundreds of dollars and still not been content. As it was, she restricted herself to picking out only a few things, and she allowed Adrienne to get a coloring book based on scripture stories and a little bracelet with a charm that said CTR on it. Whit explained to the child that it was a reminder to always choose the right, and that Heavenly Father would always bless her and be with her as long as she did her best to do so.

After they'd sufficiently perused the majority of the store, Whit guided them to the corner where the scriptures were displayed. Mary gasped when she saw them in different sizes, with different colors of leather covers available. "Oh, they're lovely," she said.

"I want you to pick out the type you like best," Whit said, "and I want to get them for you."

"Why?" she asked, astonished. "They're so expensive."

"There are many reasons," he said, "but mostly because just watching you at church yesterday, and the way you absorbed everything with so much awe and joy, was probably one of the most gratifying experiences of my life. I want you to have these because I believe they will become your most treasured possession. I want to share with you how much the scriptures mean to me, how they have saved me over and over. So . . . just be gracious and let me do this."

Mary became too choked up to speak. She just hugged him, then wiped at her eyes as he said, "Which color do you like best?"

"Oh, I love the blue!" she said.

"And the size?"

"Not too small," she said. "I'm getting too old to read tiny print." She laughed after she said it, and he picked up the display model of the standard-size, blue-covered quad. She held it reverently, thumbed through its pages, then told him it was perfect.

At the counter he insisted on paying for the other things that she had intended to purchase for herself and Adrienne. He was so insistent that she couldn't argue in front of the clerk without making a scene. He then arranged to have her name embossed on the cover of her scriptures.

"I'm thinking simply *Mary Jane*," he said, "because I know you're not fond of either of the surnames you've had. I'd like it to say *Mary Jane Eden*, but on the off chance that you *don't* marry me, that could be awkward."

"*Mary Jane* would be perfect," she said. "Maybe we can add the *Eden* later."

While they were waiting for the name to be embossed, they wandered around the store some more. Adrienne was surprisingly calm and well-behaved, entranced as she was by looking at all the things that connected into her time in Primary the previous day, which she had talked about over and over.

Adrienne insisted on carrying the bags, minus the little box that contained Mary's new scriptures, which Mary held in her arm. Once outside the store Mary stopped Whit to say what she felt needed to be said, while Adrienne skipped up and down the sidewalk, holding the shopping bags out at her sides.

"You didn't have to do that," Mary said.

"I enjoy doing that," he insisted. "I have a very good job. I can afford to buy you and Adrienne a few things."

"I have my own money."

"*How* do you have your own money?" he asked. "As long as we're getting personal about money, why don't you tell me. I know your father wouldn't give you a dime, and you told me there was no life insurance and you moved home because you had no choice."

"We had a home, if you must know. It didn't amount to much, but I couldn't afford to keep paying the mortgage, and I sold it. So I do have some money in the bank—enough to meet our needs for a long while as long as I don't have to pay rent and utilities."

"Okay," he said. "I'm glad to know that. But that still doesn't mean I can't buy you and Adrienne some nice things if I choose to. I have a very good job."

"And you're supporting your mother and—"

"My mother gets Social Security, which is enough to meet *her* needs, since the house has long been paid for. I have a reasonably large amount of money put away. I'm pretty well-off for a gang kid, *if you must know*—and I even came by my money honestly."

"I'm glad to know that," she said in return, then smiled at him with the hope of easing the tension. "If my father kicks me out, I assume we can manage to keep each other from starving or living on the streets."

"Yeah," he said, "I think we can manage." He smiled as well, then he surprised her with a long, tight hug. "I will never let you go without, Mary. No matter what I have to do." He then drew both of her hands to his chest and looked at her firmly. "It feels good to me to help you, to think of providing for your needs."

"Well, it feels good to know that you feel that way," she said. "I must admit I love the way you take the role as protector and provider very seriously."

"Yes, I do," he said.

She hugged him but kept her eyes on his. "Well, if you must know, it makes me feel loved. Thank you."

He kissed her and said, "Making you feel loved is the easiest and greatest thing I've ever done."

\* \* \* \* \*

During the remainder of the week, Mary began to feel more comfortable with Whit being a part of their lives. He gracefully integrated being her gardener with making himself a part of the family in a way that was both natural and comfortable. Janel was thrilled about the whole thing, and they all got along famously. Mary knew that she and Whit both needed time before they could appropriately decide whether or not marriage was the right course for them, but each day she felt more and more unhappy about him leaving every evening to go care for his mother and sleep under a different roof, in a neighborhood where she couldn't even visit.

Mary was thrilled when Sunday came again and they all went to church together. With her new scriptures in hand, she enjoyed the meetings even more than she had the previous week. Whit had arranged for a meeting with the branch president right after church, and Ida sat on the couch in the foyer with Adrienne while Whit and Mary went into his office. President Martinez spoke English as well as Spanish, and he was a very nice man. Whit had offered to let Mary speak to him alone if she preferred, but she made it clear she would rather have him with her, and she certainly had nothing to hide from him when it came to a conversation with an ecclesiastical leader. Whit opened with a brief explanation of how he had come to work for Mary, then he explained that they were now dating, and how they both hoped that it might lead to marriage. President Martinez seemed pleased and made no comment about their age difference. Whit also explained that Mary had been baptized at the age of eight because her mother had been a member, but she had never been active because her father had been against it. Whit wanted to see if Mary's Church records could be located so that she could officially be a member of this branch. Because it was a Spanish-speaking branch with broad boundaries in the city, she would have attended this particular branch whether she came with Whit or not. The president said he would get right on it and let them know when everything was official. He then asked Mary some specific questions about her knowledge of the gospel and her present feelings about it. He was pleased with her conviction and her desire to make it fully a part of her life.

Afterward they all went together to Mary's house, but this time she did the cooking, gently suggesting that Ida might enjoy playing a game with Adrienne; however, she did let Whit help her. Whit was insistent about that, and Mary didn't mind his help at all. In fact, his presence and involvement heightened her enjoyment of anything and everything. She felt so happy with the evidence of his growing love for her that she sometimes feared she would burst out in joyful sobbing. Their budding relationship, combined with her newfound interest in the gospel, just seemed too wonderful to hold inside her heart.

Later that day they went again to visit Claudia, and again Mary didn't want Whit and Ida to leave. But reality intervened, a reality that was worsened that night when Mary had a difficult episode with her father. She was up half the night with him and had to exercise great patience when he was especially cranky and resistant to allowing her to give him the help that he needed. She was tempted more than once to just leave him to suffer, but she couldn't bring herself to do it. He needed her assistance, and she had to consider—at the very least—that he was giving her and her daughter a place to live. At least she was able to turn him over to the care of a nurse in the morning, and she was able to get a nap that afternoon while Janel watched Adrienne.

Later that week they celebrated Adrienne's fifth birthday. Rachel, her new friend from Primary, and Rachel's mother, Cinda, went along on their outing. They had a glorious time and talked about what it might be like when the girls started kindergarten at the end of the summer. The following week they celebrated Whit's birthday. They took Ida with them and went out for pizza and to a bowling alley. Whit had insisted that was what he wanted to do the very most for his birthday, but Mary knew he was only saying that because Adrienne had been distressed on her own birthday because they couldn't go to a movie *and* go bowling, and she had chosen the movie. Mary gave him a nice pair of leather work gloves, since she'd noticed his were looking worn. She also gave him a tie, which he declared that he loved. Adrienne gave him a framed picture of herself with her mother. He declared that he loved that most of all, and Mary knew by his eyes that he meant it. He really did love her; he loved both of them. It was a miracle.

Weeks passed, and they all settled more comfortably into the pattern and routine of being as much a part of each other's lives as it was possible under the circumstances. Not once did Whit encounter Mary's father, and not once did she venture anywhere near Whit's neighborhood. She told Whit that she felt like they were living some twisted version of Romeo and Juliet, but he assured her that they would have a much happier ending. She prayed every day that he was right, that a happy ending for both of them was truly in their future.

Kristi never came back to work; as it turned out, helping her mother merged into some other work opportunity that was more suited to her college schedule. Mary was more than fine with that, since she'd managed with little trouble to take over Kristi's cleaning tasks, and she preferred not having her around. She couldn't help wondering if Kristi's preference to work elsewhere had something to do with the fact that there was no longer any reason to flirt with the gardener. Whatever the reasons, Mary was glad for the change.

Mary had become especially comfortable in her daily routine of helping around the house, caring for her daughter, and remaining actively involved in the humanitarian efforts that were so close to heart. Almost every day Whit asked her what she was doing and how it was going. She knew from his comments that he'd started to closely follow her blog, and she was tenderly amazed by his genuine interest in the things that were important to her. They talked about saving their money and someday going back to Mexico together, where they could take a more active role in making a difference for the people there who needed so much. In the meantime, they talked about things they could do to make a difference from a distance. While it was still mainly Mary's project at this point, she felt Whit's support and enthusiasm in every way.

Mary loved seeing evidence of the garden coming together—at least the part that could be seen from the house. She especially loved the fact that Whit was focusing on that particular area of the garden because she could almost always see *him* from the house during his working hours. She caught glimpses of him laying the stones to form a new walkway that wound away from the patio. The flat rocks encircled the little rosebush he'd planted, and she wondered what it would look like when it finally bloomed. Right now it looked scrawny and showed no sign of ever sprouting a bud, but she knew that it would come to life under Whit's careful tutelage.

The flowers Whit had planted brought color and pattern to the view from the house, and Mary felt more excited every day to see how it was coming together. She often had a feeling that her mother would be very pleased, and once in a while she could almost swear that her mother was there beside her, watching the progress. She shared her feelings with Whit, and he completely agreed that it was more likely true than not.

Whit asked her at one point if she wanted to pick out a fountain to replace the one that had deteriorated. He showed her a few options online, but she felt overwhelmed and finally told him to surprise her. "You know me; you know my taste. I want something simple. Surprise me."

"Okay, I will," he said, as if the prospect was utterly delightful.

A few days later he started work on the plumbing and electrical that would make a fountain work properly, and then he told Mary that it would be delivered the following day. He said that he wanted her to go somewhere else or stay away until he finished installing it because he wanted her to be surprised. She did as he asked, but her curiosity made it difficult. At the end of the day it had been delivered; he then told her it was safe for her to look but she couldn't peek. She then realized that he'd covered the fountain with a large tarp, which was held down on the ground by rocks and bricks so it wouldn't fly away if the wind should blow. It was late the following afternoon before Whit came to find her to tell her that it was ready. He actually blindfolded her with a dishtowel before he led her outside, guiding her along carefully.

"Are you sure you haven't peeked?" he asked.

"I said I wouldn't and I didn't," she said and laughed.

"Okay, we're here," he said, and they stopped walking. "Are you ready?"

"I'm ready, already." She laughed again.

"Ta-dah!" he said and pulled away the blindfold.

Mary gasped, then unexpectedly started to cry. She didn't know what she'd expected, but she loved it more than she could have imagined. It was a three-tiered fountain, with water flowing down from one tier to the next. There was an old-fashioned look about it, as if it might have originated from some European town square. And at the top was a lovely little angel with a beautiful face, flowing hair, and turned-down eyes.

"In honor of your mother," Whit said, and Mary threw her arms around him.

"Oh, it's perfect," she cried. "I love it!"

"I'm glad," he said, and then he just held her while she cried. "Are you missing her?" he asked, as if he suspected there was more to her tears than the pleasure she felt over the fountain.

"Yes, but also . . . I think she's very pleased. I'd like to think it actually means something to her."

"I'd like to think so too. If it means something to you, then I'm sure that makes her happy."

After she'd admired the fountain for a number of minutes and from every angle, Whit showed her the switches that were near the back door: one for the water, and one for a light that came from beneath the water, which could be turned on at night for a glowing effect. Mary called Adrienne down from her room to see the fountain, and she was every bit as thrilled as her mother.

"Now the most important part," Whit said and pulled some quarters out of his pocket. He handed one to Adrienne, one to Mary, and kept one in his hand. "This is a wishing fountain. If you throw in a coin and make a wish, it just might come true."

"Can I go first?" Adrienne asked.

"Of course," Whit said, and she tossed her coin in with a great deal of flair, which made the adults laugh.

"You next," Whit said to Mary. She closed her eyes for a long moment, then opened them and threw in her coin.

Whit did the same with his coin, then he pulled Mary and Adrienne close to him and declared that his wish had already come true.

"Mine will come true when we're officially a family," Mary said, then added with mild alarm, "It's not bad luck to tell what you wished, is it?"

"Not in my opinion," Whit said. "If we each know what the other is wishing, we can help make those wishes come true."

"And a sincere wish combined with prayer is surely a good formula."

"It surely is," Whit agreed.

That very night Mary insisted that Whit go home and get his mother and come back so they could barbecue on the patio and enjoy the loveliness of the garden.

"The view from here is *very* nice," Mary said in Spanish, relaxing in a patio chair next to Ida, while Whit checked the chicken on the grill.

"Yes, it's very nice," Ida said. And then Adrienne gave Ida a quarter and insisted that she make a wish in the fountain that very minute.

\* \* \* \* \*

The same week that Adrienne started kindergarten, Whit told Mary that he'd noticed a sudden decline in his mother's memory. He was worried about her, and also worried about how he might care for her while he worked. Mary suggested that he bring her with him when he came to work, and she and Janel could help watch out for her. He was reluctant to put that burden on Mary, but when Ida had a particularly bad morning, full of confusion and worry, Whit *did* bring her with him. Mary didn't feel that Ida was any trouble. She mostly watched TV in the common room, dozing now and then. She rode with Mary to take Adrienne to school. The child had been cautioned and instructed in regard to Ida's occasional loss of memory, but for some reason Ida seemed more lucid with Adrienne around. Mary observed some bouts of confusion, but she was able to just gently remind Ida of what was going on, which would take care of the problem.

Mary had felt some concern over the possibility of Ida wandering up the stairs and making Walter aware of her presence in the home. Janel suggested putting up a baby gate with a complicated latch at the foot of the stairs. Mary remembered that one had been purchased and the brackets installed back when her mother had owned a little dog that her father hadn't wanted to go up the stairs. The gate was in the basement, and Janel knew right where it was. Whit was able to fasten it firmly onto the brackets, and the latch to open it was meant to confound even a clever child; therefore, it was unlikely that Ida could figure it out unless she was shown how to do it. Mary just felt better knowing that she could leave Ida alone for a few minutes occasionally and not have to worry about any unfavorable encounters with her father.

"Thank you," Whit said at the end of the day when he was getting ready to take Ida home.

"It was no problem," Mary said firmly. "I love your mother."

"She loves you too, and she trusts you."

"I'm glad," Mary said. "And I'm glad to help. I think you should just bring her every day, so you don't have to worry."

"We'll talk about it," he said, kissed Mary, and left for home.

Mary watched them go, considering the ridiculousness of them leaving at all. They were both comfortable here. It was a huge house, and it was easy to pretend that her father wasn't even there when he never left his room. His nurses came and went with very little fuss. They were all friendly with Mary and Janel, and had no trouble with *not* telling their patient about any of the goings on in the house. They'd dealt with Walter long enough to know that keeping him ignorant was more blissful for everyone. In spite of this being Walter's home, and him still actually living there, Mary wished it were possible for Whit and Ida to just move in here—once she and Whit were married. And given the course of their relationship, she was finding it more and more impossible to see her future without Whit as a permanent part of it. He'd said they would talk about his mother's care, and she wondered if their situation might come up in the conversation.

Whit called her later but couldn't talk long since he had things at home to take care of. Again Mary felt frustrated, thinking they should be sharing one household and not having to do double duty by running two. He called the next morning and asked if it would be all right to bring Ida again. She assured him that it was, but he insisted that she be honest with him and tell him if there was any reason at all that she wasn't comfortable with this arrangement.

"I would never be anything but honest with you," Mary said, "and I consider it a privilege to help care for your mother. Just bring her."

"You're precious, Mary. I don't know what I ever did without you."

"The feeling is mutual." She paused, and he didn't hurry to get off the phone. Impulsively she just said what had been on her mind. "Maybe both of you should just move in here . . . permanently."

There was another long pause, and her heart quickened, wondering what he would say. "How can it be permanent, Mary, when it's your father's house?"

"Then let's rent a place where we can all be together."

"Are you asking me to marry you?" he asked. "Because that's my job."

"Have you changed your mind . . . about wanting to marry me?"

"Not even a little. I'd marry you tomorrow if I thought we could manage our living situation."

"Why can't we?"

"Renting another place would pretty much eliminate my job, wouldn't it?"

"Not necessarily."

"Okay, but it doesn't make a lot of sense."

"Let's . . . talk about this later," Mary said, hearing Ida talking to him.

"Okay," he said. "I'll see you soon." He paused for a second and added, "I love you, Mary. We'll figure something out."

"I love you too," she said and hung up, grateful she would see him shortly.

She felt better just seeing Whit when he arrived. His embrace filled her with love and hope, and she had to believe that they *would* figure something out. The day went well, but they didn't get a chance to talk since Ida was always with them, and she would get frustrated when they didn't speak Spanish in her presence.

Whit called Mary late that evening after his mother had gone to bed. They talked for more than an hour about the situation and possible solutions, but nothing was any better at the end of the conversation than It had been at the beginning. They could only agree that they loved each other, they wanted to be together, and they had to keep praying and not give up hope that they would find a solution.

The following morning Mary answered the phone while she was fixing breakfast. Whit sounded in better spirits and said that his mother was more herself than she'd been in days, and she very much wanted to stay at home and get some things done there. She'd promised to stay near the phone because he would be calling her frequently to check on her, and if she didn't answer, he would be going straight home.

"Anyway," he said, "I'll be there soon."

"Looking forward to it, as always," she said.

Mary was very glad to hear that Ida was doing better, even though a part of her preferred to have Ida here in her care, and she couldn't help hoping that Whit and his mother would be able to live in this house so they could move forward with their lives.

Ida continued to do better, and her bad spell of dementia seemed more like a distantly disturbing memory. Mary saw her on Sundays, but that was all. Adrienne thrived in school during her first month, and a schedule had been established for her to have regular playtime with her friend Rachel. Mary liked Cinda, and they enjoyed visiting occasionally as they took their daughters back and forth to each other's homes. Since the friends Mary had been in touch with from her previous home had pretty much stopped calling, she was glad to have found a connection with Cinda, especially given that they had their religion in common.

Mary had developed a habit of doing a great deal of gospel study during her free time, and she enjoyed having long conversations with Whit about all that she was learning. She grew to admire him all the more with the evidence of his vast knowledge and deep convictions in regard to the gospel. She couldn't deny it was one of the biggest reasons she believed that marrying him was the best thing she could do with her life. There were many other reasons; he had many fine qualities, and there was the indisputable attraction between them. But most of all, she recognized that he considered his own standing with God more important than anything else, and this helped her believe that he would not commit himself to becoming a husband and father if God's hand was not in the equation. Given her own growing religious convictions, she knew that as long as God would be a part of their lives, they could find a way to make it through anything.

# Chapter Nine

ON A PLEASANT AFTERNOON IN late September, Mary heard the buzzer that indicated someone was at the gate. She pressed the button on the intercom and said, "Can I help you?"

She was surprised to hear Ida's voice say in Spanish, "It's me, dear. I've brought Claudia for a visit."

"Oh, how nice," Mary said. "Of course." She then pushed the button to automatically open the gate. She went out the front door and immediately knew that Whit would not be pleased with this situation. The car in the driveway was flashy and souped-up in a way that was typical of those Mary had seen parked on the street Whit lived on, and behind the wheel was a young man that looked exactly like the kind of person Whit had emphatically told Mary to avoid. She knew immediately that one of Claudia's sons had probably been taking the sisters for a drive when these two elderly and partly senile ladies had decided a visit to Mary's home, where Whit was working, would be a grand idea. She tried to be nonchalant as she opened the passenger door to help Claudia out of the car. She wondered if this was a cousin that Whit could trust, or if there was such a thing.

"Oh, thank you, dear," Claudia said in English. "My Carlos took us for a drive. I thought it would be nice to come and see you, and to see what Whit's been doing with your garden."

"What a wonderful idea," Mary said, while the words rang with a sarcasm in her mind that she didn't allow to come out in her voice.

Claudia was slow getting out of the car, and Mary looked up to see Ida and Carlos waiting patiently. Mary examined him discreetly while she was helping Claudia get steady on her feet. Carlos took his mother's other arm and seemed very kind and attentive with her.

While Whit didn't necessarily look Hispanic, Carlos definitely did. He had features that were much like the people of Mexico that Mary had lived among off and on for many years of her life. The number of tattoos visible on his neck and arms was shocking, as was his extreme clothing. But Mary put her best acting skills into place and smiled at him as if nothing were out of the ordinary. Once Claudia was steady, Mary held out a hand and offered a smile, saying kindly, "It's so nice to meet you, Carlos. Your mother is very dear to me."

"Yeah, she's a good lady," Carlos said with an accent that made it evident he'd mostly spoken Spanish all his life, contrasting distinctly with what Whit had told her concerning his own efforts to refine his speech as part of leaving his old life behind. And perhaps he'd also been affected more by his father's American influence. "You must be Mary," Carlos said with a handsome smile. "While we been driving I heard nothing from Mama and Aunt Ida except how great Mary is."

"I'm sure they're exaggerating," she said, and he gave her a crooked smile that she found endearing. "Please come in." She motioned them into the house and took hold of Ida's arm while Carlos followed, helping his mother with great attentiveness.

Mary led them all down the hall and into the common room while she wondered how she was going to tell Whit that his keen desire to keep secret the whereabouts of her home—and his place of employment—had been compromised. She also wondered how he would react, although instinctively she knew he would be angry. She'd seen him agitated and frustrated, but he'd always remained dignified and in control in those cases. She'd only seen him really angry once, and that had been the day she'd gone to his home in an effort to help his mother. The compromising of her safety was an unmistakably sore point for him, and she knew this wasn't going to go well.

Janel met them in the common room, curious to see who their company was. She greeted both Claudia and Ida with great fondness. She also seemed to know Carlos. It became quickly evident that Janel had kept in fairly close touch with Claudia, whom she often visited at the care center. She'd obviously crossed paths with Carlos there occasionally. Of course, Janel had worked with Claudia here in this house many years ago, but Carlos would have been only a very young child then. He surely wouldn't have known or remembered where his mother had worked. But he knew now. And Whit would not be pleased.

Mary made certain everyone was comfortable, got them all a glass of water with Adrienne's help, then left them in Janel's care, saying as she backed toward the patio door, "I'll go find Whit and tell him you're here."

Mary walked slowly while she prayed and carefully considered her words. She finally found Whit; he turned and smiled, saying, "Hello, gorgeous. What are you up to?"

"I have something to tell you that you're not going to like," she blurted out immediately as a warning.

"Okay," he said, putting his sunglasses on top of his head. "What?"

"You have to promise to stay calm and hear what I have to say."

"Okay, you're scaring me. Get to the point."

"Will you stay calm?"

"I'll do my best," he said, but that didn't necessarily give her the reassurance she was seeking. "Just tell me."

"Claudia and your mother are here," she said.

For the flicker of a moment she saw pleasure in his eyes, then he asked the obvious question. "How did they—"

"Carlos brought them," she said quickly. "His mother talked him into it." She saw rage rise in Whit's face, mirroring what she'd seen that fateful day at his home. "It'll be okay, Whit. You need to stay calm."

"How do you know it'll be okay?" he demanded. "What I need is to make it absolutely clear to Carlos that if he so much as breathes any hint to anyone about this place, I will tear him apart."

He began to walk in the direction of the house as he spoke, but Mary stepped into his path and put her hands on his chest to stop him. "So, you'll resort to the same kind of violence that you abhor?"

"Or at least the threat of it," he growled. "It's the only communication these kind of people understand."

"Maybe you've never tried any other way, because you don't know anything different," she reasoned. "Maybe it's time to start a new trend. Carlos didn't come here of his own choosing."

"Oh, but I can assure you there's a great deal of damage he could do with what he knows now, no matter *why* he came here!"

"Maybe you're jumping to conclusions. Maybe you're not giving him any credit. He actually seems rather nice."

"You met him five minutes ago. You have no idea what Carlos is like."

"Well, he's kind to his mother, and to *your* mother as well."

"Yes, I'll give you that."

"Then there's got to be some good in him somewhere, right?"

He said nothing, but she sensed it was a result of biting his tongue very hard. She saw the muscles in his cheek twitch with tension.

"What's done is done, Whit," she said. "Now that it's happened, you need to deal with it appropriately. Getting angry with Carlos is only more likely to make him angry in return, isn't it?"

"Maybe."

"Maybe?"

"Mary, you have no idea what it's like to deal with this kind of stuff. Carlos has to know that I mean it when I tell him that his knowing where you live will never be revealed to *anyone*."

"I understand that, but you can still give him some respect, can't you? I know it's in you to behave like a Christian, even if you *are* angry."

"Oh, don't bring Jesus into this. He would not want my family exposed to danger."

"No, but He would want you to treat your cousin with respect. Surely you can communicate with him about this without being angry. Who can you be angry with, anyway? He was just doing what his mother asked him to do. You've told me your cousins respect you, and they respect your mother."

"They do, but gang loyalty will *always* override family loyalty. When those loyalties clash, it's a dangerous situation. Family won't shoot you because you have a disagreement—unless that disagreement upsets the sanctity of the gang."

Mary pressed her hands down his arms. "I know I don't understand all of this; with time you can help me understand. But right now, I'm asking you—while you're in my home—to be cordial with Carlos. Don't give him a reason to be angry with *you*."

Whit took a deep breath as if it were a great effort to breathe in air that would calm him. "Okay, you're probably right. I'll . . . be cordial. I promise."

"Okay," she said and stepped back. "We can talk more about this later."

"You said that as if you're going to ground me," he said, not entirely serious but with a subtle bite that Mary didn't miss.

She felt tempted to dismiss it, but something stronger made her call him on it. "Don't get angry with me because I'm trying to talk some sense into you. If you think I'm treating you like a child, it's because you're acting like one. Age has nothing to do with it."

He glared at her, then moved past her and went into the house. She followed after him, praying that this would go well, and that she and Whit wouldn't be arguing over it later.

Whit came in through the patio doors to see his mother, Claudia, and Carlos all sitting in the common room, visiting with Janel, who was being very kind and hospitable. Adrienne was sitting between Claudia and Whit's mother. Just having her in the same room with Carlos made his skin crawl. If Mary only knew the crimes that Carlos had committed, the kind of life he'd lived, she probably wouldn't be so quick to be kind. While Whit was wondering how to have a minute alone with Carlos, he bent over and greeted both his mother and aunt with a kiss on the cheek. He turned around to see that Carlos had come to his feet.

"Hey, bro," he said quietly. "Can I talk to you somewhere else?"

"Sure," Whit said and led him into the kitchen, which was technically an extension of the same room but far enough away from the women to offer some privacy. He reminded himself that he'd promised Mary he'd be cordial while in her home; it was her home and he needed to respect that. But he was imagining everything he *wanted* to say to Carlos, and how he would make a point to do so the next time he talked to him.

"Hey, man," Carlos said before Whit could get a word out. "Don't be ticked because I came here. I told Mama it wasn't a good idea, but she was wanting to come here real bad. It's been good between us, bro; I don't want no trouble and I know you don't neither."

"No, I don't," Whit said, humbled by the realization that if Mary hadn't cautioned him, he would have uttered aggressive threats before Carlos even had a chance to speak. As it was, he didn't have to say anything beyond a firm clarification. "You've got to know, bro, how important it is that *no one* knows where Mary lives . . . where I work. You understand?"

"I do, man. I'll never tell no one. I swear it."

"Okay," Whit said and let out a strained breath, "thank you."

"Mary's a cool lady, man. You got it in good with her, eh?"

"Something like that," Whit said, trying to hold on to that *cordial* feeling. "She's white."

"Yeah, I noticed that, bro." Carlos chuckled, as if it were funny. "I'm cool with that. You know how I loved your dad, man. If you wanna hook up with a white woman, it don't bother me none. I just wouldn't be sending out announcements to the homies, if you know what I mean."

"I know *exactly* what you mean," Whit said, trying not to sound aggravated. "That's why you've got to never break that promise. If anything ever happens to them—"

"It won't be on me, bro; I swear it! I love ya, man. I won't let ya down."

"Okay," Whit said. "Let's go . . . in here."

He led Carlos back to where the women were all seated and visiting as if they were having tea in china cups in a parlor. Then Whit and Carlos sat down among them, and to Whit it felt like tainting clear water with crude oil. He exchanged a glance with Mary and knew he owed her an apology. He just hoped that she would accept it, and that she wouldn't judge him too harshly by the anger he'd exhibited earlier. He clearly had some growing up to do, or perhaps it was growing out of beliefs and habits that just weren't appropriate. If he claimed to be a changed man, he had to live that in every respect. It was certainly something he needed to work on.

Long after Carlos left with his mother and aunt, Whit couldn't stop thinking about the encounter, the point being that his thoughts were entirely different than what he might have expected. He didn't feel nearly as afraid of the possibility of Carlos betraying him as much as he felt a need to trust in the Lord and believe that everything would work out according to His plan. Overall, his most prominent thoughts were focused on how Mary had brought to his attention a fallacy in his own thinking that had never occurred to him before. He felt humbled and a little off balance. He focused intently on his work, finding fulfillment in his labors more than he ever had in his life. But while he worked, his mind wandered through many thoughts, bringing him to the solid conclusion that he needed to talk to Mary. In fact, they needed a good, long talk—alone and uninterrupted. It occurred to him then that he'd not taken her out on a date in a few weeks. They did things together a great deal, but it was usually with Adrienne along, or with his mother around, or both. There was nothing wrong with that, except that two people who loved each other needed time to nurture that love, and he had a feeling that some quality time dedicated to that would serve them both well—especially him. He quickly found Mary, then Janel, then Mary again, and arranged for them to go out that very evening for dinner. He went home long enough to clean up and change and to make certain all was well with his mother, then he came back to pick up Mary.

"This is nice," he said, helping her into his truck.

"It *is* nice," she agreed and slid across the seat to the middle as he closed the door. He got in next to her, and they both fastened their seat belts. "Everything all right at home?"

"Yes, thank you. Adrienne got off okay with Janel?"

"She did. She was thrilled; they were *both* thrilled, actually."

"Well, I owe you an apology," he said. "In fact, I owe you more than one apology."

"What for?" she asked, sounding genuinely surprised. After what had happened earlier with Carlos, and the things she'd said to him, he would have thought she'd be counting the minutes until he apologized. And yet she was so quick to forgive and think the best of him. It was one of many reasons why he loved her.

"First of all," he said, offering her a warm glance before he looked to the road as the gate to the grounds and house closed behind them, "we haven't had a formal date for a while, and that's something I never want to neglect. When we've been married for decades, I still want to take you on dates and make sure we have time together, just the two of us."

Mary smiled at him, then chuckled. "When we've been married for decades, I will be a very old woman."

"And I will love you more every year."

"You say that with such confidence."

"Because I know it's true."

"Maybe God is giving you practice with caring for your mother, because you'll be taking care of me when I get old."

"Maybe your age is more a state of mind," he said.

"Oh, I can assure you that I really am eleven years older than you. It's a fact."

"Only ten until your birthday," he said lightly.

"So . . . ten and a half years."

More seriously he added, "What I mean by a state of mind is . . . well, I think that maybe you started feeling old as soon as you married Simon. I think maybe you're comfortable *feeling* old. Now that your life is starting over, maybe I can help you feel young again."

Mary was quiet for a minute. "Maybe you're right. I must confess that I *have* felt old for a long time. I really started to feel it after I lost my mother." She put her hand on his knee. "You *do* make me feel younger."

"You make me happier than I've ever been," he said, and hoped that she knew he meant it.

"That feeling is mutual," she said and smiled at him again.

After a couple of minutes of silence, he got to the next important point. "I also need to apologize for the way I behaved earlier today."

"I understand your anger, Whit; I really do."

"I understand it too, but that doesn't make it right. You said some things today that have made me think . . . a lot. I don't think I realized how much anger I was still carrying around. Maybe I've believed that it was the only way to protect myself and my family, but what you said made me realize that I need to behave more charitably and trust that the Lord will protect us." He chuckled without humor. "I'm not saying that's easy, given my experience with the kind of people that Carlos associates with, but . . . when were the truly valuable lessons in life ever easy?"

"I don't know what you said to Carlos today in the kitchen, but it must have been good because you both seemed fairly relaxed while we were visiting."

"Yeah, I think it went well. He apologized and promised he wouldn't betray me. If you hadn't said what you did, I would have threatened him before he would have ever had a chance to say a word. So . . . thank you. And . . . I'm sorry for behaving badly."

"I'm proud of you, Whit," she said, putting both hands around his upper arm. "It takes a lot of courage to make the changes you've made in your life; and the way you dealt with Carlos today took a lot of strength and discipline."

"I'm afraid you give me more credit than I deserve."

"I'm afraid you don't give yourself *enough* credit."

"Maybe. Maybe not."

They arrived at the restaurant where he'd made reservations. It wasn't as elegant as the place where he'd taken her on their first date, but it was still nice. After they had ordered their food, Whit took Mary's hand across the table and said, "There's something I want to share with you. We've had many conversations about spiritual things, but I haven't shared this with you yet because . . . well, it's very tender for me. I mentioned it when I told you about the changes I'd made in my life, but . . ."

"Is this about that line you crossed? You told me we could talk about it some other time. I've wondered, but I didn't want to push you to share things you consider personal."

"Mary, you can ask me anything you want."

"I figured you would talk to me about it when you were ready. Apparently you are."

"I guess I am," he said.

Right at that moment a large group was seated nearby that made the restaurant more noisy. Whit smiled at Mary and said, "How about if we enjoy our meal, and we'll talk afterward when it's a little more private . . . and quiet?"

"Excellent plan," she said. "Janel told me not to hurry. She said Adrienne can go to sleep on the couch if she gets tired, and Janel always stays up late reading anyway—or so she tells me."

"I don't think we'll be *that* late," he said, "but it's good to know we don't have to hurry."

They enjoyed their meal, interspersing it with conversation about the gospel, which brought up some missionary experiences Whit had in Mexico that he'd not shared before. The mention of Mexico always brought up their common love for the country and its people, and they always marveled at the many commonalities in their lives. In the midst of marveling—for what seemed the hundredth time since he'd met her—Whit looked at Mary and felt overcome. Since they'd finished their meal, he reached across the table and once again took her hand, saying, "I want to ask you to marry me."

"Then why don't you?"

"There are just so many . . . obstacles."

"That's just logistical," she said.

"It might *just* be logistical," he countered, now overcome more with a growing frustration that was smothering his warm feelings, "but it is what it is. How can I make you my wife when I don't know where we would live, or *how* we would live, and that's just—"

"It's okay, Whit," she said earnestly. "We both know I'm too old for you anyway. Maybe this was all just . . . a nice temporary thing, but—"

Whit felt mildly angry and leaned closer to her to avoid being overheard when he feared his voice would betray how he felt. He growled in a whisper, "I want to marry you. Why can't you believe that age has nothing to do with this? Marry me because you love me, Mary; because you believe that I would devote my life to making you happy and taking good care of you. Marry me because you know I love you and I love your daughter and I will be a good husband and father." She said nothing, and he asked, "Do you know that everything I just said is true?"

"Yes," she answered firmly.

"But you're still hesitating," he pointed out. "Why? Because I'm a poor spic who—"

"I can't believe you'd call yourself that!"

"Honey, I've been called that too many times to count—always with hatred."

"*I* would never call you that!"

"No, but your father would. He has; I've heard him."

She was understandably astonished. "*When* has my father called you that? I didn't know that you'd ever spoken to him."

"When I was a child," he admitted. "You'd moved out by then, but I came to your home with my father, and *your* father was . . . well, his usual self."

"I had no idea."

"I know. And I didn't think it was relevant."

"Until now?"

"It just . . . came out. I'm trying to make a point. *You* hear your father in your head more than you hear your own voice. I'm not asking you to marry me because I want to be *his* son-in-law. If anything, that should convince you all the more of my love for you. *No one* would want to be his son-in-law—especially someone like me who has several reasons to be the target of his bigotry. I don't want anything to do with him any more than he would want anything to do with me if he had any idea that I was even around, or what my intentions are. The difference is that I choose to avoid interacting with someone like him because he's like toxic waste. He makes people sick by simply being in his presence. He chooses not to interact with someone like me for reasons that are deplorable and reeking of hypocrisy. He's not going to change, Mary. You know that in your heart. And the sooner you separate yourself completely from him and his toxicity, the sooner you can discover who you really are—not who he has taught you to *believe* you are."

He was startled when she smiled slightly. "I knew you would say that."

"What?" he asked and leaned back.

She leaned over the table to compensate for the distance. "The moment I bring up my concerns about our age, you jump to assure me that you love me no matter what; but when it comes to working out a way for us to be together, you're entirely stuck. Sometimes your faith is inspiring, and sometimes I can't even see it. You just said you were not asking to marry me because you want to be his son-in-law, but as I see it, you're not asking me to marry you at all. So, do you trust in the Lord or not? You've taught me a great deal about applying the gospel in my life, and you should know that I've prayed very earnestly about this situation, and I know what God wants me to do. Do you?"

He felt completely stunned and utterly silenced. She stood up and took her purse. "I'm going to the ladies room," she said. "I'll meet you out front."

Whit sat there for a couple of minutes, trying to take in the very confusing conversation that had just taken place. But one point stood out plainly, and that was the one he needed to focus on. He signed the bill and put his debit card and the receipt in his wallet before he went outside to find Mary sitting on a little bench near the door.

"It's a lovely evening," she said, making it clear she wasn't at all angry, but they certainly had a lot to talk about.

"Yes, it is," he said and sat down beside her.

"I just have one more thing to say."

"Okay."

"I've been reading some articles online by General Authorities, and I've read some things that have given me a lot to think about. I've never told you this, but I actually used to be an excessive worrier; it got worse after the accident. My mother was also that way. But as I've learned more about the gospel and endeavored to take it into my life, I've realized that I don't worry so much. I think that worrying is contrary to faith. I understand we have a difficult situation, but . . . maybe we're trying too hard to work out every little thing when we should just have enough faith to take the first step, and then allow the Lord to guide us to the next step. Just think about that, okay?"

"Okay," he said, knowing he *did* need to think about it. His brain felt entirely overloaded at the moment.

"Now," she said, taking his hand, "I'm afraid I may have gotten us off on a tangent that could have waited. Let's just . . . forget about all of that for the moment. I want to hear whatever it is you want to share with me. Can we just . . . shift gears and put the rest away for now?"

"Yeah, okay," he said, but he knew it would take a few minutes for his mind to actually make that shift and get back on track. He stood up and urged her to do the same. "How about a walk on the beach?"

"Sounds divine," she said, and he helped her into the truck. He drove a short distance and parked the truck, then they walked to the beach where they took off their shoes and carried them while they strolled hand in hand.

They walked for several minutes in silence before Mary said, "Are you okay?"

"Just a lot to think about."

"Will you tell me . . . about the changes you made in your life?"

He sighed and pushed everything else out of his head, taking himself back to how he'd planned this conversation before he'd found her earlier in the day to ask her out. "I'm sure you've already put enough pieces together to know what my youth was like. I saw my father shot down in the street, and then I watched my older brother deal with his grief by becoming actively involved in the gang and acting out with senseless violence. It was easy to follow in his footsteps as soon as I was old enough. I got my first tattoo when I was thirteen."

"Thirteen?"

"Yeah. Pathetic, isn't it."

"Sad," she said. "It's very sad."

"Yes, my mother's cried many tears over the grief her sons gave her."

"Is that why you take such good care of her now?"

"I take care of her because she's my mother and she deserves my respect. But I have no temptation to feel frustrated with her, or feel cheated out of anything because she needs me. After what I put her through, she deserves the very best I can give her."

"You know they say a woman can judge how a man will treat his wife by the way he treats his mother."

"Do they?" he asked.

"If that's true—and I believe it has some validity—then I have nothing to worry about."

"I hope not," he said and sighed again. "Anyway, when Joseph was killed I spun out of control. I'd always been able to avoid getting arrested, but I look back now and I think I *wanted* to get put away. I wanted to pay for my crimes. I wanted to suffer for the things I'd done. Or maybe a part of me knew I had to serve my time if I had any hope of redeeming myself. I was tried as an adult and sentenced to five years. It could have been a lot worse, given a variety of counts they had against me. Ironically, a man in our branch who was a very good attorney helped me—pro bono—only because he cared for my mother, I believe; he made all the difference. He stuck with me through parole hearings. I got out in two years for good behavior.

"Eventually I started working very hard at good behavior. Initially, I knew it was common for prison to turn hardened youth into harder adults, and initially that's what I expected. I was almost prepared to bring it on and make it happen. I think that's all I believed I was capable of. But this attorney was far better to me than I deserved. He visited me at least once a week, just to keep track of me. And the branch president at the time started doing the same. They brought me things to read, they wrote long letters of encouragement and guidance, they believed in me and taught me that I could change my life. I read the New Testament and the Book of Mormon all the way through more than once, and by the time I got out, I was a different person. I started going to church with my mother and I wanted to be like these men who had done so much for me. I had a probationary period in regard to my privileges in the Church, but because I had done my time and I came clean with my leaders over *everything*, earning my way back didn't take as long as I'd expected. When I was reassured by my leaders that my spirit was as clean as if I'd been baptized again, I set out to fully forgive myself, and I made the decision to go on a mission."

"That's quite a story, Whitmer Eden."

"Yes, I suppose it is, but . . . there's one thing I haven't told you about. No one but my mother and the men in the Church that helped me find my way back have heard this part. But you need to know, because . . . it's very close to my heart."

"I'm honored that you would want to share it with me," she said.

He gave her a timid smile and sat down on the sand, a safe distance from where the waves were reaching as they eased toward high tide. She sat beside him and leaned her arms on her knees so that she could turn and see his face while he talked.

"There were a lot of stories in the scriptures that inspired me, but it was the story of Paul in the New Testament that really got to me. The language of the Bible can be difficult to understand, but there are certain aspects to his story that are unmistakably clear. I was so deeply troubled over the people I'd hurt—directly or indirectly—and all the damage I'd done. I remember laying on my poor excuse for a bed, staring at the ceiling of that prison cell, and wondering how I could ever turn my life around when I had inflicted so much hurt. And then I read about Saul, and the miraculous experience that changed his life. He changed so dramatically that he changed his name to Paul, and he devoted the rest of his life to being a disciple of Christ. I pondered the story *a lot*, and I read parts of it over and over, praying to understand. And one night, I was just lying there in the dark, reliving all the horrible things I'd done, and I heard a voice. It wasn't literal; I didn't hear it with my ears. But I still heard it as clearly as if someone had spoken to me . . . the same words that the Lord had spoken to Saul."

Whit had to pause to try to gather his composure. He still couldn't say the sentence aloud without getting choked up, because it always brought to mind how he'd felt when the experience had happened. In spite of his efforts, his voice still broke when he spoke, and he felt his chin quivering as he said the words. *"'Why persecutest . . . thou me?'"*

Whit cleared his throat and regained his equanimity while Mary took his hand and squeezed it; but he avoided looking at her, afraid it would only make his emotions more fragile. "That was the moment," he said. "That was when I began to understand. If the Lord says that when we do it unto the least of these, we do it unto Him, I realized that it not only applied to simple acts of kindness and service, it also applied to the contrary. All the cruelty I had inflicted on other people had been the same as if I had inflicted it personally upon the Savior, because in the end He's the one that suffers for all of His children. I struggled and wrestled with that for days . . . weeks maybe. I cried at night, glad that I was alone in my cell. And then one day my perspective changed. I realized that Saul had changed. He'd changed completely, and he'd devoted the remainder of his life to doing whatever God required of Him. He became the man who said with firmness and conviction, 'I can do all things through Christ, which strengtheneth me.' And that's when it happened. That's when I drew the line. Everything in my life before that moment was a part of the old me, the lost and angry me. I vowed to be a changed man, a good man, the man that God wanted me to be."

Whit looked firmly at Mary and tightened his hold on her hand. "I can give myself credit for coming a long way since that time, but of course I give most of the credit to the Lord for helping me make that journey."

"You *have* come a long way."

"Yes, but . . . I'm far from perfect and I still occasionally feel the residue from the damaged years of my life resurfacing. What I'm trying to say is . . . you taught me something today that I'd never considered before. I've never hurt anyone since I got out of prison—not in any way. But I'd convinced myself that I had to be tough in order to protect myself. I understand the concept that a soft answer turneth away wrath, but I'd totally missed that it could apply to my cousins who are still actively involved in gangs. I believe now that it's possible to have better relationships with them, even though we disagree so strongly on our way of life. I have to be careful with those boundaries, but . . . I can let them know I love them. I can give them trust—at least to some degree— because I do sincerely believe that they would never let anything happen to me or my family. And I can respect them for the good they do, even if it doesn't amount to much. I have to remember that God loves them, and only He can understand their way of life and how hard it is to know anything else with the way they grew up."

Mary drew his hand to her lips and kissed it. "I love you, Whit."

"I love you too, Mary."

"And I'm proud of you."

"I'm glad, because I would never want you to be disappointed in me. Changing my life was never more worth it than when I met you and I considered the possibility that you might actually want to get involved with someone like me—only because I was not the kind of man I used to be." He leaned forward to kiss her, then looked into her eyes and said, "Will you marry me?"

"What?"

"I know you heard what I said."

"Yes, I heard what you said, but . . ."

"You said earlier that we should have the faith to take the next step and trust that the Lord would *show* us the next step."

"I did say that. You've thought about it since then?"

"It didn't take much thinking. You're right. I figure the next step is to be officially engaged. If we both know that getting married is the right thing, then that's the next step. If we make that commitment and trust in the Lord, then surely He will provide a way."

Mary smiled, which somewhat eased the pounding of his heart that had begun the moment he'd heard a proposal pass impulsively through his lips. Except that it wasn't impulsive in principle. He'd pondered it for many weeks; for as long as he'd known her, really. And he knew it was right. He knew it with all his being.

"So, what do you think, Mary Jane?"

"Yes, Whit, I'll marry you. The sooner the better, in my opinion. We're not getting any younger."

He laughed and kissed her, then they laughed together and kissed again. He'd truly never felt so happy.

# Chapter Ten

THEY LEFT THE BEACH AND found a jewelry store that stayed open late. Whit insisted that they needed to make it official right then and there. Together they picked out a ring that elicited Mary's delighted laughter every time she looked at it on her finger. Whit knew that was the right one. He paid for it with a credit card that he knew he could pay off before it accrued interest, because he could transfer the money from a savings account the following day.

"I love you, Mary," he said in the truck.

With her head relaxed on his shoulder, she admired the ring on her finger and said firmly, "I love you too, Whit."

"Then we're going to get a much better ending than Romeo and Juliet."

"Indeed we will," she said.

Janel was the first to know, since she noticed the ring right off when they went in to pick up Adrienne. She was thrilled and hugged them both, and she completely understood why they hadn't set a date yet, given the sensitivity of their circumstances. But she expressed confidence that it would all work out.

Since Adrienne was still awake, she quickly picked up on the conversation and was gleefully excited to be told that Whit was going to officially become a part of their family. The child had fond memories of her father and talked about him often; therefore, no one was expecting her to be too hasty in allowing Whit to fill that role completely, but they felt confident that with time it would all naturally fall into place.

Adrienne fell asleep on the way home, and Whit carried her up to her bed and tucked her in. Both Whit and Mary placed a kiss on the child's forehead, then they kissed each other before Mary led him back downstairs and reluctantly said good night to him at the door.

The following morning Whit drove to work feeling happier by the hour. At this point he couldn't think too hard about how everything might work out. He simply focused on the joy of being officially engaged to Mary. It was a dream come true! He thought of the day they'd met, and how he'd been attracted to her immediately. If he'd known then that it would turn out like this, he probably would have made a complete fool of himself by expressing his joy like a child who had gotten exactly what he'd wanted for Christmas. He laughingly thought he might make a fool of himself yet.

As soon as he got to the house, he went inside and found Mary alone in the kitchen. He said nothing before he kissed her in greeting, then he wrapped his arms around her and lifted her feet off the floor, laughing as he turned with her wrapped tightly in his grasp.

"Will you kiss me like that every day for the rest of my life?" she asked as he set her down.

"You don't think it would get old?"

"Never!"

"I'm not dreaming, am I?" he asked, touching her face. "You really are going to marry me?"

"I really am," she said.

He reluctantly went outside to get to work, but later that morning he took Mary outside and declared that the first portion of the garden was officially completed; the view from the patio was perfect. Beautiful shrubberies stood as a backdrop to the lovely variety of flowers and made it impossible to see beyond them to the larger portion of the garden that still needed an enormous amount of work. The tops of the trees that were visible from that point all looked groomed and picturesque.

"Oh, it's perfect," she said, squeezing his hand. "The Garden of Eden."

He sounded mildly annoyed when he answered, "It's far from the first time *that* joke has come up since I began this career, but—"

"I'm sorry," she said. "I didn't mean it as a joke." She turned and looked around again, her eyes filled with fascination and intrigue. "It's beautiful, Whit. It *is* like the Garden of Eden—at least how I might imagine it to be. I love it!" She kissed him and added, "I knew you were the right man for the job."

"Which job exactly?" he asked with a laugh.

"Everything I'll ever need a man for in my entire life." She looked around again. "The garden is perfect," she said once more.

"There's plenty of work to keep me busy, but I'll be happier knowing you have a pleasant view."

They kissed and went their separate ways to get on with the business of the day. Whit had some errands to do during his lunch hour, and when he got back Mary had gone to pick up Adrienne from her half day of school. He hadn't been there long before Janel came running out to find him, obviously in a panic.

"What's wrong?" he demanded, mentally assessing that Mary and Adrienne hadn't returned yet. Had she gotten a call? Had there been an accident or something? His heart beat painfully hard.

"It's Mr. Cranford," she said. "He's fallen in the bathroom, and Doris isn't strong enough to help him up. He refuses to let *me* help, because I'm not a nurse and I'm not a man. Doris asked if it was all right for the gardener to come help, and he begrudgingly agreed."

Whit took a deep breath and tossed his gloves on the ground before he followed Janel in. "Are you sure this is a good idea?" he asked before they got to the stairs.

"Not necessarily, but it's an emergency."

"Do you think he's hurt?" Whit asked. "Maybe he needs an ambulance; maybe EMTs should be doing this."

"He's not hurt *that* badly," Janel said. "Besides, he only knows you as the gardener. He doesn't know you're going to marry his daughter."

"Yet," Whit muttered.

"Don't worry. His bark is nasty, but it's not very far-reaching."

"Not for us, but it is for Mary."

"Don't worry," Janel repeated and motioned him into the room. "Doris?" she called toward a bathroom door that was slightly ajar. "Whit is here. He's coming in."

"Oh, thank you!" Doris said with extreme relief.

Whit was surprised at Walter Cranford's old and shriveled appearance. He was also surprised that the man expressed simple gratitude for the help that Whit offered. But once Walter was back in his bed, he began grumbling at Doris, blaming her for his fall, and he snapped at Whit, telling him to leave.

"I'm going," Whit said, grateful at least that he hadn't needed to stay around long enough to let the man figure out his family connections.

Whit returned to the garden with a hovering dark cloud of worry that had been ungraciously bestowed upon him by Walter Cranford.

All these months he'd been working here and becoming involved with the man's family and employees, and he'd not once encountered the old man. Now, today, the day after Whit had put a ring on Mary's finger, he'd been slapped in the face with a reality that had been easy for Whit to ignore, given the very fact that he'd never actually seen Cranford rotting away in his self-induced solitary confinement. Whit was disturbed by the thought that he was actually employed by this man's money, even though his employment was overseen by Mary and his paycheck came from an accounting firm. He was more disturbed by the fact that Mary had to deal with this man every day. She had the patience of a saint! He thought of Mary telling him about the awful things her father had said about Adrienne—and even *to* her on the rare occasions when she had been in her grandfather's room. The idea actually made him nauseated, and it also lured his once-violent thinking closer to the surface than it had been in a long time. He quickly put his Christian conscience in place and tried to focus on his work.

Mary came to find him after she'd returned. Instead of her usual greeting, she said, "Janel told me you had the rare honor of assisting my father." Her sarcasm was as evident as her concern.

"Yeah, it was memorable," he said in the same tone.

Their eyes met for a long moment, then she wrapped her arms tightly around him as if she feared she might lose him otherwise. He returned her embrace with equal fervor.

"It's going to be all right," he said, reminding himself of the inspirational speech she'd given last night. "We're going to trust the Lord to help us work all of this out, remember?"

"I remember," she said and sighed. "I'm sorry."

"For what? You haven't done anything wrong."

"I know. I'm just . . . sorry he has to be that way. He's missing out on so many things that could bring him happiness, and he manages to make everyone else miserable if they have to go anywhere near him."

"We don't have to let him make us miserable," Whit said, glad for the way trying to encourage her was helping him feel better. "You're a marvelous example of that every day."

She sighed again and just held on to him, her head relaxed against his chest. He also recalled Janel saying that Walter's bark was nasty but not very far-reaching. If nothing else, seeing how decrepit Walter had become, Whit felt less intimidated. Maybe Mary had been right in saying that Walter might never know who was actually living under his roof. He needed to think about that. But however this all worked out, he had to believe that it *would* work out.

\* \* \* \* \*

Mary managed to avoid her father for the remainder of the day, but he needed her in the middle of the night, and she could only pray that he wouldn't bring up his encounter with the gardener. But that prayer wasn't answered in the affirmative, which she figured only meant that her father had his agency and God could not magically remove this man's odious nature.

"Who exactly is this gardener you hired?" Walter demanded with a wheezing voice while they were waiting for his medication to take effect.

"What do you mean *who*? He's worked here for several months, and you've never exhibited an ounce of curiosity."

"I met him today. He seemed nice enough."

Mary found such a statement ironic. How could a man who was not nice *at all*, have some gauge of judging another person to be *nice enough*? Of course, Walter Cranford had always lived with a double standard. People were not allowed to treat him the way he treated other people. It was the opposite of the golden rule; Mary thought of it more as a rusty-tin-can rule.

"Yes, he's *very* nice," Mary said. "I'm glad there was a man around today when you needed one."

Walter only made a disinterested noise then said, "So, who is he?"

Mary decided on honesty, but not to disclose anything she didn't have to. If she acted secretive or defensive, he was more likely to suspect there was something that wouldn't please him. "His name is Whit. He works very hard. He's polite and kind, and he's doing a beautiful job with the garden. You should come out some time and see what he's done so far. There's a fountain with—"

"I don't need to see it," he said, "even if I could get out of this room."

Mary wanted to point out that it *was* possible for him to get out of this room, but she'd tried to talk him into that before, and such conversations had always reached a hard, dead end via an ugly argument. If he wanted to stay here, so be it. Mary had her reasons for preferring it that way.

"He seems familiar," Walter said. "What's his last name?"

Mary sighed. "It's Eden."

"Eden?" he echoed immediately. "Related to the Eden who used to do some gardening here?"

"I believe so," Mary answered as if it made no difference to her.

"His son?" Walter's eyes showed a familiar spark that Mary abhorred. Her father's bigot sensors had just gone off.

"I believe so," Mary said again in a forced monotone.

"That would mean his mother's a Mexican woman." Even with the wheezing in his voice, he still spoke the last two words as if just saying them had made Whit less of a man. "A sister to that Claudia your mother insisted on keeping around here. Am I right?"

"Yes, that's right," Mary said, wishing her father could have a little less accuracy in his memory. " Janel recommended him. He's a good man. There's no need to—"

"No need for you to sing his praises." He coughed as a result of getting himself worked up. "You can keep him around." He coughed some more. "Just make sure he knows his place."

Mary watched her father coughing and made no effort to assist him. She wanted to scream out the words that were on the tip of her tongue. *I'm going to marry him!* She wanted so badly to say it. She wanted to tell her father that Whit Eden was ten times the man that Walter Cranford had *ever* been. She wanted to sing Whit Eden's praises at the top of her lungs and tell her father exactly what she thought of his hateful attitudes. But she refused to engage in such a conversation; she knew better than to waste any energy over it. After several deep breaths that calmed her emotions and reminded her of what was truly important, she helped her father to a sitting position and turned up his oxygen. Within a couple of minutes his coughing calmed down. She normally would have sat with him until he went back to sleep, but she simply said, "I think you're all right now. I'm tired. I'll come back if you need me."

She left her father's room and went to her own after peeking in on Adrienne. In her bed she cried much the way she'd cried hundreds of times through her childhood as a result of her father's brash attitudes and abrasive behavior. She wished she could stop caring. She wished she didn't have to deal with him. But for the time being staying in this house seemed the best—and only—possibility. She just had to pray that the Lord would work all of this together for her good, and for the good of those she loved. She couldn't be a hypocrite after what she'd told Whit. She needed to trust in the Lord and take it one step at a time.

\* \* \* \* \*

About a week after Whit had encountered the illustrious Mr. Cranford, he woke up suddenly in the middle of the night, feeling as if he'd been physically nudged. He reached over and turned on the lamp, expecting to see his mother there, needing help with something. But there was no one. He got up to check on her, shocked to find her bed empty. A quick search of the house let him know she wasn't there, and the back door was wide open. He frantically got dressed enough to go out and grabbed a flashlight—and his pistol. He popped the magazine of ammunition into the gun and headed out. Technically the gun belonged to his mother, since it would be illegal for him to own one—ex-con that he was. Self-protection was no small thing in this neighborhood, and he'd taught her how to use it safely. But with her sporadic memory losses, he'd kept it hidden, not trusting her to be able to use it correctly even if the need arose.

Whit didn't want to start shouting for his mother and wake up the whole neighborhood. He could only search cautiously with the flashlight and pray, listening closely to his instincts *and* the possibility of the still, small voice guiding him. Or perhaps they were the same. He searched for nearly half an hour before he found her sitting on the ground crying—in the yard of one of the most violent and high-strung gang members in the neighborhood. When he wasn't selling drugs he was using them, and both activities could send him out of his mind with violence.

Whit silently thanked God for guiding him to his mother. He whispered to her to calm her down and gently urged her home. Once she was back in her bed and the doors were locked up tight, Whit paced the house, frantic over what *could* have happened. Clearly his mother's sporadic bursts of dementia were not something that could be ignored or left unattended. How could he leave her alone for even an hour and wonder if she wouldn't lose contact with reality and do something to harm herself? Or burn down the house? Or bring on a random violent act from one of the neighbors? He prayed while he paced, but it was nearly dawn before an answer occurred to him that definitely *was* the still, small voice. He knew then that this was the opportunity he'd been wanting for years. With his mother's condition, he could legitimately move her out of this neighborhood and sell the house. *If* he could sell the house, they would have enough money to rent a place elsewhere. And he already had a fair amount of money in the bank. If he needed to hire help for his mother— which he surely would need to do eventually—he would be able to come up with the means to do it. Somehow it would work out. He recalled what Mary had taught him, that he needed to take the next step, then trust in the Lord to show him where to step after that. Right now, he knew beyond any doubt that it was time to get his mother—and himself—out of this neighborhood. But he needed Mary's help, and he felt indescribably grateful to know that she *would* help him, and that she would be glad to do it.

While his mother slept, Whit started packing the essentials. He started with his own things, then went on to his mother's, managing to do so quietly enough that she kept on sleeping. He knew his mother's needs and habits enough that he knew what she needed, what she commonly used, and what had meaning for her. He filled every piece of luggage they owned and every box that was on hand. For the first time in his life he was thankful that his mother had a thing about keeping boxes *just in case.* When he couldn't find any more boxes, he filled laundry baskets. He moved his truck right next to the back door and started loading it all up. He had the back of the truck covered with a tarp that he tied down tightly before the sun even came up. His mother was still asleep when he walked through the house giving it a careful inspection and a silent farewell. He was filled with mixed emotions; he certainly had good memories in this house, but there was a great deal of grief and fear mixed into them in such quantity that the bad far outweighed the good. Most of what was still here was furniture and household items and semitacky decor. Certainly nothing they would miss or that couldn't be replaced. Of course he could come back and get whatever they needed, but he intended to contact a Realtor that very day. He would never want some unsuspecting family to move into such a neighborhood, but he knew there were friends and relatives of people who already lived here who would love to be *closer to the action.* As long as he could sell the house and get out with anything that could contribute to a better life, he would be grateful.

Ida was still asleep when Whit knew it was no longer too early to call Mary. He knew she kept her cell phone close, which would prevent having a phone ring that would disturb anyone else in the house. He knew that Janel wouldn't have arrived yet.

"Good morning," she answered. "How are you?"

"That's a complicated question to answer right now," he said.

"Is something wrong?" she asked, panic in her voice.

"No . . . not now, but . . . I've been up most of the night. I have a lot I need to tell you, but I'd rather do it face-to-face. For the moment I just need your help. I've prayed about this and it feels right to me, so I'm just going to say it. If you have a problem with any of this, in any way at all, you need to stop me and speak up. We need to be clear on that, because I can't do this if you have any reservations whatsoever. Do you understand? Do you know how important it is that I know you're being completely honest with me and not holding anything back?"

"I understand, Whit; I promise. Now, tell me."

"I've packed up all of our things that matter; the stuff is already in the truck." He heard her take a sharp breath. "We can't stay here any longer, Mary. I can't have my mother here and feel safe. Taking any drastic steps to move her out of here just didn't feel right before now. But today it feels right. I would like to bring her there, and I'm asking if we can stay. You've said many times we could make it work. If you don't want us to—"

"Whit, you don't even have to ask. I wouldn't want you to go anywhere else. I'd consider it a privilege to have your mother here, and to be able to take care of her. And I know you'll take good care of all of us."

Whit was silent while he struggled to swallow the knot in his throat. Being on the phone, he didn't have to fight to hide the tears that stung his eyes, then soothed them. "I'm very grateful, Mary," he said, his voice cracking in spite of his best efforts to control it.

"I love you, Whit."

"I love you too, Mary." He sighed. "I don't want to even think about what might happen if your father figures out we're under his roof."

"We'll be careful, and if it happens, we'll deal with it the best way we can. If the worst happens and we have to move out, we'll make it work."

"Okay." He exhaled with force, breathing out his fears and concerns. "We'll make it work," he repeated. "I know that we're not being completely honest in not letting your father know, but I must say that I feel the Lord's approval in that . . . for now. I think He understands our predicament and He is merciful. We'll just take it one step at a time."

"I couldn't have said it better myself."

Reverting to the necessary practicality of the moment, he said, "Technically I'm taking the day off. I have a number of things to take care of, and you and I need to have a long talk; there's a lot to work out. So . . . I'll see you in a while . . . as soon as Mother is up and dressed and we get a few more things together."

"I'll be here," she said. "Well, other than taking Adrienne to school I'll be here."

"See you soon," he said and they once again shared I love you's before getting off the phone. Whit got down on his knees and expressed his gratitude to Heavenly Father, he also pleaded for continued guidance, assurance, and protection. Then he stood up and checked on his mother, who was still sleeping.

With time to kill, he made some calls until he found an Hispanic Realtor whose specialty was selling homes in such neighborhoods. Whit came right out and told him the situation and his feelings concerning the type of people he *didn't* want moving into this neighborhood. The guy on the other end of the phone obviously understood, since he'd grown up in a similar neighborhood and he was savvy on dealing with the kind of people who might be interested.

"You know," he said to Whit, "once a For Sale sign goes up in the yard, all the neighbors will be calling their friends and relatives. It might sell quicker than you think, especially if the price is reasonable."

"Good," Whit said. The Realtor was pleased that the house wasn't mortgaged and that Whit had full ownership, which would make everything very uncomplicated. The house had been put into Whit's name years earlier, soon after he'd returned from his mission, and his mother had insisted that it would be better that way. His sister had been glad to give up her share in the home if he agreed to care for their mother, since she lived far away and preferred to keep her distance. At the same time, his mother had also given him full power of attorney over any decision to be made concerning her life and her care. Now that she was slowly losing her mind, he was glad to have that in place. He would hate to have to fight for that decision-making power now when she often couldn't even remember their conversations. He was glad his mother trusted him enough to know that he would take good care of her. He was certainly trying, and he hoped that this decision was in her best interest. He thought of having Mary being a part of his mother's everyday life and he couldn't imagine any better decision on her behalf. He thought of the way that Ida loved Adrienne—and the other way around—and his confidence regarding the situation deepened.

Now that he had an appointment with the Realtor this afternoon, he gathered their few remaining things, knowing he would come back later and clean. As soon as his mother started to stir, he sat beside her and explained that they needed to go and stay at Mary's for a while so that she would be safe. She didn't remember what had happened in the night, and he didn't know if she'd remember this conversation, but for the moment she was agreeable and seemed to understand. He gave her a few minutes in the bathroom while he went out to the truck with a few odds and ends that he put in the backseat. He came back in to find her wearing slippers on her feet and her bathrobe over her nightgown, holding her big purse that she rarely let out of her sight. He guided her out to the truck, and they drove away. He didn't tell her that she would never see her home again, and he didn't let her see that he was blinking back tears.

He was halfway to Mary's house before he remembered that he hadn't locked the door. He'd always been so careful with that; it was such an ingrained habit. Then he realized that it had always been more for safety reasons than any concern for valuables, since they hadn't owned any. Now that everything of any real value was there in the truck with him, locking the door hadn't seemed relevant.

After Whit drove through the gate at Mary's house, he was surprised to see the garage door coming open. Mary was standing there and motioned for him to drive his truck inside where there was plenty of space for him to park it and then some. He pulled up beside her and opened the window. She kissed him and said, "We can unload everything here in the garage and still have room to keep your truck here. It's huge, as you can see."

"Thank you," he said.

"Good morning," Ida said in Spanish, waving at Mary.

"Good morning," Mary said back to her and blew a kiss. "Have you eaten breakfast? I hope not, because I made way too much."

"Actually . . . we didn't," Whit said, realizing he'd forgotten more than just locking the door.

Mary insisted they both eat first thing. Ida was sad that she'd missed Adrienne before she'd gone to school, but Mary promised that Ida could ride with her to pick Adrienne up later that morning. As soon as Whit was finished eating the bacon and scrambled eggs Mary had made, she took him by the hand and led him across the common room and down a short hallway, past the bathroom he often used. He'd never been this far before, however. They left Ida eating her breakfast from a little portable table while she watched the television.

Mary opened a door, and he felt some sweet relief at what he saw. "Back in the old days," she said, motioning him into the room, "this was used now and then as a guest room. Having previously lived in this area, long-lost relatives loved to have a place to stay when they'd come back here for vacations. My father hated that, of course, but my mother loved it. Until I came back earlier this year, I don't think the door had even been opened since my mother died. I thought it would be perfect for your mother. I've already dusted and vacuumed, and the bedding is being washed."

Whit looked around at the spacious, empty closet, the dresser, the desk, and the queen-size bed. Then he looked at Mary. "It's perfect," he said, and she smiled as if nothing could make her happier than to share her home with an old lady who was going senile. "And you're amazing," he added.

"I'm so happy I can make a difference," she said.

"I know. That's why you're amazing; one of many reasons, actually."

She picked something up off the dresser and handed it to him. It looked like some kind of walkie-talkie, except it was white with a bright-pink antenna. "What is this?" he asked, then he recalled Mary having a similar one nearby late in the evenings when there was no nurse with her father.

"It's a baby monitor," she said. "Well, it's your end, at least." She motioned to the little matching piece on the bedside table. "We bought two of these when we brought the twins home from the hospital, because we kept them in separate rooms so they wouldn't wake each other. I now use one of them to hear my father in the night, and you can use this one to hear your mother. The two monitors are on separate frequencies so they don't interfere with each other."

"Wow!" he said and laughed softly.

"I'm afraid until you marry me you'll be sleeping on the couch in the common room, but you can keep your things here in your mother's room, if that's all right."

"It's more than all right, Mary. Thank you." He took her hand and urged her to sit beside him on the mattress that was waiting to be made up with clean linens. "No, wait," he said and stood up again, so she did the same. He set the monitor back on the dresser and led her back through the common room, where they could see that Ida was still eating slowly and enjoying the program she was watching. Janel was in the kitchen and waved at them as they went past. They went out the patio door, and he flipped the switch to turn on the water flow in the fountain. By the time he was standing beside it with both Mary's hands in his, water was cascading from the little angel and over the three tiers.

"Mary," he said, "I need to tell you more about what happened last night and why I made this decision, but . . . right now . . . I just have to say that somewhere in the middle of the night, when I knew beyond any doubt that it was right for us to come here . . . and stay here . . . I also knew that it's time for you and me to move forward. I need to stop being afraid of your father and the aspects of this situation that I can't control, and I need to trust more fully in the Lord. I've known for a long time that it's right for us to be together, and that God's hand is in our relationship. I know now that I'm done waiting."

"What are you saying?" she asked breathlessly.

"Marry me . . . soon. As long as we're already living under the same roof, I would think the sooner the better."

She smiled. She laughed. She hugged him and he hugged her back, lifting her briefly off the ground. She took his hands again and asked, "*How* soon?"

"As soon as possible. As soon as we can get a marriage license and—"

She laughed and hugged him again.

"And I thought I'd have to talk you into it," he said.

"No, you didn't," she said and laughed again.

He laughed with her. "No, I didn't." More seriously, he said, "There's just one thing I need to clarify. I must confess that I feel most concerned about my past life, and some of my family associations, and the possible impact of those things on your life. I need to know that you can live with that, and that you can trust me completely when I tell you that I've done everything in my power to put it behind me."

"I *do* trust you, Whit—in every possible way. Moving forward together means taking on whatever comes—together—with faith. That's what we're doing."

"Okay then," he said with a sigh, then a laugh. "I can't figure that there are many people either of us know that would care to be involved, or that we would *want* to be involved, so . . . we can make a few phone calls, buy you and Adrienne and my mother new dresses, and . . . just do it."

"And we can be married right here," she said, glancing toward the fountain.

"Actually," he drawled with some severity, "we could . . . and we will if . . . well . . ."

"What?" she asked, her brow furrowing with concern.

"I think we should talk to the branch president first. He can marry us if we get married here, but . . . it might be possible for you to go to the temple." She gasped and put a hand over her mouth. He saw tears gather in her eyes, but he kept talking. "You're a member in good standing. You've been active for months, and your convictions are evident. I know you can pass the recommend interview, so . . . unless the men who have to sign off on it have some objections that I don't understand, we should get married in the temple." He took a step closer and softened his voice. "I want to do this right, Mary. I want to be with you forever."

"Do you really think it's possible?" she asked after removing her hand from over her mouth.

"To be together forever? Of course! It's the—"

"I know *that*," she said and laughed through more tears. "I mean . . . is it really possible that I could go to the temple . . . so soon?"

"You've been a member for years," he said. "It can't hurt to ask."

After another long hug, they went inside and started a list of everything that needed to be done, both in regard to Whit and Ida moving in and to prepare for the wedding. They divided the phone calls, then Whit unloaded the truck and took into the house only the minimum of what they needed right away. The rest he left stacked neatly in the garage, thinking it would be better to sort things more thoroughly after he and Mary were married and he wouldn't be sleeping on the couch. As he went in and out of the house, he was pleased to note that his mother was doing fine and seemed to be completely comfortable. He hoped she remained that way, and that the old man upstairs remained completely ignorant of their presence.

# Chapter Eleven

WHILE WHIT WORKED, HE THOUGHT about everything that was happening and all he needed to do. He'd been putting off taking his mother to a doctor for an official diagnosis in regard to her memory losses. But Mary had gently insisted earlier that he needed to do it, and he knew she was right. He stopped what he was doing and called to make the appointment. Since it wasn't an emergency, they couldn't get her in until the end of the following week. He felt a little giddy to think that he'd probably be married by then. He wrote down the date and time of the appointment and stuck it to the fridge with a magnet, then he went back to work.

In the middle of sorting through a box of his own clothes, a thought struck Whit that made him a little queasy, a stark contrast from the giddiness he'd felt earlier. Mary had gone to pick Adrienne up at school and taken Ida with her, so Whit hurried inside to tell Janel he was leaving for a while. He drove toward the house as quickly as he could manage without breaking any laws, all the while praying that it would still be there. *The gun.* He'd left it out after he'd taken it with him in his nighttime search for his mother. He'd seen it several times while he'd been packing and perusing the house, thinking he'd pick it up last thing because he didn't want to leave it in the truck while it was unlocked for loading. Then he'd gotten distracted with talking to his mother and getting her out the door, and he'd completely overlooked actually picking it up. And he'd left the house unlocked! He couldn't believe he would be so careless, when being *careful* was a way of life. Once he had the gun in his hands, he would breathe easier and everything would be fine.

When he got to the house he noticed immediately that the back door was open. The screen door was closed, but the other door had been left ajar, and he *knew* he'd pulled it closed. He hadn't been *that* absentminded. He pushed the door open cautiously, his heart dropping into his stomach. He already knew the gun would be gone. He wondered if kids on the street actually snuck around and checked doors on a regular basis to see if they were unlocked, which might offer opportunities for theft or mischief. Of course they did. How ridiculous that he would think otherwise! He crept carefully into the house, not wanting to surprise any intruder who might still be there. He found the house devoid of any person, the gun nowhere, and the television and DVD player both gone as well. The electronics ticked him off, but the gun—that scared him. His carelessness had put a weapon into the hands of someone capable of using it to commit a crime. That *really* scared him. In fact, it made him sick to his stomach. And there was only one thing he could spend the rest of the day doing.

Whit locked the house and drove back to his *new* home. He called Mary to tell her what had happened and what he needed to do, and talked to her up until he pulled into the driveway and she came out to meet him with a tight hug, a warm kiss, and sweet words of encouragement. He helped his mother out to the truck while he explained what had happened, but she seemed somewhat lost, and he wondered if she understood what he was telling her. Since the gun legally belonged to her, she needed to be with him while he did what he could to remedy the problem. They went to the police department where he filed an official report, so that if the gun showed up—especially if it were involved in a crime—he couldn't be held responsible. Not legally, at least. He was interrogated by a grumpy officer, who sounded suspicious when he looked up Whit's police record. But Whit had expected that, and he just held his ground, declaring firmly that he wasn't like that anymore. He explained that the gun had belonged to his mother and he'd taught her to use it for self-protection. He wasn't going to say anything about his mother's failing memory, or of his moving out of the neighborhood, but when Ida became confused and couldn't answer the officer's questions accurately, Whit was forced to explain. The entire ordeal, as miserable as it was, didn't take as long as Whit had expected, and they got back to the house in time for Whit to do a little more sorting and unpacking while Mary made up the bed in his mother's new room and showed her around. Whit felt safe and grateful, and he told Mary so. He just hoped and prayed that they would be able to move forward with their lives in a good way, and that his past wouldn't come back to haunt them.

Along with that, he hoped that Walter Cranford remained oblivious and they could live here in peace, at least for the time being.

Whit felt everything fall into perspective after Janel left for the day. He and his mother helped Mary and Adrienne put supper on, then the four of them sat down together to share a meal. It was a simple thing, but it had never happened like this before. They'd shared many Sunday dinners, and he'd eaten many lunches at this table. But this was a weekday evening meal, and they were gathered as a family, a *new* family that would soon be officially joined—forever. And it was the first of thousands of meals they would share together. He had to fight to keep from getting emotional as his ugly past seemed to fall further away, and the hope of a bright future spread out clearly before him. He felt so deeply grateful that it was a challenge to eat, but he didn't want to alert the others to his deep thoughts. He could talk to Mary about it later, but for now, he just wanted to savor the experience. There was plenty he could worry about if he chose to, but he figured it was best to try to put those things into the Lord's hands and avoid worrying as much as possible.

Whit was pleased that Mary had been able to get hold of the branch president, and he had agreed to meet with them that evening. They took Adrienne and his mother along, and, as usual, they chatted in the backseat in Spanish while they drove to the church. He and Mary talked in English while she sat close to him, so they could have a somewhat private conversation. Mary informed him that she'd spoken personally to each of the four nurses that took shifts with her father. They were all thrilled with the upcoming marriage, and were sworn to secrecy about who was living in the house and why. Not one of them enjoyed working for Walter, and they certainly didn't converse with him beyond what was absolutely necessary. It was not a problem to convince them that his ignorance was best for everyone.

Mary reported that Janel was thrilled with the opportunity to help with a simple open house, which would appropriately be held in the garden. She would make some refreshments and pick up everything that would be needed. She had asked Mary what they would do for a honeymoon. When Mary had told her that it would be impossible to leave, due to caring for both Walter and Ida, Janel had insisted that she would stay at least one night so that they could have a proper wedding night away from the house. Whit and Mary both agreed that such an opportunity would be wonderful, but they were both good with a twenty-four-hour honeymoon. Just being able to live under the same roof and share the same room would be heavenly.

At the church, Ida sat with Adrienne in the foyer. Ida liked to be left in charge of the child, but Adrienne knew that sometimes Ida became forgetful, and she had permission to come and knock on the branch president's office door if there was a problem.

President Martinez was thrilled to hear of their plans to be married soon, and he felt that they were being wise in their decision. He also felt good about Mary being ready to go to the temple, and he spent some time with her alone to go over the recommend questions. When they were leaving the church building, Mary stopped Whit and put her arms around him, holding him tightly.

"Everything else falls into place with this," she said, and he wondered if she had been reading his mind earlier during supper.

"What?" he asked, suspecting what she meant but wanting to hear her thoughts.

"I've learned through these months just a little bit about the blessings of the temple, and I've grown to love you so deeply. To have you forever . . . and to have all else the temple offers . . . I couldn't ask for anything more."

"Amen," he said. "It *does* put everything into its proper perspective."

They drove to another church building where they waited a short while before they were able to speak with the stake president. Since the branch president had called him, he'd been expecting them. He spoke with both of them, then he too spent a few minutes alone with Mary, and they were all set to go to the temple to be married.

The next morning Whit called the temple and made arrangements to be married the following Tuesday, early in the morning. By the end of the day, with Janel's help, they had a little open house planned for early that evening in the garden, and a short guest list that mostly consisted of people with whom they went to church.

Janel was happy to watch out for Ida while Whit and Mary went together to pick Adrienne up from school, then they all went to lunch together before they took her with them to get a marriage license. They'd checked online to make certain they had everything with them that they needed, and they weren't surprised at the amount of time they had to wait. But Adrienne had things in her backpack to keep herself occupied, and she had many questions about the upcoming wedding and how it would affect their lives. She declared more than once how glad she was to have Whit and Ida living with them, and she asked if Ida could be her grandma now, since she didn't have a grandma. This made Whit and Mary exchange a warm smile, then he told her that it would be more than all right, and they would tell *Grandma* about it when they got back. Whit felt sure she would be pleased. And she was.

That night when Whit settled down once again on the couch of the common room, he pondered the changes that had so recently occurred in both his and his mother's lives and found a deep relief in being under the same roof with Mary and her daughter. He felt greater safety for himself and his mother. The property was surrounded by a high fence, and the house had a security system that was activated at night once the nurses had gone off their last shift and everyone was in until morning. If anyone tried to come into the house, an audible alarm would sound, and if it wasn't deactivated with the proper code in less than a minute, police would be on their way.

Whit also felt better just knowing that he was there for Mary and Adrienne. He liked being the man around the house, so to speak, since Walter Cranford certainly wasn't. Even when he'd been younger and healthy, he'd never been someone that Mary could look up to and rely on, and Whit wanted to be that for her. He also knew her husband had never filled that role, but Whit took it very seriously, and he was glad to be here in her home where he could make more of a difference. Knowing it would only be four more days until he could marry her just added to his peace, and it also gave him a deep thrill. Nothing could make him happier! As for any challenges that might arise after that, he was determined to just take them on as they came and hope for the best.

\* \* \* \* \*

Mary had trouble sleeping, which was less common than it used to be but still happened occasionally. Tonight, however, her thoughts were focused in an entirely different vein than usual. She felt secure and happy just knowing that Whit and his mother were there in the house, and thoughts of her upcoming wedding filled her with delightful butterflies. She even felt less intimidated by her father, just knowing that Whit would officially be a part of her life. She'd come a long way in not allowing her father to affect her adversely, and she intended to keep Whit's presence in her home—and her life—a secret from her father for as long as she could get away with it. But just knowing that Whit was here, and that he loved her and would take care of her, made it easier to think of facing her father with whatever might happen. She sincerely didn't care what he thought; she just hoped he didn't have any opportunity to hurt the people she loved.

Mary was needed by her father in the night, but it went better than it usually did, and she was grateful. She planned to tell him the day before the wedding that she would be having a little party in the garden the next day, so that he wouldn't wonder about the noise. Since he usually had his television on and the volume up high, it generally wasn't a problem. But she still intended to mention it, which would allay the likelihood of any challenges. Beyond that, she didn't intend to tell him *anything*. Once again she reminded herself that she was grateful for him giving her a place to live—and she even told him so—but beyond that he'd never done anything to earn her respect, and she couldn't remotely think of anything he'd *ever* done—beyond providing a living for her and her mother—that qualified him as a father.

Mary was able to get a few hours of sleep before morning, and she felt happy before she even got out of bed, just knowing that Whit was already here and they were a day closer to being married. After sharing breakfast he went back to work, having already taken two days off to deal with all the changes in their lives.

Mary took Ida with her when she went to pick Adrienne up from school, then they went to lunch and went shopping for new dresses. Ida settled happily on a floral print with many bright colors, and Adrienne wanted the pink satin dress with a wide, white sash around the waist and little white flowers appliqued on the skirt. Mary didn't want any kind of a fancy wedding dress for the open house, but she found something perfect on a closeout rack at a wedding shop. It was Grecian style with simple but very flattering lines. Whit had told her where to go to get what she needed for the temple. By showing the kind ladies there her recommend, they helped her get everything she needed, including a lovely white dress that she would be married in and that she could use for years to come each time she attended the temple.

When the women returned, Whit was glad to hear the report of their successful shopping. Then he had to leave work early to go to the old house and do some cleaning. Mary wished she could go with him and help him, but they both knew that was impossible. He assured her it didn't amount to much since he and his mother had both been pretty meticulous about keeping things clean all the time. He admitted that he was a little OCD about keeping things clean and tidy, and a counselor had once told him it was a typical way for a person to exert control when there were hard things in life over which he had no control. So, he'd kept the house clean and pristine, while the neighborhood beyond the walls of the house had been reeking of evil.

They had talked about the situation and had decided that he would rent a storage unit for the furniture and other things in the house that they might need if they could no longer stay in her father's home. But Whit had no reason to move them out of the house at this time. When the house sold, he would deal with that, and he felt sure he could get some help from a few men in the branch who could go with him into the neighborhood and not arouse any attention.

Mary sent some food with Whit to get him through the evening, and he came home just before Adrienne went to bed, reporting that the house was ready for a Realtor to be able to show it and expressing his hope that it would sell quickly. They read a few verses of scripture together as a family, then knelt to pray before Adrienne smothered her new grandmother with hugs and kisses that made Ida giggle like a child. Then Whit carried Adrienne up the stairs and Mary followed. As always, they were careful to latch the gate at the foot of the stairs so that Ida couldn't absently wander to the second floor and cause any problems. When she was lucid she completely understood the reasons, but they never knew when she might forget where she was or what she was doing.

Once Adrienne was put to bed, Mary walked back downstairs with Whit, who went outside while she helped make certain Ida had everything she needed. This woman who was about to become her mother-in-law surprised Mary when she expressed sincere gratitude to Mary for all that she did.

"Whit is such a good boy," she said in Spanish, as she always did, "and he has always taken such good care of me since he came back from his mission, but it's nice to have a woman helping me. You're so very kind, my dear."

"It's a pleasure, I can assure you," Mary said and hugged her tightly.

After Ida had gone to bed, Mary found Whit standing on the patio, his hands in the pockets of his jeans. "Are you all right?" she asked, noting his somber expression as she stood beside him.

"Yeah, I'm fine," he said. "There's just something I'm dreading that has to be done."

"What?" she asked, unable to imagine what it could be.

He took a deep breath as if he were gathering courage. "You need to see the tattoos before we get married."

"Do I?" she asked. "Do you think they'll make me change my mind?"

"Maybe," he said, and she scowled. "No, not really, but . . . I don't want the first time you see them to be on our wedding night. They're hideous and repulsive, and I'm just hoping you can look past them."

"I can," she said. "I've seen the ones on your arms."

"But you haven't seen my chest and back, and you need to."

"I must admit you're very skilled at keeping them covered," she said. They'd been swimming together, and to the beach many times, but he always wore a T-shirt when most men would have gone bare from the waist up.

"Yes, I am," he said, as if showing them in public might be mortifying. "I used to be proud of them. I wore tank tops a lot, or I went without a shirt whenever I could get away with it. Now I can't even imagine what I was thinking. It's like there was some crazy person living inside of me."

"It doesn't matter, Whit," she said firmly.

"It isn't who I am anymore; I know that. And I know *you* know that. But it still matters—at least it matters between you and me."

"Okay," she sighed, "if you're worried about this, then let's get it over with."

"Okay," he said, then took a deep breath and pulled his shirt and undershirt off over his head. He held up his arms as if he might have expected her to hit him or at least yell or something.

Mary took a good, long look at the artwork spread over his chest and upper arms, knowing that he wanted her to. She didn't want to admit that she was more preoccupied with his muscular appearance. She knew he was expecting her to say something, so she stated a fact, "That's a lot of ink, I must admit."

"That's it?" he asked.

"What did you want me to say?"

"Tell me what you think. They're disgusting, I know. Tell me."

He turned around to show her his back, and she added, "It must have been painful to have all that done."

"Yeah, it was painful," he said. "Not as painful as looking at them in the mirror every day. Every time I shower I wish I could scrub them off."

"I can understand why having a permanent reminder of that part of your life is not pleasant, but . . . I'm not shocked or horrified." He turned back around to look at her. "I've known for a long time they were there, so I got used to the idea months ago. It's not like you've got vulgarities there or something."

"No, but . . . it's . . . ugly. I don't know why you're not repulsed or disgusted. Or maybe you're just too polite to say so."

"I'm being honest with you, Whit. I wouldn't be anything less. If I had a problem, I would tell you—not that it would change anything." He looked as if he didn't believe her, and she added, "What if I'd had breast cancer and I had nothing left but hideous scars? Would you be repulsed or disgusted by me?"

"No," he insisted.

"I know you wouldn't because you're not that shallow. So, give me some credit. I'm not that shallow either."

"But this is different."

"In some ways, yes, but it's also the same. Because you know what I see when I look at that?" She glanced at his chest, then back to his eyes. "I see battle scars. I see a man who survived things I cannot even imagine. Given the changes you *have* made, and the man you've become, I don't see them as ugly. I see them as a part of who you are, and I love the whole you. Get used to it." She smiled as she repeated this expression that he'd often said to her.

Whit put his shirt back on, then hugged her tightly. "You're too good to be true."

"It's the other way around," she said, returning his embrace with fervor. She loved him so much!

Whit broke the silence by saying, "Can we talk?"

"Of course," she said, looking up at him. "We can talk about anything. Obviously you have something on your mind."

"I do." He took her hand and went inside, locking the patio door behind him. They sat together on the couch and turned to face each other. "I've told you," he began, "that you can ask me anything you want about my past, and I will tell you—even though I'd rather not."

"Yes, I know. We're good with that."

"Good," he said. "If you decide you need to know more, we can talk about it."

"Okay," she said, knowing that he was leading up to something else.

"Well, I'm wondering if the same applies the other way around . . . because you've told me practically nothing about your past with Simon. If there are things you don't want to talk about, that's your choice, but . . . if I'm going to be your second husband, I'd like to know a little more about your first. I don't want you to feel like you can't talk about him . . . or your relationship with him."

Mary took a deep breath and mentally brushed away the bristling defensiveness that often accompanied thoughts of Simon. She admitted readily, "I don't really like to talk about it, but I'm not trying to hide anything. You can ask me anything you want."

"Okay," he said. "What went wrong?"

"I wondered about that myself . . . for years. If you must know, I too have been through a fair amount of counseling, even if it was for entirely different reasons than yours. To just get to the bottom line, I learned over time that I had been attracted to Simon because subconsciously I felt comfortable with a lack of love and attention, because that's what I'd been raised with. Consciously I believed that our common causes were enough to sustain a marriage. Obviously I was very naive. He never loved me, and I don't believe I ever really loved him; not the way a woman should love her husband. I think I was in love with the idea of marriage. I think I projected a potential on to him that he never possessed. The very fact that he was not a bigot and he was not unkind to me somehow made him so much better than my father that I assumed he would be everything I'd hoped for in every other way. Obviously I was wrong. He was content to have a woman in his life who fit comfortably into his world, and who would support him in his endeavors. I fit the bill. He was married to the humanitarian work he did, and he was passionate about serving the people of Mexico and making a difference for them. As long as we worked together in those things, we were great as a team. Beyond that, I was of little value to him, except as a cook and a housekeeper. Of course, we shared a lot of years and it's more complicated than that, but . . . well—maybe it's *not* more complicated than that. Truthfully, that sums it up. Simon had many good qualities, but he was a very uncomplicated man. So, there you have it."

"Okay," Whit said. "Thank you. I'm glad to understand it a little better. I can't say I understand how *any* man could be that way . . . especially with a woman like you in his life, but everyone is different, and who am I to judge?"

"That's how I saw it. For all that I disagreed with him over so many things, I couldn't possibly judge why he was the way he was. Now I've given all that to the Lord. It's in the past, and I'm ready to go forward."

Whit smiled and squeezed her hand. "I like the sound of that very much." He kissed her, then looked contemplatively into her eyes. "Speaking of not judging . . . do you ever wonder *why* your father is the way he is?"

"I've wondered about that a great deal, actually."

"Do you know anything about his childhood? His history before he married your mother?"

"Practically nothing. The very fact that there seems to be no information, very few photographs from his early years, seems to imply that it's a past he doesn't want to look at. *Or* maybe he's just terribly unsentimental and it's simply a part of his character."

"Maybe," Whit said, "but I believe that bigotry and meanness are more learned than inherent. I can't help wondering if there wasn't something in the way he was raised, or something that happened to him when he was young, that might have impacted his thinking."

"I've wondered the same," Mary said, "more times than I could count. Whatever the case, I know it's too deeply ingrained to be changed now. Sometimes you just have to accept that a person is a certain way and you have to make peace with it. I'm doing my best to turn *that* over to the Lord as well."

"As we both should," Whit said. "I just can't help wondering."

"And we may never know," Mary said and kissed him the way he'd kissed her a minute earlier. "Now let's talk about something else, like . . . how we're getting married in a few days. It's so wonderful, I feel like I'm living a fairy tale."

"I don't think I'm any Prince Charming."

"Oh, I do," she said and kissed him again. "Maybe you should try seeing yourself the way *I* see you!" After another kiss she added, "Get used to it."

\* \* \* \* \*

Sunday came and went, and Monday was filled with making certain everything was under control while Whit actually put in a fair amount of time in the garden and in cleaning up the patio area so that everything was party ready. He also mowed what little lawn there was and pulled some weeds so that it was all perfectly groomed.

Late that night when the house was quiet, Whit and Mary sat on the couch, holding hands, with the two little monitors on the coffee table in front of them.

"Tomorrow will be a dream come true," he said and kissed her brow.

"For me too," she said and snuggled close to him. "I love having you here. I can't even find words to tell you how happy it makes me."

"I could say the same . . . if I could find words." They both laughed softly, then he added with more seriousness, "I want you to know, Mary, that whatever happens, we'll find a way to manage, and we'll get through it together." He exhaled loudly. "What I really mean is . . . if your father finds out . . . kicks us out . . . fires me . . . whatever happens, we'll manage. We'll get an apartment if we have to. I've got money in the bank to fill in the gaps. I'll find another job. I know how to work hard, and I'll do whatever it takes to provide for my family."

"I know you will."

"I know you know, but I want to clarify that we don't need to fear what your father can do. He has no power over us if we have options. Do you understand what I mean?"

"I do, yes. Thank you; I know you're right."

"For now we'll be grateful for what we have here, and hopefully it will last. The longer we can stay here and I can do this work, the more money we can put away to get a home of our own, given that it's not likely your father will leave you this one when he dies. But it's okay. We'll be happy together wherever we are, and I'll make a new garden."

Mary smiled at him, then put her head on his shoulder. "You really are very good to me, Whit Eden."

"I think it's the other way around," he said, "but I will be *so* glad to share the same last name with you."

"Amen," she said with another laugh.

They sat together in warm silence for several minutes before they both had to admit they were getting sleepy and they had an early morning ahead of them. He kissed her good night at the foot of the stairs, then he locked the little gate after she'd gone up, glad that it was the last night he'd ever have to sleep alone, hopefully for the rest of his life—because he couldn't imagine life without her.

Mary was awake the following morning before her alarm went off. She was barely dressed when Janel arrived hours earlier than usual to take care of Adrienne, who would miss school this morning. Janel would bring the child to the temple and arrive before the estimated time when Whit and Mary would come outside for pictures. Janel wasn't LDS, but she was respectful of their beliefs and had been ever since she had worked for Mary's mother, who had shared things about the gospel with her many years ago.

Mary left Adrienne with a kiss on the forehead while she was still sleeping, her pink dress all laid out and ready to put on after breakfast. She helped Ida with her hair, ate a simple breakfast, and tried to keep herself from staring at Whit while they both made certain they had everything they needed. Mary's stomach fluttered with pleasant intensity as they headed out for the temple while it was still dark. Once they arrived, Ida went with Mary as her escort, and Whit said he would see them both in a little while. Mary discreetly whispered to the sweet lady helping her that her soon-to-be mother-in-law struggled with memory loss, and she promised to pass that carefully along to the other ladies who would be helping Mary through all the steps of the process that would lead up to the wedding.

The entire experience was glorious for Mary. Some of it felt overwhelming, but she'd been well prepared by Whit and their kind leaders, and she took everything in with joy and gratitude. The culminating moment was kneeling across a temple altar from Whit, feeling more blessed than she ever had in her life. A short while later they walked through the temple doors together, holding hands as husband and wife—for time and all eternity. Ida was at their side, beaming with pride and happiness. Adrienne squealed with excitement when she saw them and came running. She hugged Mary, then Whit picked her up with a burst of laughter.

"We're a real family now," he said in Spanish, then he kissed Adrienne on the forehead, his mother on her cheek, and Mary on the lips before he declared, "I love you, Mrs. Eden."

"I love you too," she said and kissed him again.

The remainder of the day went according to plan, and it all worked out beautifully. Janel was amazing at keeping everything running smoothly for their little social gathering and at keeping Adrienne occupied and supervised. Walter never even noticed the little party going on in the garden on the other side of the house from his room. Elaine, the nurse on shift at the time, came down for some refreshments while her patient was engrossed in the television, and she assured them that everything was fine.

After all their guests had left, Whit and Mary changed clothes, then left everything in Janel's capable hands and drove into the city to a fine hotel where Whit had reserved a honeymoon suite for the night. Mary's memories of her previous honeymoon were mostly negative, and she was glad to be replacing them with a new life, a new perspective, and the first real love she'd ever experienced. She felt so perfectly happy that she couldn't imagine life ever being hard again. As long as she had Whit, she believed that they could get through anything.

\* \* \* \* \*

Whit and Mary returned home to find that everything was fine. Of course, they knew that Janel could have called either of their cell phones if there had been an emergency. But all was well. Walter hadn't needed any help in the night, and therefore he hadn't even realized that Mary had been gone.

By evening, Whit had moved most of his things into Mary's room, which was spacious enough that they didn't feel at all cramped—unlike the home he'd been living in, where he'd felt cramped even having a room to himself. But he told himself not to get too comfortable. He had a feeling that this was only temporary, and they would eventually end up living in an apartment until they were able to get a home of their own.

Within a couple of days, married life took on a comfortable rhythm for everyone involved. Whit was able to come and go from the room he shared with Mary and not get anywhere near Walter's room. Ida seemed content and rarely had any anxiety. Once in a while she asked about her home or mentioned missing something about it, but those moments passed quickly. Having Mary and Adrienne and Janel all around her to help care for her and keep her company seemed to compensate for any misgivings she might have had.

Mary went with Whit when he took his mother to the doctor. He was the family doctor they'd gone to for many years. He was kind and bright and he spoke Spanish fluently. Ida was given a thorough physical, including blood work, which was long overdue. But the majority of the doctor's time was spent asking questions, both of Ida and those who had been caring for her. At the conclusion of their visit, the doctor told them that there was no specific test to officially diagnose Alzheimer's disease, but with the information he had gathered, he could determine with 90 percent accuracy whether it was present. And he felt relatively certain that Alzheimer's was the reason for Ida's increasing memory loss. There were specific things about her behavior and the patterns of her memory lapses that were strong indicators of the disease. Ida was completely lucid during most of the exam, especially when the doctor talked to her about what he believed. She couldn't deny her own awareness of forgetting things, and she admitted that it frightened her. They were assured that medications could help slow the process of memory loss, and that other associated symptoms were treatable. But she would need watchful care for the rest of her life, and a time would come when her family would no longer be equitably capable of taking care of her and keeping her safe.

Once they were back in the truck, all three of them in the front seat, Ida started to cry. Mary got teary herself and wrapped her arms around her mother-in-law.

"It's going to be all right, Mama," Whit assured her. "I know it's frightening, but we're going to take very good care of you."

She told them she wasn't worried about that, but she didn't want to be a burden, and she was afraid of what she might do when she wasn't in her right mind. They both offered as much reassurance as they could possibly give, then Whit insisted they were going out to lunch; they needed to do something fun and normal and they would talk more about it later. Cinda would be picking Adrienne up from school so she could spend the afternoon with Rachel, which meant they didn't need to hurry home.

They enjoyed their lunch and did a little shopping, but Ida was obviously disheartened, as anyone *would* be with such a diagnosis, and they found it impossible to distract her completely from her dismal thoughts. That evening she seemed a little better, but then it became evident that she'd probably forgotten about the doctor's visit. It was difficult to tell whether that was good or not.

When Ida and Adrienne were both down for the night, Whit and Mary sat together in silence on the couch for several minutes before Mary finally got him to express how he truly felt about the news they'd received that day.

"I think a part of me already knew," he said, "but I didn't want to face it. I'm not . . . surprised, but . . . being forced out of denial can be tough."

"I think I knew as well," she said. "And it's heartbreaking."

They talked for a long while about their feelings and how they were going to manage. They concluded the only thing they *could* conclude, and that was the need to take everything one day at a time. They needed to do research, learn how to manage the situation, and be as prepared as possible for whatever challenges might arise. After they went up to bed, they talked some more in the dark, with Mary's head resting comfortably on Whit's shoulder. The irony of caring for two elderly parents sank in a little deeper.

"Yes," Mary said, "but at least your mother is kind and loving."

"Yes, she is. But we both know enough about the disease to know that it can induce personality changes, and she might not always be her kind and loving self."

"We'll just have to do the best we can."

"And we need to teach Adrienne about the disease, so she's prepared and doesn't get upset when such things start to happen."

"We'll *all* be upset," Mary said. "We just all have to be mature enough to handle it appropriately."

"Yes." Whit sighed. "I'm so grateful that you're a part of this . . . that you're here to help me through this—even though I don't like the idea of bringing burdens into your life."

Mary leaned up on her elbow and looked down at him. "I would never consider caring for your mother a burden—no matter how hard it gets."

"I know," he said, touching her face. "That's one of the reasons I'm so grateful. I can't even imagine how I would have dealt with this on my own. There's no one I trust enough to help care for her, except perhaps some members of the branch, but I don't know how they could have helped without it being a great burden to *them*."

"Well, I'm glad we're all together—and we'll get through this."

"Yes, we will," he said.

# Chapter Twelve

THE WEEKS OF AUTUMN WERE filled with many pleasant days, but also a number of rainy ones that made it impossible for Whit to work outside. But he helped Mary clean out the basement and the garage, and he did a number of little repairs around the house. He also painted the kitchen and the bathroom on the main floor, then he basically remodeled the laundry room since it had been in terrible condition. Mary was continually impressed with how hard he worked and how many different skills he had. If he wanted to do something, he figured out how to do it and he did it well.

The more time they spent together, the more she saw evidence of his kindness and patience. If not for the tattoos, she never could have imagined the person he'd described himself as once being. Ida showed signs of declining in spite of the medication, but Whit never lost his patience with her—even when she was immensely difficult. It was the doctor's opinion that the disease had progressed more rapidly in Ida than might be typical, or else it had been coming on for longer than they'd believed and she'd managed to keep it hidden. Whit had to admit she'd shown signs of forgetfulness for years, but he'd just figured it was part of aging, and she was getting on in years most of his life since she'd given birth to him at an age when most women were long past childbearing.

Adrienne had started referring to Whit as her daddy, and he filled the role well. Mary realized more and more that Simon had not been a bad father; she knew he'd loved the girls very much, and he'd never been unkind to them. But then, Mary had only been comparing him to her own father. Now she could see that Simon hadn't necessarily been a *good* father. He'd been very preoccupied with whatever his current work or project might have been, and he'd rarely interacted with the girls or spent specific meaningful time with them. Seeing the contrast of how Whit was so actively involved in Adrienne's life, Mary just couldn't imagine what she had ever done to deserve being so blessed.

Whit and Mary went out on a date once a week, and at least once a week they took Adrienne and Ida on some kind of family outing. They continued going to church, and they attended the temple with the goal of going together at least once a month. Mary received a calling in the branch to work with the young women, and she was thrilled with the opportunity. Previously she had been helping in an unofficial capacity with Relief Society activities, but this gave her a deeper sense of belonging, and she quickly grew to love the small group of girls she worked with as well as the other leaders.

They all went every Sunday to visit Claudia, and one time Carlos came while they were there. He and Whit exchanged pleasant greetings, and Mary hugged him. He congratulated them on their marriage, which Claudia had obviously told him about. Mary could tell Whit was still a little tense over the situation but he handled it well. Of course, Carlos would have known that Whit and Ida had moved out of the neighborhood, so his getting married wasn't a big surprise. Carlos reassured them that he wouldn't tell a soul about Whit's family or where he was living. And what could they do except believe him?

Whit wished that he could take Mary and Adrienne to visit his Aunt Sofia, who was homebound, but since she lived in the old neighborhood, it was impossible. Whit took Ida to see her other sister occasionally, and the sisters talked on the phone some. Mary just had to be content to maintain a certain distance from the majority of Whit's family.

The following week Whit got a call from the Realtor, who informed him that someone had made an offer on the house. Just as Whit had predicted, it came from some relatives of a family that was well-established in the neighborhood—a family that had strong gang ties. He hated the thought of the gang power becoming stronger, but not as much as he hated the thought of someone moving in who was innocent and ignorant. He gladly accepted the offer, and the following Saturday a few men from the branch's elders quorum helped him clean out the house. What didn't go to charity went into a storage unit, then these good men helped Whit do one last cleaning and he turned the keys over to the Realtor and said good-bye to the house—and the neighborhood—forever.

Whit told Mary he appreciated having the burden of the house off of his shoulders, and he also felt grateful to have the money from the sale of the house tucked away in safe investments. It could be accessed without too much trouble, and he called it their house fund—although they both agreed that the money might be needed to see to Ida's care when they could no longer care for her at home. At least the money was there so her care wouldn't become a worry. Mary secretly hoped that in the end her father *would* leave her this house, and they could stay here where they'd become so comfortable and she would never have to leave their beautiful garden. But she couldn't deny Whit's reasoning in having a plan to fall back on. The situation was too unpredictable to not be prepared for a number of possible outcomes. Since Whit had a fair amount of money put away, on top of that from the sale of the house, they both felt confident they would manage as long as they were careful with their resources.

The first week of November, Whit suddenly became excited for the holidays and wanted to go Christmas shopping. He and Mary went while Janel took care of Adrienne and Ida, and they had a wonderful time picking out gifts for his mother, and especially for Adrienne. They even got a few gifts for Walter, in spite of knowing he would probably not care. They hid gifts in the basement that had recently been cleaned and organized, and the following week they took Adrienne shopping to pick out gifts for the people she cared about. They talked about going shopping again, just for fun, after the malls all had their Christmas decorations out, and then she could meet Santa and talk to him. Adrienne was thrilled, and Whit said quietly to Mary, "I love being a dad."

Mary kissed him. "It shows. You're very good at it."

In spite of having a very good day, at bedtime Adrienne had one of those moments that happened on occasion when she missed her father and especially her sister; she cried and was slow to be comforted. It usually happened as she was going to bed, when things were quieter and memories had a better chance of creeping in. Whit or Mary—or both—would just sit with her and talk about the *good* memories and do their best to console her grief. The episodes were becoming less frequent, but Whit and Mary both agreed that she was doing beautifully overall after such an enormous loss, and it would be more of a concern if they didn't see any sign of grief.

The following day it rained again, and Whit helped Mary pull out boxes of Christmas decorations and lights that hadn't been used for years. While they were organizing and trying to figure out what worked and what was worth keeping, Janel declared how good it would be to have Christmas again in this house. Since Mary's mother had died, there had been no sign of it. She had been coming and going, keeping the house in order and cooking meals for Walter and his nurses, while the house had been way too quiet and depressing. They all agreed that it was good to have this house be a home for all of them—even for Janel during her working hours. And she was happy to admit that they had become her second family.

Whit got out some Christmas decorations he'd brought with him when he'd moved, and his mother was thrilled to see her own things. They talked about getting a tree as soon as they'd celebrated Thanksgiving.

The evening was pleasant, and everything felt as good as it had ever been. In fact, the thought occurred to Mary so strongly that it drew her attention away from everything going on around her. It was as if she were meant to stop and take note of this moment. A cold chill accompanied the thought that perhaps something was going to change, or something bad was going to happen. She promptly dismissed such a possibility, certain that even thinking such a thing was probably bad luck—even if she didn't really believe in *luck*. She believed that their lives were in God's hands, and He had a plan for them. As long as they did their best to live close to the Spirit and make righteous decisions, then luck had nothing to do with the events of their lives—good or bad.

Mary didn't give the matter another thought until she was awakened in the night by a loud thud she could hear through the monitor on her bedside table. The thud that made her immediately coherent was followed by the sound of her father groaning, then cursing. Mary ran out of the room and down the hall, flipping on the light in her father's room as she entered to find him on the floor.

"What happened?" she demanded, then gasped when she saw blood spewing from a gash in his forehead. "Good heavens, you're bleeding!" she said, then tried to calm herself even while she argued with her father. He was not cooperative about her trying to hold a clean rag over the cut to stop the bleeding. He rejected the idea that he might need stitches, even though they could get a nurse to come to the house and do it so that he wouldn't have to leave his room. He insisted that he had no idea what had happened. To Mary it was evident that he'd fallen and had hit his head on the corner of the bedside table, but she couldn't imagine how it might have occurred since it had never happened before. He was too frail to get out of bed on his own, and he knew it, so he always demanded help before he even considered trying to stand. He was wheezing, and she had to try to calm him down since she couldn't maneuver the oxygen so that it was easily within his reach. Mary finally got him to breathe more evenly and to hold a gauze pad over the wound while she focused her attention on helping him get back into his bed. Then she realized that it wasn't just his head that he'd hurt. One of his legs was not working well, and her efforts to help him back to bed were completely pointless. While she was considering how to find a way to make him comfortable on the floor until a nurse arrived at six to help her, she looked up and saw Whit come into the room. Only then did it occur to her that he would have been hearing the entire drama on the monitor in their bedroom.

"No!" she said and frantically tried to motion him out of the room, knowing that nothing was worth having her father know that he was here in the middle of the night.

Whit completely ignored her and said softly, "I'm not going to let him lay on a cold floor all night." He promptly scooped Walter off the floor and set him on the bed with very little trouble. Then the expected outburst occurred.

Walter demanded to know what Whit was doing there at this hour, but his demands were accompanied by more than one offensive word. He yelled with a force and volume that Mary wouldn't have believed possible, given all his health problems. To Whit he shouted, "Are you sleeping with my daughter?" Whit said nothing, and Walter demanded of Mary, "Are you *sleeping* with *him*?"

Mary cringed as the emphasis on the word *him* made it clear that he probably wouldn't care *who* she was sleeping with, or under what circumstances, as long as he was white. She took a deep breath to calm herself, then she looked at Whit. "Let me handle this," she said. "If Adrienne's awake, let her listen to music on my iPod so she won't be able to hear any of this."

She saw the muscles tighten in Whit's face and knew that he didn't want to leave her alone with the dragon, but he turned around and left the room. Mary drew courage and turned to her father, saying firmly, "I'm married to him." She fully expected the rage and ranting that followed, and could only be grateful when he began to cough, permitting her to slip an oxygen mask over his mouth and nose. She could still see the anger in his eyes, but he couldn't do anything about it. And she just waited, trying to be a dutiful and caring daughter and stay with him until he was breathing properly. He obviously wasn't in much pain from the wound on his head or the temporary weakness in his leg, or he would have been more distracted from his anger.

Whit felt himself shaking as he left Walter's room. He couldn't say for sure what had made him step boldly past their clearly established boundaries in order to help Walter. And he knew he'd have trouble explaining it to Mary. But listening to her trying to deal with this cantankerous, difficult old man, he'd suddenly felt fed up with the sneaking around and hiding. He'd suddenly felt like it would be better to live elsewhere than to live like this. Now he wasn't so much questioning his decision as he was regretting the fact that Mary had to take the brunt of Walter's anger. He checked on Adrienne and found that she *was* awake. He did as Mary had suggested and quickly got her listening to music that would block out the shouting down the hall. He assured her that everything was all right and promised to check on her in a few minutes. She nodded and seemed fine, but Whit knew she'd probably heard her grandfather shouting many times—one more reason for Whit to feel completely disgusted. He got her settled, then he paced the hall while the shouting continued, and he could not believe the things this man was saying to his daughter. He said horrible things about Whit, but he was used to that kind of thing and he really didn't care. But the way he insulted Mary, questioned her judgment, and completely demeaned her made him absolutely furious.

When the old man started coughing, Whit felt some relief in hoping the worst was over. He went downstairs to check on his mother and found her in bed asleep. He went back upstairs, closing the gate behind him, and walked again into Walter's room to find Mary sitting on the edge of his bed, wiping away the blood from his forehead with the gauze she held in one hand, while she held the oxygen mask to his face with the other. Her compassion and charitable nature were incomparable, especially when he felt tempted to inflict bodily harm on this man. Walter tried to tell Whit to leave the room, but he started coughing and gasping and couldn't speak.

Whit took advantage of the moment to say what he felt he needed to say; otherwise, the words would go around and around in his head until they drove him mad. He put the kind of calm façade in place that he used when he had to face any of the violence-prone people from his past. "Just listen to me for a minute," he said. "Then I'll leave, and you never have to see me again." Walter tried to protest again, but Whit lifted a finger, saying, "Just be quiet and listen, or you can sit here and cough and bleed the rest of the night all by yourself, and no one will ever know about it."

He glanced at Mary to gauge her reaction, but he had no idea what she was thinking. He focused instead on getting this over with. "I know we deceived you by not telling you we're married and that I've been living here, but as you can see, we knew that you would be very angry if you knew, and you would never understand. I don't expect you to understand, and I don't really care whether you do. If you want us to leave, we will. We'll start packing tomorrow and we'll leave your house, and you can get a nurse to come in here at night the way you used to, someone who can deal with your pathetic belligerence so your daughter won't have to do it anymore. She deserves better, you know. She is a fine and amazing woman, and you don't even know her. She is everything you are not, and she became those things in spite of you. I just wanted you to know that, because you *should* know it. She's far better to you than you deserve, but that's the kind of woman she is."

Walter pushed away the oxygen mask and snarled in a raspy voice, "I want you all out of my house. I want you to leave and never come back."

"That will not be a problem," Whit said.

"You've got twenty-four hours to leave or—"

"Or what?" Whit demanded. "Are you going to get out of that bed and throw us out? We'll be out as soon as we can pack our things, but we won't be leaving in the middle of the night. So make it thirty-six hours. That's all I have to say."

Whit tossed an apologetic glance to Mary, on the chance that he'd disappointed her, then he turned and left the room, surprised at how relieved he felt to have the truth out on the table and to no longer have to stay here. He'd find work, they'd find a place to live, and they would all be fine. Better, in fact. He just hoped Mary saw it that way. He took a few minutes to calm down, then he checked again on his mother, who was still sleeping. Adrienne was sleeping as well, and he carefully turned off the iPod and moved it without disturbing her. He would be glad to have his wife and daughter and mother away from here. He didn't even want them breathing the same air as Walter Cranford.

Once Whit had left the room, Mary courageously met her father's eyes, feeling surprisingly *more* courageous after what Whit had just said on her behalf. She was startled by the intensity of anger and hatred she saw there, and the way he hissed through his breathlessness, "You have no idea what you've done. You have no idea what those kind of people . . . are capable of."

Mary felt chilled by the comment, mostly because it made her wonder all over again *why* her father was this way. But she knew it wouldn't do any good to ask him. He would never talk about his past; she knew that well enough. Instead she said, "Whit is a good man. You cannot judge him by the color of his skin. I know you and I will never agree on such things, and that's okay. But I'm an adult and I've made my choice."

"You bet you have!" Walter said and coughed several times. "And you can live with it—anywhere but here."

"Fine," she said and felt glad that he was overtaken by more coughing so that he couldn't speak. But she knew she hadn't heard the last of it, at least for the amount of time she felt obligated to stay in the room.

Whit paced the bedroom for nearly an hour before Mary came back. He knew from the sounds on the monitor that her father was probably asleep, only because Mary would have given him medication to ease the coughing and that would have made him drowsy. If not for the coughing and the need for medicine and oxygen, he'd probably still be shouting. Whit stopped pacing when she entered the room. Their eyes met for a only a moment before she closed the door and leaned against it, sighing loudly with her eyes closed.

"I'm so sorry," he hurried to say. If she was angry with him he wanted to get his defense in as quickly as possible. "I just . . . couldn't take it anymore. I haven't said anything, but . . . I've hated the sneaking around, knowing we were deceiving him. Maybe we did what we had to do; it felt right and I believe it was. But maybe it's time to do something different . . . something better. I can't bear the way he talks to you, Mary; the way he treats you. Every time you go in there it just makes my skin crawl." She said nothing, and he went on, if only to fill the silence. "Beyond that, I couldn't sit in here and know he was hurt and lying on the floor and that you were unable to help him."

"So," she said and that one word hung in the air for several seconds while he held his breath, "you were concerned for *his* comfort in spite of everything else."

"I suppose I was," he said, "but—"

"Don't say anymore," she said and held up a hand. "I . . . was angry at first, but . . . after what you just said to him, I . . ." She looked directly at him and tears filled her eyes. "I've wanted to say those things to him for years, and I never had the courage. Simon would never stand up to him—

especially on my behalf. He was always trying to placate my father, like one of the spineless employees of his company who would do anything to stay in his good graces."

She sighed and Whit did the same, deeply relieved that she wasn't furious with him. When she said nothing more, he felt the need to clarify that very point. "I wouldn't blame you if you were angry with me. I should have talked to you about how I was feeling; I've intended to, but . . . it just never felt like the right time, and . . . then he needed help, and . . . I shouldn't have done that without us talking it over first, and—"

"It's all right, Whit," she said. "I've been feeling the same way."

"You have?"

"It felt like the right thing to keep him ignorant when we got married, but I've been feeling recently like we needed to come clean."

"Then you forgive me?"

"There's nothing to forgive," she said and stepped toward him, easing into his arms. He held to her tightly, grateful beyond words that they were on the same page and he wasn't arguing with her *and* her father—even though she would have been justified in being upset. His respect for her grew more every day. And his love for her grew in proportion to his admiration. "I love you, Whit. I'll go anywhere as long as we can be together. I'll be most sad to leave the garden."

"We'll buy our own home, and I'll make you a new garden; a *better* garden."

"I don't know if that's possible."

"Is that a challenge?"

She looked up at him. "Maybe. But let's talk about it tomorrow. I think we need some sleep. I'm calling the home health care company tomorrow and arranging for a nurse on the night shift. I'm not going into that room again—ever."

"Not even to say good-bye?"

"Can you think of a reason I should?" she asked as they got back into bed.

"Not really, no."

"There you have it," she said.

He turned off the lamp and eased her into his arms, feeling a deep relief.

"Do you think we can find a place to rent so quickly?"

"I don't know. We'll stay in a motel if we have to. We'll manage. You mustn't worry."

"I'm *not* worried," she said. "That's the best part. I don't feel worried. I have you to take care of us. Why should I worry?"

"Can't think of a reason," he said and they drifted into silence, then into sleep until the alarm went off when it was time to wake Adrienne to get ready for school.

Whit woke Adrienne while Mary spoke quietly to the nurse who had arrived at six about what had happened to Walter in the night. He was sleeping now and seemed fine but the nurse would make certain all was well after he woke up.

At breakfast Whit explained to Adrienne and his mother why they would be packing all day and moving out tomorrow. Adrienne seemed fine with it. As long as she had the people she loved and she could keep going to the same school and the same church, she didn't care where she lived. She admitted in her childlike way that she would be glad not to have to live in the same house with her scary grandpa.

After Adrienne went to school, Whit's mother wanted to talk to him about what had happened and why. He tried to explain it in a simple way that skirted around the core of the real issues—which was nothing but pure bigotry and meanness—but his mother was in one of her especially sharp moods and she kept asking questions, wanting to understand. She was worried that she had done something to cause a problem, and he assured her repeatedly that it had nothing at all to do with her. He hoped that she believed him, and he hoped that in a memory lapse she might forget the whole thing.

Packing their things didn't prove to be terribly complicated, given the fact that they'd all come here with minimal belongings. They set aside some things to go to the storage unit until they were settled. Since Whit was still trying to find a suitable house or apartment to rent, they had to go forward on the premise that they might be confined to a motel room for at least a few days.

Janel was heartbroken over what had happened, and she couldn't imagine going back to working in such a lonely and bleak environment after all the joy she'd gotten from helping care for Adrienne and Ida, and working side by side with Mary and Whit. Of course they all promised they would keep in touch, and since she was the only person they trusted to care for Ida or Adrienne, they would still be seeing each other often. This made her feel better. In fact, she insisted that if they couldn't find a place to rent they could stay with her until they did.

"It would be cozy," she said, "but I've got a couple of spare rooms since the kids left home. It would be better than a motel room, and there's no need for you to be spending money for an expensive room when you could stay with me."

"We might take you up on it," Whit said and gave her a loud smooch on the forehead, which made her laugh. Then he went back to his packing. He was glad that his mother had spent most of the day preoccupied with the television and seemed to have forgotten about the issue at hand. She seemed oblivious to the work that Whit and Mary were doing and the reasons for it but Whit preferred it that way. For all of her memory lapses, she seemed to trust that the people around her would take good care of her, and she had no need or reason to fear. When she started to forget *that*, they could really have a problem.

Whit got a call on his cell phone and had to leave because Jose, Carlos's brother, had gone to visit his mother while he'd been either drunk or stoned. He'd caused some problems at the care center and had been arrested. Whit had no intention of doing anything to help Jose, who didn't have even a degree of the redeeming qualities that Carlos possessed. If he'd gone to the care center, he'd probably gone with the intention of trying to get money out of his mother. He never went to see her for any other reason, as opposed to Carlos, who actually loved his mother and put some effort into caring for her. Whit's only intention in getting involved was to visit Claudia and to help calm her down.

Carlos was there, seething with anger at his brother, and Whit had to try to calm *him* down as well, fearing there might be another shooting in the family if Carlos didn't keep his senses about him. Carlos agreed, but Whit sensed that he was agitated for reasons beyond what he was willing to disclose. Whit felt uneasy over it, but in truth he didn't want to know. He felt uneasy for different reasons when Carlos mentioned how sorry he was that Whit and his family had to move due to the old man being so difficult. Whit was astonished that Carlos would know about their situation until he realized that his mother had talked to Claudia on the phone, and both of the women were too forgetful to be discreet. Claudia's forgetfulness was normal for old age, but it was just enough to create problems that these women were oblivious to. Whit just tried to keep his conversation with Carlos casual and not let it bother him.

He visited with Claudia for a while, assured her that everything would be fine, and stayed with her until she drifted into a late-afternoon nap. Whit spoke to one of the managers of the care center and suggested they file a restraining order against Jose, but they feared that would only bring on more trouble. And Whit couldn't argue with that. He hated it, but he couldn't argue.

By the time Whit got home, he felt deeply exhausted. It had been a long night and a long day, and the drama from both sides of the family felt overwhelming. He laid down on the couch, near where his mother was sitting in her usual chair in front of the TV. He'd intended to just lay there for fifteen or twenty minutes, but he came awake to Adrienne nudging him, her little face close to his.

"Hey, Daddy," she said. "Mommy says it's time for dinner, and you should wake up."

"Okay, precious," he said. "I'll be there in a minute."

He sat up and tried to get his bearings.

"Sorry to wake you," he heard Mary say in the distance, "but I was afraid you wouldn't be able to sleep tonight if you slept any longer."

"It's okay," he said, glancing at his watch, surprised to realize it was even later than he'd thought. They usually ate earlier than this. He stood up and went into the kitchen where he hugged all three of the women he loved who were there working together to put supper on the table.

When they sat down together to eat, Whit felt much as he had the first time they'd all sat here together for supper the first night he and his mother had stayed here. He felt reassured that as long as they could be together, they could be happy anywhere. But when he'd been sorting out Christmas decorations the previous day, he hadn't imagined that tonight would be their last supper at this table.

After Adrienne had finished eating and had left the table, Mary told Whit that she'd phoned Mr. Lostin, the man who handled most of her father's personal business matters. Whit knew him mostly as the man who signed his paychecks.

"I told him what happened and that we were leaving. He said that he was very sorry to hear it, and he wished us all the best. He told me to let him know where to send your last paycheck, and he said you had a bonus coming."

"A bonus?" Whit asked skeptically.

"I don't know." Mary shrugged. "He's a good man; he's always trying to figure out legal ways to work around my father's stinginess. If he comes up with a bonus, I'm not going to argue with him."

Whit made no comment.

Later that evening when the nurse from the late shift left, she told Mary that Walter had specifically charged her to tell his daughter that she and her family had better be out of the house by the following day or he would be calling his attorney.

"Okay, you've delivered your message," Mary said. "I'm sorry you had to deal with that."

"It's all right," Doris said. "I'm just sorry that you have to go."

"Me too. Did he say anything else?"

"Oh, he's had *a lot* to say today, but I'm not repeating such awful things."

"Okay," Mary sighed, "enough said. Have a good night." They shared a hug when it became evident Doris wouldn't be back until the family had left the house. Mary watched her go, grateful for these saintly women who were so gifted at dealing with the most difficult patient on the planet.

That night Whit *was* able to sleep, but he came awake abruptly to a terrible sound. He'd heard the alarm system go off before, always due to someone forgetting to punch the code in when they were supposed to. As long as the code was put in within a minute of the alarm going off, no law enforcement would be dispatched. Whit just had to find out if there was a reason he *needed* law enforcement.

"Stay here," he said to Mary and hurried down the stairs, wishing he still owned a gun. He thought of his uneasiness earlier today in regard to his cousins. He thought of a thousand fears in regard to his past catching up with him, and he prayed that this would not become a moment he'd been dreading. He found the patio door open, and he knew he'd locked it. He *always* double-checked *every* door, but he'd also known of his mother trying to go outside after the security system had been set for the night. Maybe that was all that had happened, he reasoned, liking that idea. But he found his mother in bed, surprisingly unaffected by the noisy alarm. She could certainly be a deep sleeper.

With evidence that the house might have been invaded—even if he couldn't imagine how someone could have unlocked the door—he hurried back upstairs to make certain Mary and Adrienne were okay. He found them together in Whit and Mary's room, the child holding her hands over her ears.

"It's okay," he said to them, "the police will be here soon and they'll make sure everything is all right." He sat on the edge of the bed, thinking it would be best to just stay here and keep an eye on his wife and daughter until he knew everything was okay. He spoke soothingly to Adrienne, who took her hands away from her ears since he'd closed the door and the alarm wasn't so loud.

He felt proud of himself for remaining so outwardly calm while his insides were churning with the possibilities of gang violence coming into his home. Given his train of thought, he could almost believe he had some power of premonition when a horrible noise interrupted his gentle words to his daughter.

Gunshot sounded from nearby. The sound was distinct and surprisingly loud. Mary gasped. Adrienne winced and again pressed her hands over her ears even more tightly. Whit felt sick to his stomach. He took a long moment to ascertain whether or not he should investigate or wait for the police. Would he be putting himself in danger if he went looking for the source, being unarmed? For all of the bad things he'd imagined possibly happening to him or his family, he couldn't begin to imagine *why* they'd just heard a gun go off. The possibilities were as confusing as they were frightening. After a few minutes had passed, he finally crept quietly down the hall, admonishing Mary and Adrienne to stay put. He flipped on light switches as he went, needing light to give him the advantage of being able to see what was going on. As much as he didn't want to, he went into Walter's room and flipped on the light, certain the noise would have awakened him long before now anyway. He wondered why the old man hadn't been grumbling about it; they should have heard him over the monitor. Whit felt a little dizzy and had to lean his shoulder against the door frame to remain upright. No wonder the gunshot had been so loud. They'd heard it over the monitor. The weapon had been fired in this room. Walter Cranford had been shot in the chest. Whit didn't even have to touch him to know he was dead. The ghastly way his eyes were half open, and the stark absence of his noisy breathing were sufficient proof.

Whit distanced  himself from the shock enough to take stock of the situation. He knew better than to touch anything; the police would handle all of that, and he suspected they would arrive at any moment. But he did notice that the sliding glass door was open. He stepped out onto the little balcony but saw nothing below—no movement, nothing. But it was completely dark, and he wondered what he might have expected to see.

He panicked at the thought of Mary possibly coming to investigate his reason for not returning quickly. He took one more glance at the ghastly body of Walter Cranford and wondered how he would be feeling right now if he'd actually cared about the man. But even his deep feelings of animosity toward this man could not erase the horror of what had just happened, and he knew somewhere deep inside that he was somehow responsible. He didn't know exactly who, or how, or what had happened, but he knew that this *wouldn't* have happened if he had not become a part of this family. He felt sick. But right now he had to deal with what was right in front of him.

The alarm stopped blaring as he walked down the hall; apparently it was set to stop after so many minutes if it wasn't disabled. He took a deep breath and went back to where Mary and Adrienne were clinging to each other, looking frightened. He forced a calm voice and said, "Adrienne, honey, there's nothing to worry about. Something bad has happened, but the police will be here any second, and nothing bad is going to happen to *you*. I promise. Okay?" She nodded firmly, and he hoped her trust in him had not been misguided. He looked directly at Mary, whose eyes were now even more filled with dread. "I need to talk to you privately for just a minute, and then you should stay with Adrienne."

Mary nodded and followed him into the hallway. He closed the door, looked at her firmly and said, "Your father is dead, Mary."

She sucked in her breath and teetered slightly. He took hold of her shoulders to steady her.

"I don't know what happened, or who is responsible, but the police will be here any second, and they'll take care of everything. You just watch out for Adrienne and see if you can get her to go back to sleep." She nodded, with tears shimmering in her eyes. He hugged her tightly for a long moment, aware that she was gasping for breath and near to sobbing.

"I . . . can't believe it," she muttered. She looked up at him. "Who would do such a horrible thing?"

"I don't know," he said.

"But you have an idea?"

"I don't know," he repeated firmly. He couldn't help noticing that her focus was more on the shock of the event as opposed to any grief over the announcement of her father's death. Perhaps some of that would come with time. At least he didn't feel alone in his emotions on that count.

"The police will be here any second," he said. "I need to go. Everything's going to be all right." She nodded stoutly, and he urged her back into the bedroom.

Whit hurried down the stairs, still wearing pajama pants with a T-shirt, but he figured the police had seen worse. He checked on his mother and found her still tucked in her bed, apparently oblivious. He wondered for a moment if she was awake but huddling there because she was frightened. He was about to check further when he heard an officer shouting at the door to announce their arrival. Whit stepped into the common room and shouted back, "I'm Whit Eden. I live here." A flashlight beam struck his face and made him squint. "We've had an intruder, and my father-in-law has been shot. That's all I know."

"Where is he?" an officer asked, and Whit saw them lower their guns.

"Upstairs," Whit said and motioned. "He's dead. The light is on in his room. My wife and daughter are in another room. Please try not to frighten them."

"Did you touch anything?" an officer asked as two men rushed past him, and he saw two others moving through the house to make certain it was clear.

"Nothing but the light switch," Whit said, then hurried to add, "My mother is in a room down that hall." He followed the officer heading that way to make certain she was all right.

"Anyone else in the house?" he was asked.

"Not unless the shooter is still here," Whit said and opened the door to his mother's room, turning on the light so the officer could check the room. "It's all right," he said in Spanish as his mother looked up at him, clearly terrified. She *had* been awake and hovering in her bed in fear. Of course, how could anyone have slept through that alarm? He sat on the edge of the bed and put his arms around her. "We had an intruder," he explained gently, "but the police are here now and everything's going to be all right."

Within a minute the police declared the house to be clear, and a couple of officers went outside to check the yard. Backup was called in now that they had a murder to investigate. Whit was informed that he and his family needed to remain in the house until the police could talk to everyone and thoroughly comb the house and yard for evidence. He knew that would take several hours, but all he said was, "May I get dressed?"

"Of course," he was told. "But please hurry. I want to talk to you first."

Whit hurried and put on some jeans, then he checked on Mary and Adrienne.

"Are you okay?" he asked.

"It's hard to say," Mary said, her voice trembling.

"The police checked this room?" he asked.

"Yes," Mary answered and left Adrienne's side to move closer to Whit so they could speak privately in whispers that the child wouldn't overhear.

"I have to go talk to them," he said. "They'll want to question you too."

"Okay," she said, and he hurried to add something that he knew had to be said.

"They're going to be suspicious of me, Mary. As soon as they figure out my background, they're going to believe that it has something to do with this, and maybe they're right. They're *probably* right. But I don't want you to tell them anything but the absolute truth about everything. Do you understand?"

She nodded, looking afraid. "It's going to be all right," he said. "Try to get Adrienne back to sleep, then get dressed and come downstairs."

"Is your mother all right?"

"A little shaken, but fine. How are you?"

"In shock," she said. He nodded and kissed her brow, then he left the room, not wanting the police to have any reason to be *too* suspicious of him.

# Chapter Thirteen

WHIT HURRIED BACK DOWNSTAIRS. AT the kitchen table he was rigorously questioned regarding exactly what had happened, and every step he had taken from the moment the alarm had awakened him. He'd been questioned by police before—many times—and he knew from experience that the best thing to do was to be completely patient and cooperative, no matter how many times they asked the same question and no matter how long it took.

By the time they'd gone over the events from Whit's perspective three times, a detective arrived, and Whit waited while the officer filled him in. Then the detective sat down across from Whit. "I'm Detective Wilson," he said.

"Whit Eden. Thank you for coming."

"It's my job, Mr. Eden, but we'll do everything we can to figure out who did this."

"I know you will," Whit said, but he felt doubtful they would ever be able to pin the crime on anyone enough to make it stick. That's how it was with gang crimes. In that vein, he knew it was better to come clean than to wait for them to figure it out. "There's something I need to tell you that may be relevant."

"Okay, I would be happy to hear *anything* that might be relevant, even if it might seem insignificant."

"I have a personal history with gang violence. I did time, and I've had nothing to do with it since then."

"Okay," the detective drawled with a dawning skepticism in his eyes. But Whit had expected that and he went on.

"My mother and I just moved a few months ago from the neighborhood where I grew up; it has heavy gang control. I have cousins who are actively involved." He explained a few more specific details about the specific gang to which he had belonged and where exactly he had lived. He explained how his mother communicated with his aunts, one of whom had once worked in this house, and that information concerning his whereabouts and circumstances might have leaked through inadvertently. He also mentioned how completely uninvolved he had remained for several years. "But it's not easy to get away from the consequences," he added.

"Do you think any of your former . . . associates . . . would have a reason to do this?"

"To be frank, it's impossible to understand what might motivate some of the things they do. In your line of work I'm sure you know what I mean."

"I do."

"I will tell you that my father-in-law was well known as a bigot. He overtly hated Hispanics and hated the fact that his daughter had married one."

"You think this was a hate crime?"

"Looks that way, but I don't know."

"Can you tell me the names of those who might have known of your situation?"

"Detective Wilson," Whit said with perfect respect, "I'm absolutely certain that it would take very little effort for you to figure out the identity of my cousins who have gang affiliations. For the safety of my family, I would far prefer to be able to look my cousins in the face and tell them honestly that I did not give their names to the police."

The detective was silent for a long moment, then said, "Okay, I get that."

"Thank you," Whit said and felt some relief. He couldn't even imagine where all of this might go if his *former associates* started getting questioned about this. And he was sure they would be. The nightmare was likely only beginning.

"One more question." Detective Wilson motioned toward the boxes against one wall in the common room. "Is somebody moving?"

"My family was in the process of moving out," he said.

"Why?" the detective asked.

Whit felt some hesitant trepidation in formulating his answer. But he said it coolly, "My father-in-law didn't want us here."

"Because . . ."

"He was a bigot, Detective. Anyone who knows him will tell you that. He didn't try to hide it."

"So . . . you *won't* need to move out now that he's dead?"

Whit felt sick at the implication; he knew what this man was thinking. But he answered with a straightforward lack of defensiveness. "As far as I know, my wife was cut out of her father's will years ago. We have nothing to gain by his death . . . if that's what you're wondering. We'll be moving out regardless."

"Where will you go?"

"We haven't figured that out yet, but we'll manage."

With the interview apparently completed, Detective Wilson thanked Whit, then told him to stay close by. Whit checked on his mother and found her sleeping. A few minutes later Mary came down the stairs, now dressed. She reported that Adrienne was asleep with the iPod playing softly in her ears to block out the noise. Mary was rattled by all of the people in her father's room and still in shock over the fact that he was dead. When Whit put his arms around her he could feel her shaking. He was about to guide her to the couch where they could talk when the detective approached her and said, "Mrs. Eden?"

"Yes."

"I need to ask you some questions."

"Of course," she said, and Whit paced back and forth at the far end of the common room while Mary was questioned at the dining table, beyond his range of hearing. He saw Mary glance at him a few times, and he felt sick to consider how utterly horrible this was for *her*. He just hoped and prayed that it would all be wrapped up quickly and they could feel safe. He felt some small measure of comfort in realizing that if someone with violent tendencies had been in the house and they'd only harmed Walter Cranford, the implication leaned toward that person trying to protect Whit and his family rather than harming them. But he was freshly stunned by this distorted gang mentality, as if murder could be the solution to *any* problem.

Once Mary had been thoroughly questioned, she and Whit sat together on the couch while the police continued their work. They had little to say to each other, and Whit finally said, "You should try to get some rest."

"As if I could," she countered. She looked around. "How long do you think they'll be here?"

"Hours," he said, and they both sighed. Since it was still dark, they knew it was going to be a terribly long day.

Mary decided to make coffee. She and Whit didn't drink it, but Janel and the nurses did, so it was kept in the house. She thought the officers might appreciate some, and it would give her something to do. Whit helped her, then he took it upon himself to inform all the people working in the house that they could help themselves to the coffee in the kitchen.

Daylight finally came. Ida and Adrienne continued to sleep, and Whit urged Mary into the kitchen when he realized the body was being brought down the stairs. While they were in there, she realized that they didn't need a nurse to come, so she called the home health care company to inform them that their patient had died. The person on the other end of the phone expressed condolences, didn't ask questions, and said they would inform the scheduled nurse so that she wouldn't come. She was likely en route, but they had a cell phone number.

Whit felt some relief when the coroner's van drove away, and he hoped that meant the episode was winding down. He didn't know whether to feel comforted or terrified with the way that every inch of the house and grounds were being so meticulously searched. A deeply uneasy premonition kept nagging at him, a feeling he didn't dare voice to Mary. But he suspected this was going to get a lot worse before it got solved.

Mary felt exhausted and her eyes were burning. She kept going up the stairs to check on Adrienne, always relieved to find her still sleeping, but she preferred hovering close to Whit, who was mostly pacing the common room when he wasn't sitting on the couch, deep turmoil brewing in his eyes. She wanted to talk about what had happened. She wanted to know whatever he might know that he hadn't told her yet. But she could hardly think, let alone speak. And her preference for privacy outweighed her desire to try to begin a conversation when officers were constantly going in and out, walking past them, and sometimes examining details of the room. One of them asked about the reason for the gate at the foot of the stairs, and Whit explained its purpose in regard to his mother's Alzheimer's disease. He didn't say anything about keeping her presence in the house a secret from the murder victim; he simply said that they hadn't wanted her to wander upstairs unsupervised. The police asked questions about other things as well—things that Mary couldn't imagine had anything to do with a murder investigation, but Whit assured her that they needed to be thorough.

The police wouldn't let Janel into the house without first questioning Mary, then Janel, then Mary again. When she was finally allowed through the door, her eyes were wide with terror.

"What's happened?" she asked Mary in little more than a whisper.

Mary swallowed hard and said in a raspy voice, "We had an intruder last night, and . . . my father was shot."

Janel gasped. "Is he . . ."

"He's dead. Shot through the heart; that's assuming he had one." She heard the words come out of her mouth and immediately regretted them. She squeezed her eyes closed and said, "Sorry. That was entirely inappropriate."

"Maybe it's inappropriate to speak ill of the dead, Mary, but being dead doesn't change the kind of man he was."

"I know," Mary said and had to sit down. She hurried to the couch, and Janel sat beside her, putting a hand on her shoulder. "I just . . . feel so guilty for being relieved . . . that he's dead, at least. The reasons for it are frightening, however. I can't even imagine how someone got in and out like that."

"Do you think it has anything to do with . . . well . . . Whit's former . . . associations?"

"He thinks it does. He tells me they're capable of jumping fences, picking locks, and taking a life without blinking. The very idea makes me feel so . . . unsafe. Except that . . . it almost seems that someone was trying to . . . *protect* us."

"What do you mean?" Janel asked quietly.

"Claudia knew about my father kicking us out . . . and so did Carlos." She looked hard at Janel. "Whit thinks there's a connection, but . . . I don't know what to think. He tells me I have no idea how these people think. I'm sure he's right about that, but . . ." Tears finally came into the conversation. "I'm scared, Janel. I have a feeling this is far from over."

"At least you won't be moving out."

"Not yet, at least. I'm relatively certain he didn't leave the house to *me*. It's probably just a matter of time before we have to go, and you could be without a job. I guess we'll see."

"Don't you worry about me," Janel said. "Whatever happens, we'll all be okay."

"Yes, I'm sure we will," Mary said, but she didn't feel much conviction on that count at the moment.

An officer came into the house and spoke to Detective Wilson, who was leaning against the counter, drinking a cup of coffee. The detective followed the officer outside as if they were on to something significant. Mary noticed that Whit's pacing became more intense, and she asked, "What's wrong?"

"I don't know. I just . . . feel sick. Something's wrong."

"I'm sure everything will be all right," she said, and Janel went to the kitchen, as if to give them some privacy.

Whit nodded, but she knew he wasn't convinced, and she didn't know what else to say.

A few minutes later the detective and a couple of officers came back in and walked directly across the room to talk to Whit. Mary stood firmly beside him, feeling definitely unsettled herself, even though she couldn't begin to imagine what else could go wrong.

An officer wearing latex gloves held up a gun with two fingers and asked, "Do you recognize this, Mr. Eden?"

"Yes," he said, and Mary's heart began to pound. "It technically belongs to my mother, but it was stolen weeks ago. I filed a report."

Mary saw subtle, skeptical glances passing between the officers just before the detective said to Whit, "You're going to need to come with us until we can get more information."

"Why?" Mary demanded, unable to disguise her panic.

"Are you arresting me?" Whit asked in a voice that betrayed he wasn't as calm as he was trying to be.

"Is there a reason we should?" the detective asked.

"No!" Whit insisted. "I had nothing to do with this!"

"Let's just go downtown and talk about it," the detective said.

Whit turned to Mary with some degree of resignation. "It'll be all right," he said, but she barely had a chance to give him a quick hug before he was escorted away. The only thing that made her believe he *wasn't* being arrested was the fact that they didn't put him in handcuffs. Mary wanted to run after them and scream at the officers. She wanted to insist that she knew her husband and she knew he would not be involved in anything like this. Instead she sat on the couch, suddenly light-headed. She put her head down and forced herself to take some deep breaths, fearing she would pass out. She found Janel beside her and felt a comforting hand on her back.

"What's going on?" Janel asked quietly.

"They took Whit," she said breathlessly.

"They arrested him?"

"Not technically, but I'm afraid they'll find a way to pin this on him. I think that's what he's been afraid of since it happened, but he wouldn't say anything."

"Everything will be all right, Mary," Janel said.

"That's what Whit said, but I'm not sure he believes it. I'm not sure I do either." She realized she was shaking.

"He's innocent!" Janel insisted.

"I know that, but it wouldn't be the first time an innocent man has gone to prison." She gasped for breath. "Oh, heaven help us!"

"Calm down," Janel said. "Getting upset isn't going to help. Adrienne will be awake soon, and she's going to need you to be steady."

"You're right," Mary said as she stood up. "I'm going to go sit with her. I don't want her to wake up alone."

"I'll watch out for Ida when she wakes up," Janel offered.

"Thank you," Mary said and hurried up the stairs.

She was relieved to find Adrienne still sleeping, the iPod still playing in her ears. She sat down across the room from the bed and wept as quietly as she could manage while she prayed that this horrible misunderstanding would soon be corrected. She wished they had left this house long before now, and then none of this would have ever happened. She felt guilty for her lack of remorse over her father's death, then she reminded herself that her inability to feel any tenderness toward him was a result of years of bad behavior on his part; she had sincerely done everything she could. And she could honestly say she had never been unkind to him. She'd been firm in standing up for herself when it was necessary, but never had she been unkind. She could find some peace in that. She thought of Whit's behavior with her father, what little interaction there had been, and she knew that he had maintained a great deal of control, especially when she'd known how angry he'd felt. Then it occurred to her that he had actually been in this room with her when they'd heard the shot fired. And she'd told the officers that. She could testify that it couldn't possibly have been him who had pulled the trigger. With that thought, she breathed in some relief and felt confident that this would all be over very soon. But then, if Whit hadn't done it—and she knew he hadn't—who had? Who had been able to get into their home and threaten their safety? The thought was unnerving to say the least, but she chose to focus instead on praying that Whit would soon be returned home to her, and they could move elsewhere and be safe—and together.

Adrienne started to stir, and Mary laid down on the bed beside her, holding her as she came awake. Once she was alert enough to have a conversation, Mary told her plainly what had happened, why there were police in the house, and that Daddy had gone to the police station to answer some questions. Adrienne was far more concerned about Whit's absence than her grandfather's death. She had barely been exposed to his presence, and those moments had been nothing but negative for her. She asked if they still had to move, and Mary told her they'd talk to Daddy about that when he got home.

Mary asked her if she wanted to go to school, praying that she would. Having normalcy in her life and getting her out of the house were surely the best things right now—for both of them. Adrienne thought about it and said that she did, and she asked if she could play with Rachel.

"What an excellent idea," Mary said and called Cinda while Adrienne was picking out what to wear. She gave Cinda a brief explanation. Cinda was horrified, but was more than happy to take care of Adrienne. She offered to pick her up after school and keep her for as long as Mary needed.

Once Adrienne was dressed, they went downstairs to get some breakfast. The child was initially a little taken aback by the officers in the house, but within a few minutes she started making conversation with them. Janel offered to take Adrienne to school, and was cleared by the police to do so. Mary focused her attention on helping Ida, since she was now awake. She explained the situation to her as best she could, then left her to get dressed. Ida seemed unsettled, but she didn't say much, and Mary wondered if she was simply in a confused state where her mind was not cooperating. Once Ida was up and about, the detective wanted to question her. Mary reminded him of what he'd already been told, that the woman had Alzheimer's, but he wanted to talk to her anyway. One of the officers spoke fluent Spanish and interpreted for him. Ida had nothing to say except that the alarm had awakened her and she'd been frightened, but she stayed in bed and put her hands over her ears. And that was all she remembered.

Soon after Mary had Ida settled in front of the TV with her breakfast, the police finally cleared out. Mary compulsively walked through the house, wondering if they'd done any damage in their searching, but she found nothing out of order. The blood on her father's hospital bed was the only sign of the horror that had taken place there, and after consulting with the police, she immediately called the home health care company and arranged for the bed and all of the medical equipment to be picked up that afternoon. She told them what had happened so they would be fairly warned about the blood. She had no intention of cleaning it up herself.

They would probably just dispose of the mattress and bedding anyway, and she was fine with that.

Reminded that the health care company was paid by her father's corporation, which was a matter that would be overseen by Mr. Lostin, she knew she needed to call and inform him of what had happened. He would be the one to inform the board members, and he would see to any necessary details related to her father's finances and the business. He was as shocked as she expected him to be by the news, but he told her straight out that he didn't think they should move out yet. He told her that it would take some time for everything to be settled, and the house was now technically owned by the company. Until the board agreed to sell it or do something else with it, the house would just sit empty.

"Eventually they might start charging you rent," he said, "at which time you could decide whether you want to stay, but for now, you can stay rent free. I can convince them to give the matter some time."

"I must admit that would be a relief," she said, not wanting to tell him that the police had taken her husband with them.

"Besides," Mr. Lostin added, "everyone who worked for your father knows what kind of man he was. I can't think of one of them who wouldn't want to help you out by letting you stay in the house for a while, at least until everything's settled."

"Okay, thank you," Mary said and started unpacking boxes the moment she hung up the phone. Unfortunately she was too restless and uptight to accomplish much, and she did more pacing than anything else.

The day wore on, and Mary wondered what to do with herself while she waited for any word from Whit. Janel kept busy and insisted that she eat something. Ida remained oblivious, preoccupied as usual with the television. Cinda called to tell her that she'd gotten Adrienne from school and the girls were now eating lunch. Mary was grateful to have her daughter in someone else's care, and she told Cinda so. Cinda reassured her once again that she was glad to keep Adrienne for as long as she needed, and she could even spend the night if it would help.

A short while later Mary gasped when the phone rang. A glance at the caller ID told her it was the police department. She wanted it to be Whit rather than more questions, but on the other hand she didn't like the idea of him calling her from that number as opposed to using his cell phone. She only had to hear him say, "It's me," before she knew something was horribly wrong.

"What's happened?" she demanded.

"Is everything all right there?"

"Yes, we're fine. Adrienne is with Cinda. Your mother is fine. What's happened?"

"They've arrested me, Mary. I have to stay."

"No, Whit. No. This can't be happening. What evidence do they have?"

"I can't talk about that," he said. "Listen, I need you to call Brother Vega. You know who he is?"

"Yes, of course," she said. She'd encountered him many times at church, and she knew he was the attorney who had helped Whit before his mission. He'd also become a very good friend of Whit's, and he'd been greatly responsible for helping Whit turn his life around.

"Call him and tell him where I am and what's happened. Nothing else can happen without his help. Okay?"

"I'll call him. What can I do?"

"Nothing," he said. "Pray."

"I can't believe this is happening, Whit."

"Me neither, but . . . I have to go, Mary. I love you. No matter what happens, never forget that I love you."

"I love you too, Whit."

Their call ended, and she sat down and cried like a baby, barely able to mutter through her tears what had happened while Janel did her best to offer comfort and assurance. Mary pulled herself together when she remembered Whit's request. She quickly found Brother Vega's number, but there was no answer. Of course, it was his home number. She looked in the phone book for the number for his law office and found it without any problem. A secretary answered, and Mary explained that it was very important that she speak to Mr. Vega, since her husband had been arrested and Mr. Vega was his attorney. A minute later she was able to speak to Donald Vega, and he listened with compassion while Mary explained what had happened.

"I'll make arrangements to speak to him right away," Donald said. "I'll do everything in my power, Mary, to prove him innocent and to do it as painlessly as possible. I promise. Do you understand?"

"Yes," she said. "Thank you. We'll find a way to pay you whatever you need. We will"

"Don't worry about that, Mary. Just take care of yourself. Do you need anything? Can the branch do anything to help or—"

"We're fine," she insisted. "Just . . . help Whit."

"I will," he said. "I will call or come by later when I know more of what's going on."

"Thank you," Mary said, then she hung up the phone and cried again.

* * * * *

By late afternoon Mary felt so unsettled that she decided she should go and get Adrienne, hoping the child would have a soothing effect on her. But Janel talked her out of it, saying that Mary needed some time to deal with the issues at hand and get some rest. Janel offered to pick Adrienne up at Cinda's. She would take some of Adrienne's things with her so the child could have a sleep over at Janel's house. She would take Adrienne to school in the morning before she came in to work, and Mary could have until school let out the following day to pull herself together. Mary had to admit the plan was wise, and she wouldn't have to worry about Adrienne overhearing any difficult conversations, especially while Mary was so upset and could hardly stop crying.

A little while after Janel left with an overnight bag for Adrienne, Mary got a call from Donald Vega. "I just have a minute now," he said, "but I'd like to come over in about an hour, if that's all right with you, and I can tell you everything I know."

"That would be great, thank you," she said.

Certain this could be one of the longest hours of her life, Mary got herself cleaned up, then got Ida her supper and made certain she was doing all right. She still seemed oblivious to any problem, and didn't seem to notice Whit's absence. She did ask about Adrienne, and Mary simply said she was sleeping over at Janel's.

"Oh, that will be fun for her," Ida said and turned her attention back to the television. Mary knew it wasn't good to use the TV as a baby-sitter for children, but she wondered if that rule applied to elderly people. She didn't figure they needed to worry about its impact on Ida's mind, and she could only be grateful that it kept Ida occupied and that there were several channels available that were entirely in Spanish.

Mary felt so full of nerves by the time she heard the buzzer at the gate, she felt sure she would burst into tears the minute Brother Vega came through the door. She pushed the button to open the gate, then went to the front door to greet him. She opened it to see Brother Vega and President Martinez approaching.

"I asked the president to come with me," Brother Vega said. "I hope that's all right."

"Of course," she said and motioned them inside. She didn't know if his intention was based in it being more appropriate for him to not visit her alone, or if the news was so bad he felt that she would need the support of their ecclesiastical leader. She invited them to sit with her at the dining table, which was far enough away from where Ida was watching TV that the sound didn't interfere.

"Okay, tell me," Mary said. "I need to know everything."

"Right now," Brother Vega said, "the main reason they're holding him is the fact that his fingerprints are on the gun. His are the *only* prints on the gun." Mary sighed, and he added, "The gun was found in the shrubbery just outside your father's bedroom window. It appears to have been dropped from the balcony, as opposed to being discarded by someone running from the premises."

"How can they possibly know that?" Mary demanded.

"They're working on theories until the facts come together. They still need to do a ballistics test to match it officially with the bullet that killed your father, and that will take a few days. But they *can* keep Whit in jail given the present facts."

"Which are?"

"He had motive, means, and opportunity. His record is only working against him."

"I was with him when the shot was fired," Mary said.

"I know that, and they know that, but . . ."

"But what?"

"They want to talk to you in the morning. They called *me* because I told them you were my client and you wouldn't talk to them without my being present. I hope that's okay."

"More than okay," Mary said. "I've already told them everything I know. And I don't understand *why* he's even a suspect when he was *with me* when the shot was fired."

"I'm not sure, Mary, but given the full scope of the situation, they could present this to a jury with the scenario that you're covering for him, or that . . ."

"What?" Mary insisted, trembling from the inside out.

"Or they could present the possibility that the two of you were in on it together; that it was premeditated." Mary gasped, and he added, "I'll be frank with you, Mary. If he gets convicted of premeditated murder, he'll get put away for life. And if they believe you had something to do with it, you could serve time as well."

Mary found it difficult to swallow, then to even breathe. She was suddenly overcome with such a rush of nausea that she had to run into the bathroom to throw up. How could this have happened? How could it be this bad? She couldn't even fathom life ever being right again!

She forced enough composure upon herself to go back out and face these men who were trying to help her. As soon as she sat down, Brother Vega said gently, "Forgive me, Mary. I'm giving you the worst-case scenario. I just think you have to know what the people on the other end might be thinking. To be a good defense attorney, I have to consider every possibility."

"I understand," Mary said.

"And I promise you I'm going to do everything in my power to get this to go away."

"Thank you," she said, then she looked him in the eye. "Do you believe he's innocent?"

"I *know* he's innocent, Mary. I know Whit, and I know he wouldn't have done something like that."

Mary let that reassurance sink in and felt a little better.

"I know it too, Mary," President Martinez said. "I know his heart. He's a good man, and we're going to help you get through this. I wonder if we could give you a priesthood blessing."

"Oh," Mary said with pleasant surprise. "I would like that very much. Thank you."

Mary sat beside Ida and explained that these men were here to give her a blessing, and asked if they could turn off the television. Ida was eager to do so, and pleased to be present. In the blessing Mary was offered love and comfort from her Heavenly Father, and the promise of great blessings in her life. She was promised that Whit's life was in God's hands, and she was also reminded that they were sealed for eternity and as they remained true to their covenants, nothing could keep them from having the desire of their hearts, which was to be together forever. Mary had hoped to hear a specific promise that this would all turn out favorably, but she couldn't deny feeling a great deal of peace and hope, even if she didn't know the outcome.

Ida had tears on her face when the blessing was over, and Mary quickly realized that as Ida had listened to the words of the blessing, her mind had put the pieces together and she was more mentally alert than she had been all day. She asked questions, and the three of them did their best to answer in a way that offered her reassurance while remaining completely honest. Mary promised to take very good care of Ida while Whit was gone. Ida asked if she too could have a blessing, and the men gladly complied. Brother Vega gave this blessing, since President Martinez had given the other. Ida was told that her Heavenly Father knew her heart and that her sins were forgiven and she would be watched over with great care from both sides of the veil. She was promised that she would see her son return home, which made Mary cry.

After the men left, Mary made sure everything was locked up and the security system activated, although she wasn't sure what good that might do. Last night all it did was wake them up *before* someone got shot. Mary sat with Ida for quite a while. They talked and cried together, then Mary made certain Ida was safely in bed before she went to bed herself. In spite of her utter exhaustion, she slept only periodically throughout the night, her sleep littered with awful dreams and her time awake plagued with fear that she tried to pray away. Knowing that God was with them and that He knew the truth was the only true source of comfort that Mary could find, and she held to it tightly, wondering how she had ever managed before she'd had the gospel in her life.

# Chapter Fourteen

The following morning, Mary had to leave the minute Janel arrived in order to meet Brother Vega at the police station. He insisted that she needed to call him Donald, since they were possibly just getting started on a long journey together. He also told her that his wife would be coming to visit her this evening and bringing some supper. Mary couldn't deny feeling very blessed, in spite of the nightmare into which they had been catapulted.

"Do you think they'll let me see him?" she asked as they went into the building together.

"I don't know, but I've already put in a request for that."

"Thank you," she said, wondering what she would have done without him.

"I need to warn you that the detective is probably going to be very hard on you. He's going to try to get you to let something slip that might incriminate Whit—or you."

"I have nothing to hide, Donald, and neither does Whit."

"I know. Just . . . be warned, and . . . he's going to bring up Whit's past. I'm certain of it. Are you prepared for that? You do know about his past, don't you?"

"I know enough."

"Just understand that when he came clean, he really came clean. And there are some things he got convicted for that he didn't do. One of his gang buddies purposely framed him."

Mary stopped walking and looked at Donald hard. "Is that what someone is trying to do now?"

Donald's expression was grave. "I don't know. But if that's the case . . ." He didn't finish his sentence, and Mary had to start walking again to keep from repeating last night's episode of unexpected nausea.

She and Donald were seated in an interrogation room with a mirror opposite them that she knew had to be an observation window on the other side. Detective Wilson came in with another plain-clothes officer, and they sat across the table. She was glad for Donald's warning when the detective immediately opened a folder in front of Mary that was Whit's police record—including mug shots of a young man with angry eyes and a hard countenance. The photos were chilling evidence of how much Whit had changed, and she took that to heart. After the detective reiterated Whit's gang history and his reasons for serving time, he slammed his hand down on the table and insisted, "Mrs. Eden. I'm not sure you know your husband *at all.*"

"He's not the same man he used to be, Detective. I know my husband better than anyone."

"Don't you find it even a little suspicious that a man so much younger than you would set out to marry a rich, white woman in order to get access to the house, the money, the—"

"You are out of line, Detective!" Donald said. "You have no idea what you're talking about, and the marriage has no bearing on the case."

"A jury might not agree."

"Until we're in front of a jury, keep the marriage out of it."

"Fine," the detective said, then he asked Mary all of the questions he'd asked her yesterday, except that today he was not even remotely kind. When the interview was over, Mary had to find a ladies room and throw up again.

Donald was waiting for her in the hall, and told her that although she was going to be able to see Whit, they had to go to a different building, and their visit would be brief. Mary felt like she was participating in a nightmare with all she had to go through just to get into a room where she was on the other side of the glass from her husband. She started to cry when she saw him wearing bright orange and being treated like a criminal. They were only able to talk through a phone headset, but she put her hand on the glass between them, and he put his against it.

"I'm so sorry I brought this into your life, Mary. You deserve better."

"You're not responsible for this, Whit," she insisted.

"Not directly, but—"

"Listen to me," she said, leaning closer. "We got married for all the right reasons, and I regret nothing. We're going to get through this. You're innocent and we're going to prove it."

"And if we can't?"

Mary's chin quivered and her voice shook, but she still spoke with conviction. "We will be together forever, Whit, no matter what. I will never give up on you! I will never let go! Do you understand?"

Whit nodded, and tears trickled down his face. "I love you, Mary."

"I love you too," she said with fervor, then they were given a one-minute warning.

"Listen," he said. "Donald's the only one they'll let me talk to most of the time. Do you have everything you need? Do you have enough money and—"

"We're fine. Don't worry about that."

"You call Donald . . . or President Martinez if you need anything, anything at all. Do you hear me? I don't want you to be afraid or go without for any reason. Do you understand?"

"I understand. We'll be all right."

"I'll see you at the hearing," he said, and she didn't know what he was talking about. He was taken away and looked over his shoulder as long as he could manage.

Donald explained on their way out that there would be a hearing to determine bail. He needed to get Whit's nice clothes from her before then. Mary said she'd send them with his wife when she came that evening. The implication suddenly set in, and she asked, "Does this mean he can get out on bail until this is settled?"

"Depends on what the judge says. Given his gang history, the DA's office is going to push hard to *not* let him out. But I'll give it all I've got."

"You're wonderful, Donald. Thank you."

"Glad to do whatever I can," he said, but he said it with some sadness.

Mary cried all the way home but managed to pull herself together long enough to stop at the grocery store and pick up a few things. She knew that Adrienne would be home by now, and she didn't want to show up looking like a wreck. She was proud of herself for the smile she managed to plaster on her face as she pulled the car into the garage and Adrienne ran out to meet her. After Mary answered Adrienne's questions the best that she could, she checked on Ida, updated Janel, and then she made cookies with Adrienne so the child could feel some normalcy. Mary concluded it was also good for her, when Adrienne's positive attitude and simple faith were contagious. The child believed that everything would be alright and her Daddy would come home. Mary wanted to believe that too.

While the cookies were in the oven, the medical examiner's office called Mary to ask to which mortuary she would like her father's body released. The question took her off guard and made her realize that she should have some kind of service. Funny how it had never occurred to her. She immediately thought of the mortuary that had handled her mother's funeral and burial, and that's what she told them. She then had to look up their number and call to tell them the situation. She spoke to a kind man who agreed to take care of everything. She made an appointment for the following morning when she would go in to make the arrangements.

Sister Vega came that evening with a nice meal and some sweet compassion. Mary had Whit's suit and everything that went with it ready for her to deliver to her husband. But it felt painful to Mary to let it go. Everything felt painful, and after her visitor left she once again felt sick and had to throw up.

The next morning she left Ida in Janel's care while she took Adrienne to school, then she went directly to the mortuary to keep her appointment. She ordered a simple casket, a small spray of flowers to go on the top, and indicated that she only wanted a simple graveside service. She came right out and told the mortician that she doubted anyone would come besides those who came with her, because no one liked him. He didn't seem as astonished as she might have expected, and said, "Not the first time that's come up."

"Really?" Mary asked, wishing she could become friends with other women who had been forced to deal with a loathsome father. But she doubted any of them had their husbands on trial for murder, so they wouldn't have *too* much in common.

With everything arranged for her father's burial, Mary focused on putting one foot in front of the other, and she prayed more than she ever had in her life. Since she couldn't talk to Whit or see him, she started writing him a long letter, which Donald promised to deliver. It felt good to at least get her feelings out, since she could confide in him more than she had ever confided to anyone else in her life. She also told him details of sweet things about Adrienne, and reassurances concerning his mother and everything else that was going on.

After she finished the letter very late in the evening, she felt sick again, and a thought occurred to her that seemed completely absurd and ridiculous. But the more she thought about it, the more she had to conclude that it might be a possibility. When Mary took Adrienne to school the next morning, she stopped at a drugstore on the way home. Then as soon as she got to the house she went directly to the upstairs bathroom to use the pregnancy test. She sat on the edge of her bed holding it in her hand, waiting for the answer to appear. Then she nearly passed out from hyperventilating. The conclusion was amazing. The timing was horrible.

Needing to share the news with *someone*, she hurried downstairs to the kitchen and said to Janel, "There's something I have to tell you . . . show you."

"What?" Janel asked, turning toward her fully when it became evident this was serious.

Mary held up the little plastic device, and Janel asked, "What is that?"

"It's a pregnancy test, Janel. And it's positive."

Janel gasped, then she laughed. "That's incredible!"

"Janel! I'm forty years old."

"I know. It's incredible!"

"My husband is in jail!"

"It will still make him very happy." Janel laughed again. "Oh, it's incredible! I guess this means that the lack of children was Simon's problem, not yours."

"I guess it does," Mary said and had to sit down. "I can't believe it. I just can't believe it."

Janel sat across the table from Mary and put a hand over hers. Tenderly she said, "Mary, honey, this is a miracle. No matter what else is going on, or what else happens, it's a miracle."

"I know," Mary said tearfully. "I just wish that Whit was here to . . ."

"Everything will be all right," Janel said, and Mary tried to believe her.

The hearing was scheduled for that afternoon, and once again Mary was immeasurably grateful for Janel, who kept Ida and Adrienne well cared for when she needed to be elsewhere. In the courtroom, Mary wanted to run into Whit's arms when she saw him, but she had to keep her distance. She wanted to tell him the miraculous news, but this hardly seemed the right time or place, even if she *could* get close to him. Their eyes met across the room and locked. She could feel his anguish, and she knew he could feel hers. She also hoped that he could feel her love, and her hope, and her prayers.

They had to look elsewhere when the judge came in. Mary felt a sense of doom as the prosecutor stated in a few sentences the criminal history of

Whit Eden in the very worst light, insisting that he should not be let out on bail due to his tendency to violence. She felt a little better when Donald had his turn and stated plainly that Mr. Eden had a perfect record since he'd come out of prison years earlier and that he had no gang affiliations. He talked about Whit having a wife and daughter that loved him very much and needed him, and a mother with Alzheimer's, for whom Whit had been the primary caregiver for many years. He assured the judge that Mr. Eden was not a flight risk and that he was well respected in his church and community.

The judge listened and considered, then she pronounced bail at $500,000. Mary gasped and saw Whit hang his head. They both knew they could never come up with that much money, and he was destined to spend months in jail while waiting for a trial. Mary believed his thoughts were likely the same as hers, and when their eyes met again, she absolutely knew it. If he *did* end up getting convicted, he would spend his life in prison. If he could be out on bail in the meantime, at least they would be able to have some time together. But she could only stand there and watch helplessly as he was led away. And once again she cried all the way home. She put on a stoic face before going into the house to tell Adrienne and Ida that Whit wouldn't be coming home until after the trial was over—and then only if he were proven innocent.

Ida got very emotional, but Adrienne said, "It will be all right. I know how we can get Daddy to come home."

"How?" Mary asked.

Adrienne ran out to the garden, turning on the switch for the fountain on her way. She waited for it to begin flowing freely, then she pulled a nickel out of her pocket, closed her eyes, and threw it in. She smiled at Mary and said, "Now Daddy will come home."

Mary smiled at her daughter and tried not to cry. She squatted down to look at her directly and said, "Making a wish is a lovely idea, but we must remember that even if it doesn't come true the way we want, Heavenly Father is still watching out for Daddy—and for us. I think we should pray for Daddy, too."

"Okay," Adrienne said and ran into the house and up the stairs as if she intended to do so that very minute. Mary wanted to follow her and eavesdrop, but Ida was upset and needed Mary's attention.

The next day was the funeral service, and it was indeed a lonely event, as Mary had predicted. Janel went along to support her and to help with Adrienne and Ida. President Martinez was there, since he'd been asked to dedicate the grave. Donald Vega came as well as Mary's visiting teachers. And Mr. Lostin came, but no one else from the company could take any time away from work for the event. It was over in less than ten minutes, and Mary thought how very sad it was that a man's life would end with so little fuss. She remembered her mother's funeral, when the mortuary had been packed with people whose lives had been impacted by her kindness and charity. It was too bad Walter Cranford couldn't have been humble enough to learn a little more about life from the woman he'd married. Mary felt some sadness over her father's death, but she felt even more sad about the life he'd lived that had been so wasted. Mary's sadness quickly shifted to Whit's absence. He should have been here with her. He should have been beside her. It was all just so wrong!

The following day Mary felt downright depressed, and since the illness from her pregnancy was settling in, she felt physically more horrible than she ever had in her life. When she got back from taking Adrienne to school, she sat to visit a few minutes with Janel before she intended to go upstairs and lie down. Janel took Ida out for a walk in the garden, then Mary heard the buzzer on the gate and Donald's voice on the intercom. She hoped he had perhaps come with a letter from Whit, or any little piece of good news. She didn't know if she could bear any more bad news.

She opened the door to see him smiling, and she immediately demanded, "What?"

"It's a miracle, Mary!"

"What?" she asked, holding to the door frame.

"I think we should sit down," Donald said, and they moved inside and to the couch.

"Tell me," Mary insisted.

"I did some legal tap dancing, and members of the branch pitched in and came up with bail."

"What?" Mary said breathlessly.

"I got bail lowered with some conditions, and the members cleaned out their savings to get the money together."

"I don't understand," Mary said.

"They all know they'll get the money back, because they know Whit and trust him."

"I can't believe it," Mary whispered. Then she recalled what he'd said, and asked, "What conditions?"

"He'll be under house arrest. They're coming here this afternoon to set up the equipment. He'll be wearing an ankle monitor that can't be removed. If he steps off the property, he'll go back to jail. But he can be here at home with his family until the trial, which, at this rate, will probably be sometime next spring."

"Oh," Mary said, "it *is* a miracle." She put her face in her hands and wept. It wasn't freedom, but it was so much more than she'd dared to hope for. She was so grateful she could hardly breathe.

"Are you all right, Mary?" Donald asked.

"Oh, I'm good," she said and laughed. "Thank you. Thank you for everything!" She sighed and wiped her eyes. "When will he be able to come home?"

"Maybe tonight; if not, tomorrow morning."

Mary laughed again, thanked Donald profusely, then happily saw him off before she went out to the garden to give the good news to Janel and Ida. Whit's mother wept and wrapped Mary in her arms, then they went inside to pitch in and clean up the house before the police came to do whatever they needed to do, and especially to have everything perfect before Whit came home. And Mary couldn't wait to pick up Adrienne from school to tell her that her prayers had been answered, and her wish was coming true. Her daddy was coming home.

\* \* \* \* \*

It was almost nine o'clock that evening when Mary received a call to inform her that her husband was on his way home. She had the gate open when they arrived, and she was standing in the driveway with Ida and Adrienne when Whit stepped out of the police car. They both laughed and cried when he wrapped her in his arms and briefly lifted her off the ground. He then picked Adrienne up, hugging her tightly as he spun her around. He set her down and hugged his mother, who also cried.

"Okay," one of the officers said to Whit, "it's activated. You know the drill."

"I know the drill," Whit said. "Thank you."

Mary knew as the police drove away and the gate was closed that Whit was being sentenced to a different kind of confinement. She knew the months ahead with him being unable to leave—even to go to church— would be extremely difficult. And knowing there was a trial at the end of this journey, with so much uncertainly attached to it, was too horrible to think about. So she *didn't* think about it. She just focused on having her husband home with her. He helped tuck Adrienne into bed, and he spent some time with his mother while he helped her get settled in for the night as well.

When they were finally alone he looked at her, sighed loudly, and said, "I am so grateful to be here that I cannot even . . . find the words."

"That makes two of us," she said and took a deep breath. "There's something I need to tell you, Whit." She took both of his hands into hers. "When all of this happened, I just felt sick . . . a lot."

"That makes two of us," he said.

"And then . . . I realized I was really *sick*."

"Is something wrong?" he asked.

"No, Whit. Something is . . . wonderful." She shrugged and just said it. "I'm pregnant."

He drew in a sharp breath, then just stared at her for a long moment. "You're serious."

"Of course I'm serious. Would I joke about something like that?"

"But you're . . ."

"So old?" she guessed, then laughed, knowing he'd never say such a thing.

"I was going to say that we obviously thought it wasn't possible."

"Apparently it is," she said.

As if it had fully sunk in, Whit grabbed hold of her and hugged her tightly. "Oh, Mary. It's a miracle!" He drew back and looked at her with sudden concern. "Are you alright? You said you were sick."

"I've been feeling some sickness, but Janel says that's normal. I have a doctor's appointment next week."

"I wish I could go with you," he said with a weighted sigh.

"So do I, but we're not going to focus on the things we wish could be different. We're going to focus on our gratitude for having this time together, and that you're not rotting away in a cell somewhere while we have to live without you."

"And what if it ends up that way, Mary?"

She put on a brave smile. "We're not going to worry about that, Whit. You're innocent until proven guilty. We are going to wish and hope and pray and enjoy every minute we have together, and if the worst happens, I've already told you where I stand on that."

"Tell me again," he said.

"We will be together forever, Whit, no matter what. I will never give up on you! I will never let go!"

"Tell me that every day," he muttered and hugged her again. Mary felt so grateful to have him in her arms that she started to cry, then she realized he was crying too. The wonderful thing was that they could hold each other all night and cry together.

\* \* \* \* \*

The challenges of Whit not being able to leave the property quickly settled in. The most difficult was his not being able to go to church with his family, but he studied the scriptures and conference talks while they were gone, and he watched some religious programs on TV. And he loved it when they got back and he could help Mary cook dinner while she recounted every talk from sacrament meeting and details of the lessons.

The home teachers began coming once a week instead of once a month to give Whit some version of the priesthood lessons that he was missing, and since the branch president was confident of Whit's worthiness in the gospel—in spite of the pending criminal charges—priesthood holders came each Sunday afternoon so that he could partake of the sacrament. He was probably more grateful for that than for anything, but all of his other blessings seemed to be wrapped up in the atoning sacrifice of the Savior in one way or another.

Whit's days in jail had starkly brought back the reality of his years in prison, to the point that he'd experienced some minor symptoms of post-traumatic stress disorder (PTSD). He couldn't even imagine going back to prison, especially when he'd done nothing to deserve it. Worse than that, how could he ever survive the possibility of spending the rest of his life there, knowing he was innocent? It haunted him deeply, but he found some measure of comfort in the stories of the apostle Paul— one of his greatest heroes. He had suffered much persecution, including being imprisoned unjustly many times. And yet he boldly declared that he gloried in his suffering for Christ's sake. Whit knew his own innocence, and he knew where he stood with the Lord. He had to trust that the Lord would take care of him and his family, and that however this mortal experience might turn out for them, the promise of eternity burned brightly at the end of this long, dark tunnel. He and Mary talked deeply and extensively about such eternal principles, and they were mutually committed to living the gospel fully and making the most of whatever might happen. As long as they were in it together, they agreed that they could get through anything. But the possibility of prison still felt unbearable to both of them, and they prayed fervently that the outcome would be positive.

Whit was deeply grateful that he could continue working on the garden without compromising his house arrest. And he was also grateful that Mr. Lostin saw fit to continue paying him a salary for doing so. Mr. Lostin had also assured them that, even though Mary had not been included in her father's will *at all*, the house was theirs to use for a long while yet, and perhaps a permanent arrangement could be worked out. At some point they might have to start paying rent, but Mr. Lostin had said that might be traded for Whit's gardening services, since his work was continually raising the value of the property. And perhaps they might even be able to work out a manageable arrangement for Whit and Mary to buy the house. For now, he assured them that they didn't need to worry. He was a kind man, and they were both grateful. They also appreciated that he expressed confidence in Whit's innocence, and he even said, none too lightly, that there were times in working for Walter Cranford when *he'd* had brief inclinations to shoot the man. "But of course," he concluded, "neither of us would ever give in to such a temptation."

Mary's illness from her pregnancy became difficult to endure, but the doctor said she was healthy and everything seemed fine. He had told her that many women her age went through childbirth with no complications, and most of the babies were healthy and normal. Whit wished he could go to her appointments with her, but he was very glad to be there in the house to help take care of her and to help with other things so that her stress could be eased. Janel was available to take Adrienne back and forth to school when Mary didn't feel up to it. Beyond that, Whit found pleasure in taking over the care of their daughter for the most part, and he was glad to be able to take care of his mother and see that her needs were met. He saw more and more evidence of her failing memory, and sometimes she became very upset due to her confusion, which often made her afraid. But there were good moments here and there, and Whit was glad to be there to enjoy them and to know that Mary was not left with the burden of caring for his mother *and* Adrienne while she was so ill much of the time.

Since they couldn't go out, they found ways to enjoy time together at home. At least once a week Whit and Mary enjoyed a nice meal together and sometimes a movie while Adrienne had a sleep over at Janel's. As a family they played games, watched movies, and read together, with Mary joining in as much as she felt able. They all enjoyed Christmas preparations, and Whit was glad he'd been able to go shopping with Mary before all of this had happened. Thanksgiving had come and gone, hardly noticed amidst the drama, but they were determined to make this a great Christmas, praying all the while that it wouldn't be their last Christmas under the same roof.

They *did* have a glorious Christmas. In spite of the dark cloud looming in the future and the continual reminder that Whit couldn't leave the house, both Whit and Mary agreed that it was absolutely the best Christmas of their lives.

"God willing, we'll have many more to come," he declared.

They prayed night and day that all would be well in the end, and each day Adrienne threw a coin into the fountain, wishing that her daddy would be able to stay with them always. And she always concluded the ritual by running up to her room to kneel by her bed and ask Heavenly Father that her wish might come true.

The new year began with dismal skies and rainy weather. Whit's confinement felt more difficult when he couldn't go outside and do some manual labor. But he continued to be grateful that he wasn't alone in a jail cell, and he enjoyed every little thing he did to help care for his family. Mary's illness began to improve in direct proportion with the way she was beginning to show just a little. Whit had told her that he didn't need to have a child of his own to be happy and fulfilled, and he'd meant it. But he couldn't deny the joy he felt to think of Mary having his baby. He just prayed every day that he could be a part of the family and watch this child grow and be an active part of its life. The thought of his baby growing up with the knowledge that its father was in prison made him sick to his stomach. So he avoided that thought and kept praying.

Branch members rallied around them with love and support, including fasting and prayers that were taking place on their behalf. Whit still marveled that these people had come up with his bail money and that they were willing to put that much trust in him. He was determined not to let them down, and he often imagined how it would feel to be a free man again and to go to church and embrace them all. Just to be among them and worship seemed like a precious gift that he longed to receive.

While they all wanted to have the trial over with, they dreaded it too. Whit would need to remain in jail during the course of the trial, and if the outcome was bad, he would probably never come home again. If he were declared innocent, however, the whole thing would be over. A part of him wished that it could be postponed until after the baby was born, but on the other hand, he would prefer to actually be able to leave the house and be there when that happened. Everything depended on the outcome of the trial, and since they had no way of knowing what the outcome would be, they could only put the matter in God's hands and move forward with faith.

When the trial was officially scheduled for the latter part of April, Whit began to feel the days of his life ticking away. As much as he wanted—and tried—to believe that his innocence would be proven, he knew he had many strikes against him. He'd always wondered if his past would catch up with him, and maybe this was the price he would have to pay. He and Mary talked about it whenever they felt the need, and they both agreed that even if the worst happened, at least they'd had this time together. At least they'd shared these months as husband and wife. At least he would have a child to carry on his name. At least there was someone in his life who would care for him, even from a distance. And at least Mary would take care of his mother. She would have likely gone into a care center long before she would have needed to if Mary hadn't grown to love her as her own mother. There was no denying that they had much to be grateful for, but the entire situation just felt so ludicrous. And always in the back of their minds was the never-ending question: if Whit didn't kill Mary's father, then who did?

The day before the trial was set to begin, Donald called to say he would be coming with the police to take Whit in. Farewells were painfully difficult, but Whit was determined to have them over with before the police arrived so that he could leave with some dignity. He'd done everything he could possibly do to make certain his family was cared for. Donald had helped him with legal matters so that Mary had full access to his money, and a will was in place so that she always would. His mother's care was prearranged for the time when she could no longer be handled at home. And the house and garden were in as good a condition as they possibly could be. He'd also transferred the title of his truck into Mary's name, so that she would have a vehicle even if her father's car—which was technically owned by his company—might be confiscated.

With everything in perfect order and properly arranged, Whit forced himself away from the three women he loved—and his unborn child— and left behind life as he knew it. He could only pray that it would soon be over and that God would give them a miracle.

That night, alone in a cell, Whit felt strangely comforted to know that he was not alone in being lonely and miserable because Mary was probably crying her eyes out. He hated the irony of all that she was suffering for his sake but he could never deny how grateful he was to know how much she loved him.

The following morning Whit was able to see Mary in the courtroom, but only from a distance. And once he was seated he could find comfort only in knowing she was sitting somewhere behind him. He knew Janel was taking care of Adrienne and his mother, and he wondered what they would have ever done without this precious woman.

* * * * *

Mary felt utterly drained and exhausted after spending two long days in the courtroom, but she knew it was far from over. While Adrienne and Ida were watching TV together, Mary stepped out onto the patio and turned on the water to the fountain. She closed her eyes and listened to its gentle flow, trying to wrap herself in memories of all the beauty that Whit had brought into her life. She also tried to take hold of all the wishes that had been made in the fountain, each one represented by a shiny, glistening coin in the bottom. Mary glanced at the coins and conjured up a sad smile to think of Adrienne's tender ritual of regular wishes and prayers on Whit's behalf. Her eyes scanned the garden and tears stung her eyes. It was so beautiful! It was perfect! And she missed the gardener so much that it hurt.

Mary's eyes then came to rest on the little rosebush that Whit had planted the previous year, the one he'd built the walkway around. He'd told her that he'd paid for it himself, that it was a gift from him. It had been many weeks since she'd even noticed it or given it any thought, but something was different. She stepped closer and bent down. It was blossoming! There were four rosebuds just starting to open, and she could see them just enough to finally know what color they were. Lavender! Lavender roses.

"Oh, they're beautiful," she said to no one, hoping that Whit might feel some small sense of the love and gratitude she was sending across the city. She recalled the very first day he'd come here and his conversation with Adrienne about her favorite color. Not once had she heard it mentioned since, but he'd noticed and remembered. He loved her. And she had tangible evidence of that love in front of her, and that gave her hope.

The following day, two of Whit's cousins were put on the stand. Their obvious gang affiliation and their relationship to Whit didn't help his case, but they did both say that they thought Whit was a good guy and that they didn't believe he had committed this crime. However, the prosecutor managed to word his questions in a way that could easily lead the jury to believe Whit was still close to his cousins and active in their illegal activities—even though no actual reference or admission to anything illegal came up. The very ambiguity and vague implications felt most damaging of all, but Mary also felt vulnerable as she wondered whether one of his cousins might be guilty. It was the only thing that really made sense, but apparently it could never be proven. She also hated the implications of how they might feel about how this situation had drawn legal attention to them. She didn't like the way they looked at Whit when they were seated on the stand and she didn't like the way they looked at her. But what could she do but keep praying and strive to trust in the Lord, to believe that they would all be protected and come through this safe and together as a family?

Four days into the trial, the situation didn't look good. The prosecutor had painted a picture of Whit that made him sound devious and selfish, as if his leaving behind his gang affiliations had only been for outward appearances and he'd simply chosen a different avenue for perpetrating evil on innocent people. It was made to appear that Mary was covering for him in saying he'd been with her when the shot was fired and that they'd both wanted her father dead. Even though the possibility of this being a gang-related hate crime came up in quite a bit of detail, with the capabilities and motives of these kind of people being made very clear, the lack of evidence in that regard made it all seem irrelevant.

At that point the DA's office offered Whit a plea bargain. Whit would do less time if he admitted guilt and claimed it was impulsive and not premeditated. He adamantly refused, unwilling to admit to any level of guilt when it wasn't true. When the deal was no longer available, Whit was able to speak with Donald alone.

"It's bad, isn't it," Whit said.

"Yeah, it's bad."

Whit chuckled without humor. "That's one of the things I love about you, Donald. You're always honest with me."

"That's right, and I'm going to be honest with you now. I know you haven't wanted Adrienne to testify, but it's your only chance. You know me, Whit, and I've been praying very hard about the best way to represent you and get you through this. You've told me you're worried about the impact of Adrienne having to be in the courtroom. But what about the impact of her living without a father? And have you considered how empowering it might be for her to know, for the rest of her life, that it was her testimony that saved her daddy?"

"And what if—in spite of her testimony—it still doesn't work? How will *that* impact her?"

"We have to try, Whit. When you're doing hard time, you could very well regret not having at least tried. I'll talk to Mary. I'll make certain Adrienne is cared for and treated with respect."

"Okay," Whit said reluctantly. "Talk to Mary. And keep praying."

"Oh, I will," Donald said, and once again Whit was left alone.

* * * * *

Mary felt deeply relieved when Donald called to say that Whit had agreed to let Adrienne testify. They had discussed it a number of times, but they had always been in disagreement over it. At one point Whit had agreed that if the situation became desperate, he would consider it. Well, it was desperate, and she felt that her prayers were being answered. In her heart she believed that Adrienne could make all the difference, and she prayed now that it would all come together for their good, and that the outcome would be everything they'd been hoping and praying for it to be.

Mary had a careful visit with Adrienne, not surprised by how much she understood everything that was going on and why. She'd always been bright and perceptive, but she was also very spiritual. She'd actively prayed and wished for her daddy to come home, and she was pleased to be able to have the chance to testify about what she knew to be true. According to Donald's guidance, Mary prepared Adrienne for the courtroom experience and how she should answer questions, then they prayed together and went to bed. Mary felt so lonely for Whit that it felt physically painful, and she prayed that their nights apart would soon come to an end.

The following morning Adrienne insisted on wearing the pink dress she'd worn on the day of the wedding. She made a wish in the fountain and said a prayer before they were off to the courthouse, leaving Ida in Janel's care.

In the courtroom, Mary watched Whit closely as he was escorted in and his eyes scanned the room for her. He smiled with sad eyes when he saw her; then he saw Adrienne, and his eyes lit up and his smile widened. She waved excitedly at him, as if they were at a circus instead of in a courtroom. He waved back and blew her a kiss, then the proceedings got underway.

Mary was relieved to realize that the judge had insisted that she would question the child rather than allowing the attorneys to do so. Mary didn't like the prosecutor, and she far preferred knowing this man would not be allowed to confront her daughter. The judge was very kind to Adrienne and asked her to just look at the judge and pretend they were having a conversation, just the two of them. She didn't have to think about anyone else in the room. The judge asked questions that clearly established Adrienne's strong knowledge of right and wrong and the importance of telling the truth. Mary could see the jury softening as they watched Adrienne intently. When the events of the night in question came up, the judge just asked Adrienne to tell her what had happened as clearly as she remembered it. Mary could plainly discern the sincere spontaneity of a child who could never concoct such a detailed lie without making it obvious she was lying.

Adrienne became tearful as she talked about being frightened that night, but how her daddy had helped her feel better with the things he'd said. She talked about hearing the gunshot, and how it was louder because of the monitor nearby. She talked about how shocked and scared both of her parents had been. Adrienne was kindly dismissed, and the judge thanked her for being such a good witness. Court was then adjourned before closing statements would be given. Mary had just enough time to take Adrienne home where Janel would look after her, then grab a snack she could eat while she drove back to the courthouse.

As Donald Vega spoke to the jury with dignity and confidence about the innocence of Whit Eden, Mary felt deeply touched and filled with hope. He pointed out that there was far too much reasonable doubt to convict a man based on fingerprint evidence alone. And then he gave an eloquent speech about the power of change in a person's life, concluding with the firm statement, "Whit Eden is a man who paid a high price for the consequences of his actions in regard to the violence that surrounded him in his youth. And he went on to prove that people truly *can* change and make a positive impact on the world around them. Mr. Eden is a loving son, husband, and father. If you, as the jury, make the decision to send this man to prison for a crime he did not commit, you are making a statement to this community that there is never a way out for the troubled kids out there who might actually have a chance to become better people. I ask you, ladies and gentlemen, to show your faith in the human spirit, to believe that good things can come out of bad situations, and to trust your deepest instincts that are telling you that Whit Eden is innocent. Thank you."

Mary wiped her tears with a tissue, feeling the truth of Donald's statement course through her veins. She could only pray that the jury felt it too. Then the prosecutor stood to face the jury in order to give his closing statement, and Mary's nerves were immediately on edge. He spoke with all the passion and skill of a well-practiced attorney, determined to see Whit pay for the crime that had been committed. He recounted details of Whit's gang history and the people he had associated with during those years. He listed the crimes for which Whit had served prison time and implied that there might have been many more that he'd gotten away with. He gave a convincing speech about the ramifications of growing up in violent surroundings and the personal impact of such things on a man's life, stating clearly that he didn't believe any man could change that significantly and that the jury should not be fooled into believing that Whit Eden was innocent.

By the time the prosecutor had finished and returned to his seat, Mary felt sick to her stomach. It took great willpower to subdue her nausea, knowing she needed to be composed and strong. She realized her hands were clenched tightly into fists when she felt her fingernails biting into the palms of her hands, and she had to consciously relax and breathe deeply. She had to close her eyes and recall Donald's powerful words that had preceded this damning summation from the prosecutor. And again she prayed that the jury would do the same and recognize that Whit was not the man he used to be. Court was then adjourned. It was all over except for the final outcome. The jury had to make a decision, and then it would be over one way or another.

Mary knew that jury deliberations could go on for hours, or even days, but she didn't want to leave the courthouse. She had to be there when the verdict came in. She paced the halls but didn't wander very far, knowing that Donald would call her cell phone when they were ready. Less than an hour after the jury had left the courtroom, they came back with a verdict. Mary's nerves were so frayed she feared that she wouldn't be able to hold herself together. Whit turned for just a moment to look at her over his shoulder. Their eyes met, and she offered the best loving smile she could muster. A moment later the defendant was asked to stand, and Donald stood beside him. Mary expected a long, anticipatory pause; some kind of silent drum roll or something. But maybe that was from watching too many legal dramas on television. Before she barely had a chance to wonder what would be said, she heard the words loud and clear. *Not guilty!*

It was over! The judge thanked the jury and dismissed them, banged his gavel, and court was adjourned. The room was suddenly very noisy. Mary couldn't even get out of her chair. She pressed a hand over her mouth while she wept openly, vaguely aware of Whit and Donald sharing a brotherly hug. Then Whit turned toward her, and the expression of relief and joy on his face only intensified her weeping. She saw him coming toward her, but she still couldn't stand until he practically lifted her out of her chair and into his arms.

"Oh, Mary, Mary, Mary! It's over. It's over." He looked at her with tears in his eyes, then he laughed—either from pure joy or some humor over her inability to speak; probably both. "Let's go home," he said, and they walked out of the courtroom together. She leaned against him as she walked, and he kept his arm securely around her. They were going home. Together. He was free.

Late that evening, after Adrienne and Ida were both tucked into bed, Whit stood with Mary at the edge of the garden. The fountain was running, and the light shining from beneath the water was the only visible light.

"We could probably do something pretty exciting with all the money in that fountain," Mary said. "Adrienne made lots of wishes on your behalf."

"I think we'll just leave it there," Whit said. "The angel can watch over the wishes—and the money."

"What a lovely thought." Mary sighed and wrapped her arms around him. "The roses are blooming," she added, knowing they were scattered throughout the garden. But from where she stood, her eyes focused on the lavender roses, wide open and brilliant, even in the subtle light from the nearby fountain.

"Yes," Whit said and pressed a kiss into her hair. "The roses are blooming, and life is good."

# About the Author

Anita Stansfield began writing at the age of sixteen, and her first novel was published sixteen years later. Her novels range from historical to contemporary and cover a wide gamut of social and emotional issues that explore the human experience through memorable characters and unpredictable plots. She has received many awards, including a special award for pioneering new ground in LDS fiction, and the Lifetime Achievement Award from the Whitney Academy for LDS Literature. Anita is the mother of five and has two adorable grandsons. Her husband, Vince, is her greatest hero.

To receive regular updates from Anita, go to anitastansfield.com and subscribe.